P.S. I Hate You

BOOKS BY SOPHIE RANALD

Sorry Not Sorry

It's Not You, It's Him

Out with the Ex, In with the New

No, We Can't Be Friends

Just Saying

Thank You, Next

He's Cancelled

It Would be Wrong to Steal My Sister's Boyfriend (Wouldn't it?)

A Groom with a View

Who Wants to Marry a Millionaire?

You Can't Fall in Love with Your Ex (Can You?)

P.S. I Hate You

SOPHIE RANALD

bookouture

Published by Bookouture in 2022

An imprint of Storyfire Ltd.
Carmelite House
50 Victoria Embankment
London EC4Y 0DZ

www.bookouture.com

ISBN: 978-1-80314-118-3
eBook ISBN: 978-1-80314-117-6

For Hopi, always

SPRING 2001
YELLOW

Abbie had never been inside a house this large or grand before. The lights were dimmed, but she could make out huge, squashy leather sofas, pale in the gloom, perhaps cream or even white. Rugs with a zigzag pattern had been rolled up against the walls to clear the floor for dancing, but there would have been no way to shift the concert piano that stood by the window, its top littered with CDs and their plastic cases.

Music pounded from the stereo, the occasional shriek of laughter rising above it. A mirrored disco ball hung precariously from a chandelier, casting rainbow flashes of light onto the faces of the laughing, dancing crowd. The air was thick with cigarette smoke and the smell of Lynx deodorant.

Abbie took a swig from the bottle in her hand, which was already slippery with condensation. Her lip gloss left a sticky pink ring around its neck, and she wiped it away, feeling the stickiness transfer to her fingers. A cold ribbon of sweat made its way down her back, bridging the seemingly endless gap between where her neon-yellow crop top ended and her ultra-low-rise jeans began. She tugged anxiously at the waistband – hip band, really; crotch band, even – feeling the fabric of her thong above her jeans sticking to her skin and working its way relentlessly higher and higher between her bum cheeks.

She'd spent almost two hours getting ready, her hands unsteady as she applied her frosted eyeshadow and straightened her hair, which she prayed wasn't already frizzing in the heat. She could smell waves of Clinique Happy coming off her hot, anxious body. She took another gulp of Smirnoff Ice, knowing the sickly sweet alcohol would only make her thirstier, however much of it she drank.

Where was Matt? He'd asked her quite casually, as they walked home from school together the previous day, whether she would be at Andy's party on Saturday. It was the first she'd heard of it – certainly Andy, almost godlike in his inscrutable cool, hadn't thought to invite her. But Matt had given her the address, scrawling it on a page torn from his spiral-bound note-book, and said he'd see her there, so it must be okay.

Or was it? In the two months she'd known Matt, seeing him every day at the bus stop in the mornings and again after school (and in her head, on an almost constant Matt channel), she'd never had reason to doubt that he liked her – after all, they were mates (more than mates?). But what if this was some kind of cruel joke? What if Andy was about to appear and look at her in that uniquely withering way he had and say, 'What are *you* doing here?' And what if Matt saw her leaving, humiliated, and did nothing? Or even laughed?

Her heart pounding, feeling more like an imposter than she ever had in her life, Abbie took a cautious step into the room, balancing precariously on her white plastic flatform sandals, feeling the hems of her jeans brushing the parquet floor. If she didn't find Matt soon, she'd cut her losses and go home – after all, she'd promised her parents that she'd be back right after the fictitious movie she'd said she was going to see with her friend Chloe, who was in fact innocently at home, probably watching *Big Brother*.

Part of Abbie wished fervently that she, too, was at home watching *Big Brother*.

And then she saw him. Once her eyes found him, she couldn't believe she hadn't noticed him straight away. His head was clearly visible above the throng, his coal-black hair gleaming as the mirror ball passed over it, his white T-shirt fluorescing under the ultraviolet light. Tall Matt, they called him at school, to distinguish him from the five others in his year with the same name – Hot Matt, Speccy Matt, Arsenal Matt, Geordie Matt and Matt Jones.

But as far as Abbie was concerned, he was the only Matt who mattered. The only Matt in the world. The only boy in the world, even.

Abbie felt as if she might be sick, or faint, or as if her head might simply come loose from her body and drift up to join the cloud of helium balloons bobbing against the ceiling.

But she found herself moving, treading carefully across the room, threading her way through the crowd. Her shoes were digging into her feet, but still she felt like she was walking on air. He had his back to her; she could see his bony shoulders, stooped as they always were, as he bent his head to catch what the girl next to him was saying. The pretty girl. Abbie felt a lurch of jealousy as she noticed the girl's curtain of honey-blonde hair, the flash of her white, even teeth as she giggled at something Matt had said.

But her jealousy and apprehension melted away the second he turned and saw her, breaking away from the group to come and meet her. His face broke into a huge grin, his smile looking almost too wide for his narrow face, as always. His eyes were lighter than his hair, and crinkled at the corners as if he was laughing at some private joke. There were deep dimples in both his cheeks, and she wondered what it might feel like to run her fingers down them.

'You made it,' he said.

'I made it,' Abbie agreed. There was no way she was going to confess to the lie she'd told her mum and dad, or admit that, if they'd known she was planning to attend a house party held while the host's own parents were away in Santorini, she'd have been as grounded as a grounded thing.

'Got a drink?'

Abbie nodded, holding out her half-empty bottle of Smirnoff Ice. Matt reached out his own beer and they clinked, the rims of the two bottles meeting like a kiss.

'Want to dance?' he asked.

'Sure.' To her surprise, her voice sounded steady – casual, even.

'I'm a crap dancer though,' he warned.

'I don't mind. We can dance craply together.'

Matt laughed. 'Come on then.'

He hadn't been joking; he *was* a crap dancer. His legs were too long and he didn't know what to do with his hands, so they either hung awkwardly by his sides or flapped goofily up by his shoulders. But Abbie wasn't much better; her shoes were too high and her jeans were too long, and she had to keep hoiking up the strap of her top as it slipped down over her shoulder.

But neither of them cared. As Destiny's Child blared from the speakers, telling them that they had to work their jelly, they just stared at each other, moving their bodies more or less in synch with the music, grinning at each other. They might as well have been the only two people on the dance floor.

The track ended and another began, and Matt's eyes didn't leave Abbie's face. They kept dancing through 'Lady Marmalade' and 'Where the Party At', and then the music changed again, to a slow song: 'Yellow' by Coldplay.

Abbie's stomach somersaulted. Was he going to take her in his arms and sway slowly with her to the music, as she could see other couples doing?

But Matt just said, 'Another drink?'

Abbie nodded dumbly, and he faded quickly away through the crowd.

She stood there alone for a moment, all her bewilderment and awkwardness flooding back. Perhaps he hadn't really wanted to dance with her and was just being kind. Perhaps he was looking for an excuse to return to the blonde girl, who Abbie could see was still in the corner, surrounded by her friends, giggling and tossing her sleek curtain of hair, smiling away with her perfect teeth.

If he didn't want to slow dance with her, perhaps he didn't fancy her after all.

But, seconds later, Matt was back.

'There's no more Smirnoff Ice, so I got you a Bacardi Breezer.'

'Thank you.'

He looked at her, serious all of a sudden, his smile dialled right down from a grin to something more tentative. Abbie felt a cold jolt of worry hit her stomach along with the first swallow of cold-ish alcopop.

'Want to go outside? It's hot in here, and the garden's seriously awesome.'

'Sure. I'd like that.' Relief flooded through her, immediately followed by a potent hit of excitement.

She followed him towards a pair of tall French doors hung with heavy velvet curtains that puddled on the floor. Abbie could feel the stickiness of spilled alcohol under her shoes, and for a second she imagined the state the house would be in the next day and hoped Andy's parents weren't coming home any time soon.

And there was Andy, leaning in the doorway alone, watching the dancers. His pink Lacoste polo shirt looked almost luminous in the gloom, as did his golden hair. A bottle of tequila hung from his right hand, and his left held a joint up to his mouth.

Matt paused by his side. 'All right, mate?'

Andy nodded and smiled, but didn't say anything. He gave the smallest of gestures with his chin, as if ushering Matt outside. As if somehow giving them his blessing.

Abbie forgot all about the floor and the curtains as soon as they stepped out into the night.

A lush, emerald-green lawn sloped down towards a swimming pool, lit up so its water looked turquoise against the dark sky, a haze of steam rising off its surface. Tropical plants grew around it, their leaves like jagged samurai swords. A magnolia tree was laden with blooms as bright as stars. The air smelled of flowers and the smoke from Andy's spliff.

Abbie heard herself give a little gasp, and Matt said, 'Cool, right?'

'It's amazing.'

'Come and explore.'

They paused for the briefest second, and then Matt took Abbie's hand. His fingers were cool and damp from the drinks he'd been holding, and his grip was gentle. Her own hand felt tiny inside his; even though he was so tall, she'd noticed before that Matt's hands, like his smile, seemed almost too big for the rest of him.

She remembered what her friend Chloe had said about the size of boys' hands corresponding to the size of... well, other bits, and stifled a giggle.

'Something amusing you, Abigail?' Matt asked, in a passable imitation of Mr Burroughs, the school principal. 'Care to share it with the group?'

'Yes, sir. I mean, no, sir. I was just thinking about something funny.'

'Well, don't,' Matt barked, and now they both laughed properly together.

He led her down the slope towards the pool. Abbie trod carefully on the slippery grass, feeling the dew soaking into the hems of her jeans and working its way up. She'd be soaked to the knees at this rate, but she didn't care.

Abbie heard a series of shrieks from inside the house, and the blonde girl emerged, tearing off her clothes and dive-bombing into the pool in her bra and pants. She was followed by two other girls, and then a few of the boys. Andy watched from his vantage point by the door, still smiling to himself.

'Want to swim?' Matt asked.

'No way.' Then Abbie added, 'Unless you want to?'

She'd rather die than strip down to her underwear in front of all these people. But death would also be preferable to Matt thinking she was boring.

'Don't want to mess up my barnet, do I?' Matt grinned and raked a hand through his hair, which flopped immediately back down over his face.

Abbie giggled. It was all right.

The dying chords of 'Yellow' faded away, and there was silence apart from the splashing and laughter of the swimmers. Then someone inside started the music again.

Matt turned away from the pool, Abbie's hand still in his. They walked along a flagstone path, through an archway festooned with headily scented jasmine, and came to a paved courtyard with a fountain in the centre. Abbie could feel the last warmth from the day's sun radiating up from the stone, warming the damp legs of her trousers. It was dark here, away from the lights of the house and the pool, and the music was quieter. She could hear a bird singing, and above her in the distance she could see stars.

They stopped, and Matt let go of Abbie's hand. For a second she felt bereft, but then he slipped a warm arm around her shoulders. She turned to face him and looked up into his eyes.

He was going to kiss her. He was going to kiss her and she wanted it more than she'd ever wanted anything, but at the same time she wanted this moment, this magical second before the kiss happened, to last forever.

She'd snogged boys before, obviously. Gareth Roland, who'd tasted of cheese-and-onion crisps. Wayne – she'd never found out his last name – who'd stuck his tongue so deep into her mouth she thought she might choke. Vaughan Black, who she'd had the most enormous crush on but who'd groped her so enthusiastically he'd snapped her bra strap, and she'd had to spend the rest of the night clutching her left boob against her side with her elbow.

Matt's kiss couldn't disappoint her – it mustn't.

It didn't. From the first tentative meeting of their lips until the moment they broke away from each other, gasping and laughing, only to start again straight away, she felt only ecstasy. His mouth was warm and soft against hers – feeling so right already it was almost as if it was her own. He tasted unfamiliar, but the strangeness was exotic and addictive, like her first ever sip of espresso. His hands enfolded her upper arms, strong but tender, and as she leaned into him with the whole length of her, it felt like her heart and her body were singing.

I don't care if I never kiss anyone else in my life, ever again, she thought.

And, twenty years later, she hadn't.

CHAPTER ONE

I remember the exact moment when the thought leaped into my head, as fully formed as if it had always been there, yet alien and frightening.

Oh my God. Do I still love my husband?

In that instant, it felt almost familiar, like my wonky left incisor or the silver necklace with my name – Abbie – on it, which Matt had given me for my twenty-first birthday and I'd almost never taken off.

It felt almost as familiar as the love I'd had for Matt had become over the years – love I'd assumed would only grow and never really alter.

And it wasn't during one of our increasingly frequent, ever more bitter arguments. It wasn't when he rolled his eyes at me and said, 'Fine,' in that way he had that would make a saint – Mother Teresa, Princess Diana, even – want to do horrible things to his testicles with a Mexican elbow citrus squeezer. It wasn't even when I cried while we were having sex.

It was when I saw a discarded teaspoon on the draining board next to the kitchen sink.

I'm not an irrational person – really, I'm not. Okay, the

Mexican elbow thing... But we all think that sometimes, right? Right? But when I saw that teaspoon, right there next to the dishwasher, in a puddle of almost-dry coffee that someone – guess who? – would have to wipe up before putting the spoon in the appliance that was, as I said, *right* beside it, it filled me with an emotion so intense I thought for a moment it was rage.

Then I realised it wasn't. Rage is hot – it burns fiercely, frightening you with its intensity. Then it subsides, and you say to yourself, *God, Abbie, what the hell was that all about?* And you laugh, a bit shakily maybe, and carry on with your day.

Once you've swept up the fragments of the glass you smashed on the kitchen floor, obviously.

But this wasn't like that. It was cold and hard and it felt like something inside me had become hard and cold too. My heart, I guess. I put the spoon in the dishwasher and wiped up the puddle of coffee, and while I did it I found myself doing sums in my head.

Matt and I had been together for twenty years – that made seven thousand three hundred days. (If you didn't count leap years, obviously, and I wasn't going to do that, mental arithmetic never having been my strong point.) Over the past two decades, the teaspoon thing hadn't always been a thing. We hadn't actually shared a kitchen for all of those years, only for about fourteen of them. So that would have been – what? – about five thousand one hundred days.

Five thousand one hundred teaspoons? Not literally, of course. We only owned about ten of them: a couple left over from the original IKEA cutlery set we'd bought when we first moved in together, a few from the slightly posher set that had been a wedding present from someone, plus a random one that had appeared in the drawer one day and neither of us knew where it had come from.

And the spoon thing couldn't have happened every day. I wouldn't have put up with it in the beginning, surely? And there had been days when Matt hadn't made himself a coffee in the morning – when he'd bought a takeaway cup on his way to work, or when we'd been on holiday, or those few months when he took to drinking green tea instead, and fished the teabag out of the mug with his fingers (and left that next to the sink too).

Still, though. The figures spun pointlessly through my brain – at least two thousand times when I'd picked up the spoon, put it in the dishwasher and wiped the smear of coffee from the worktop. Say it took thirty seconds to carry out the task. That would make a thousand minutes of my life. Sixteen hours – the waking part of an entire day – that wouldn't even have been necessary had my husband just. Put. The. Bloody. Spoons. In. The. Dishwasher.

In the short time it had taken me to clean the coffee smear, and the longer time I'd been wrestling with my mental calculations, something had changed. I took a deep breath and waited, trying to work out what was different. The hard, cold thing inside me seemed to have dissolved, but it hadn't left anything soft and melty in its place.

There was only emptiness. A space where I expected to find the warm, familiar presence of my love for Matt. And with that realisation came a horrible lurch of fear and a feeling of loss so deep and intense I thought I might break into uncontrollable sobs.

I looked down at the cloth in my hand. It was the same square of microfibre towel that had been there a few minutes before – no doubt even the same one I'd used to clean up countless coffee smears before. But it, too, looked different. It was as if the colour had faded, from a rather pleasing vivid raspberry to the washed-out pink that strawberries take on when they've been in the fridge too long and are about to sprout whiskers of mould and need to be thrown away.

I squeezed the scrap of fabric dry, draped it over the curve of the tap and washed my hands. When I turned around to resume the interrupted making of my own coffee, I saw Matt standing there in the kitchen doorway, watching me. His shoulder was propped against the door frame and his head on one side, his right ankle crossed in front of his left. A shaft of sunlight from the window cast the shadow of his cheekbone down over his face but illuminated the white threads that had appeared in his dark hair – sometime; I couldn't remember when I'd noticed them first – and made his hazel eyes glow the same colour as his khaki jumper, only bright instead of shabby. As always, he seemed to be all angles and limbs, awkward as a marionette whose strings had been left slack.

The familiar sight of his face, puzzled, half-smiling, comforted me. He was still Matt, still my husband, still the man I'd loved for so long he was more like a part of me than a separate person.

But... what if he wasn't? What if the shift I'd noticed in my heart hadn't been just a wobble but the beginning of a more fundamental change – or, worse, the end of something?

'You okay, Abs?' he asked. 'You looked kind of weird back there for a second.'

'I'm fine,' I said. And I realised that I was. Or rather, that the disconcerting moment when that question had flashed into my head – *Do I still love my husband?* – and the feeling of chilly emptiness that had followed it didn't feel so strange any more. They'd blurred somehow into the background of my internal landscape, so that I wondered whether, actually, they had been there for a lot longer than I realised.

'What time do we need to head off to this school reunion thing tonight?' I asked.

'About six, I guess. If we're going to get there for drinks at seven like the invitation said. Although I guess we could just...' His words tailed off.

'Sack it off? Pretend one of us is ill?'

'Or just you go, and say I'm ill.'

We looked at each other, complicit in our anticipated guilt.

'We could.'

'But we can't. We're going to have to go.'

'It's a school reunion, after all. There'll be loads of people there who we haven't seen for years.'

Matt shifted position in the doorway and I could read the thought on his face as clearly as if it had passed through my own mind – which, to be honest, it had.

We could have seen them if we'd wanted to. We haven't seen them because we didn't want to.

'Did you see what Rosie Mallet said on the WhatsApp group?' I asked.

'Nah. I've not been reading it. And if I had been, I'd have skipped Rosie Mallet's messages on it.'

I grimaced and he winced in sympathy. I expect every school has a Rosie Mallet: the queen bee, the girl who all the boys want and all the girls want to be – the Lara Croft of the sixth-form common room. Kids had gravitated to her like wasps to honey. Or more like bumblebee to a lime tree – I read recently that the poor bees drink and drink and drink the lime nectar, not knowing that it doesn't have enough sugar in it to sustain them and quite often kills them.

But that was the wisdom of twenty years' hindsight talking. Back when I was seventeen, I'd been as star-struck by Rosie as anyone, as eager to be her friend. It was only some years later that I'd realised what a lucky escape I'd had not being one of the chosen ones.

'She said something like, "Of course, it's Matt and Abbie we all want to see. Still together after all this time – we need to know your secret, guys!" And then she put a load of emojis. One of them was the aubergine.'

Matt laughed. 'Well I'm not going to be getting my dick out for Rosie to admire, don't worry.'

'She'll probably have her tape measure handy just in case you decide to oblige.'

'Christ. Do we really have to go?'

'It's just one night,' I soothed. 'We can leave early. It'll be okay. Chloe's going to be there.'

Matt looked unconvinced. 'With her kids.'

Of course – her perfect children, one of each. I'd seen the photos of them on her social media, blowing out candles on birthday cakes, faces smeared with chocolate, adorable chubby hands reaching out for their mother.

'Yeah, I suppose with her kids. But still, it'll be great to see her.'

To see my old friend, with whom I'd shared packs of chewing gum and mix tapes, confided in about my crush on David Beckham (she'd even spent ages helping me plan Becks' and my wedding, although I'd already been going out with Matt and he'd been married to Posh Spice for two years). Chloe, whose life had diverged so far from my own it was hard to imagine us having anything to say to each other once we'd covered, *Do you remember the time we toasted marshmallows over our Bunsen burners in Chemistry?*

'How about Andy?'

Matt shook his head. 'He's in Manchester this weekend.'

A rare act of self-preservation by Andy. I supposed it was too late for me to book a train ticket and escape up north on some fictional urgent business.

'Oh well. We said yes to the original invitation so I guess we've got to go.'

'We said yes when we thought it probably wouldn't happen.'

'I know. But it is, so we're going.'

'If you say so.' He made a face like the gritted-teeth emoji.

'I suppose I'd better paint my toenails.'

'I guess I should iron a shirt.'

We brushed past each other in the kitchen doorway, but instead of the brief contact turning into an embrace as it would have in the past, and the hug turning into sex as it would have even longer ago, we kind of flinched away from each other. I headed upstairs to the bathroom and heard a thud as Matt folded the ironing board down.

I knew that it would still be there, taking up half of the space between the kitchen worktop and the fridge, when we got back later that night. It would still be there on Monday morning if I didn't put it away, or ask Matt to, earning myself another eye-roll and a 'Fine.'

But that was nothing compared to the marathon task that lay ahead: convincing a group of people we hadn't seen in decades, most of whose opinions we didn't even care about, that everything was fine. That *we* were fine.

CHAPTER TWO

You know how it is with arguments. Sometimes you know that it's going to happen – that *Shit, this thing is getting big now and we're going to have to talk about it and it's going to get messy* feeling. You can spend days waiting for the moment before it comes, while the surface of your relationship remains still and unruffled, the fight gliding along beneath like a shark.

And sometimes it lands out of absolutely nowhere. You're having dinner together or watching a movie or whatever and the other person says something so ridiculously wrong or absurd that you can't let it go. It starts as a light-hearted difference of opinion, but before you know it you're arguing furiously about whether Sean Connery or Daniel Craig was the best James Bond. And then the row segues into something else – like how the other person has always had terrible taste in music, not to mention their snoring driving you wild, and they tell you the way you never, ever close a cupboard door or a drawer is literally like being poked in the eye with a fork every single day. And half an hour later you're staring at the person you love, feeling like a tornado has just ripped through your relationship, and you're thinking, *How the hell did that just happen?*

That's how it was with Matt and me, anyway. And when I mentioned it to my friend Naomi, who'd been with her husband for ages and seemed as happy as can be, she nodded so hard her head almost fell off and said, 'Oh my God, yes, that's exactly what happens.'

So I guess it's not just us. I hope not, anyway.

The fight we had on the way to the school reunion was that kind.

I'd spent ages getting ready – longer even than when Matt and I went out to a posh restaurant for our fifth wedding anniversary. I don't know why it seemed so important that the people we'd been at school with – who I'd barely seen in the intervening years and probably wouldn't see for another ten – should think I looked good, that I'd aged well, but I did. I suppose I was comparing myself not to me on an ordinary day, or even to how I imagined Chloe and Rosie and all the rest of them would look, but to the seventeen-year-old girl I'd been, with my ultra-low bootcut jeans hanging off my slim hips and my washboard stomach, proudly adorned with a diamanté belly-button piercing I had to cover up when I was at home because my mum would freak out if she saw it.

I looked nothing like that now, of course. The hair I used to highlight ash blonde and straighten to within an inch of its life with the GHD irons I'd begged to get for my birthday wouldn't put up with that kind of treatment any more, even if the poker-straight look was still in fashion, and my attempts at natural beachy waves always ended in a frizzy mess. In an attempt to rescue its condition, I'd reverted to my natural mousy light brown, which made me feel plain and nondescript, and the long layers my hairdresser had put in had more than a whiff of Rachel from *Friends* about them. I never seemed to have the cash to invest in lash extensions or have my eyebrows microbladed or even get a proper pedicure in a salon. I told myself that all the other women at the reunion would have had all those things done, even though I should have known it wouldn't be true.

All my dithering in front of the mirror meant we left the flat way later than we should have, especially as a final crisis of confidence led me to abandon my trainers in favour of a pair of wedge espadrilles I hadn't worn for years because the straps rubbed my ankles raw every time I put them on. Matt went from sitting patiently downstairs waiting for me, messing about on his phone, to pacing up and down the way he did when he was anxious about something, occasionally saying, 'It's the three-fifteen train we're getting, right?'

Prompting me to reply, 'I'm being as quick as I can!'

It was almost ten past three when we finally left the house. Matt strode off down the road towards the station and I followed, already cursing my shoes and sweating in my polyester prairie dress, which had looked pretty and boho when I ordered it online but in the flesh made me look like one of the little Gilead girls in *The Handmaid's Tale*.

'You okay, Abbie?' Matt asked over his shoulder as he walked, his long legs taking him along at a pace I had to trot to keep up with.

'Fine,' I said through gritted teeth. If we missed the train, it would unquestionably be my fault, and therefore, we were not going to miss the train, even if it killed me.

We didn't miss the train. We made it with seconds to spare and pushed our way onto a carriage at the back, edging through a crowd of other late people. It was busy – there were spare seats here and there, but no two together. Matt carried on through that carriage and the next, ignoring a pair of seats that looked perfectly acceptable to me, and through into the next. I was falling further and further behind him, but kept going.

At last, after we'd made our way through five compartments, with me wobbling on my heels, my hips knocking into people's shoulders, a wave of tuts following me, Matt sat in a window seat facing the back of the train. I flopped down next to him, out of breath and out of sorts.

'There were loads of seats back there,' I said. 'Why didn't you stop?'

'Because you only like sitting facing the back,' he replied, with the air of a man announcing that the sky was blue.

'Huh?'

'You always want to face the back. Remember that time you made us move when we were on the way to Edinburgh for the festival, even though we'd reserved seats?'

'That was because the man sitting opposite us was eating fish curry, and the smell was making me feel sick.'

He looked at me like I'd just announced that the earth was, in fact, flat. 'No, it wasn't. It was because you wanted to face the other way.'

'Well, that's just what I said to you! I wasn't going to say in front of him that his lunch smelled absolutely bogging, was I?'

'But every time we get on a train together, we face the back. It's what you like.'

I leaned over and eased the strap of my shoe away from my ankle. There was a blister forming there already, and my dress was sticking to my sweaty back.

'Matt, I don't care. Genuinely. I can't believe you've spent years putting yourself out so I can face backwards on the train when I'm not bothered.'

His look told me quite clearly that he disagreed.

'Why are you looking at me like that?'

'I'm not looking at you like anything.'

'You are!' I heard the annoyance in my voice and took a breath, imagining the row hovering over us, its wings flapping in anticipation of the moment when it could descend and ruin our evening. 'I'm sorry. It's just these shoes really hurt and walking the whole way along the train hasn't helped.'

'Why do you wear shoes you can't walk in, anyway?'

'I can walk in them.'

'You just said you couldn't.'

'I didn't – I said they hurt.'

'Well, that doesn't exactly equate to being able to walk in them, does it? That's like saying, "Of course I can sleep perfectly well on this bed of nails."'

'It's not the same at all.'

'Really? How is it different?'

I paused for a second, stumped. How was it different, exactly? Of course, what I should have done was laughed at the misunderstanding and my stupid choice of footwear, and allowed us to move on with the afternoon. But it was already too late – I was angry and I had a blister and the line had well and truly been crossed: we were in Row Territory, our respective armies preparing for battle, even though there'd be no winner and the only casualties would be ourselves.

'Because it's fashion,' I hissed furiously. 'Maybe you don't give a shit what I look like any more, but I do.'

'Of course I give a shit what you look like. But I give more of a shit about you not having sore feet and actually being able to, you know, get from place to place without acquiring welts on your ankles.'

'I'd have been perfectly able to get from place to place if you didn't go so bloody fast.'

'I had to go fast or we'd have missed the train,' he pointed out calmly.

This implacable logic infuriated me. 'There's no need to be so smug about it.'

He looked at me, almost rolled his eyes, then stopped himself. 'I'm not being... Look, Abbie, you're not going to start a row over the shoes that you chose to wear to the event you insisted we go to, are you?'

'No, I'm not, but it looks like you just did.'

Just then, I noticed that the teenage couple in front of us, who until that point had been giggling over a phone's screen, an earbud plugged into each of their ears, their hair mingling as they leaned in close to each other, their hands on each other's thighs, had fallen silent.

The girl looked at the boy, and he looked back at her. There was a moment of connection between them and I knew that they were thinking, *We're never going to be like that. We're never going to become the kind of tragic married couple who have arguments on trains about whether they're having an argument on a train.*

Part of me thought, *Just you wait. Twenty years ago, Matt and I were you two and now look. The real world is out there waiting for you, snowflakes.*

But a bigger part of me just felt suddenly, desperately sad that we had been them and now here we were.

So I said, under my breath, displaying a level of maturity that would have brought shame on the fifteen-year-old girl earwigging on our argument, 'Okay, whatever.'

We spent the rest of the journey, and the Tube journey that followed, and the bus journey after that, in stony silence, communicating only to check that we knew where we were going, and for Matt to ask if my feet were okay and me to say, 'Perfectly fine, thank you.'

And when we got to the reunion, the first thing Rosie said, even before I got a chance to admire her eyelash extensions, was, 'Oh my God, look at you two lovebirds!'

Matt and I got kind of separated after that. Rosie pulled me into a hug (not that we'd ever hugged each other in our lives before) and said I must come and say hi to Amber, who was desperate to see me. I made small talk with the two of them for a few minutes about what a good fundraising idea it was of the school governors, charging fifty quid a ticket and laying on a bouncy castle for the kids, sour pinot grigio for the adults and a fish and chip van owned by one of the dads for the catering.

Just as we were running out of things to say to one another, I spotted Chloe and excused myself, crossing the room to speak to the woman who'd been my best friend for over a year when we were at school.

It had been generous of her, I thought with hindsight, to adopt the new girl the way she had back then. It hadn't occurred to me at the time that she might have been just as lonely and out of place as I was; we'd just kind of slipped into a friendship that had felt close at the time – although nowhere near as close as the romance that had quickly blossomed between Matt and me. But when we'd gone our separate ways to university, we'd lost touch almost immediately, staying in contact only through superficial interactions on social media.

'So,' I said, once I'd admired her children, her squashy cream leather jacket and her husband, who was chatting awkwardly with a group of other plus-ones. 'Weird to be back here after all these years, isn't it?'

'So weird.' Chloe took a gulp of wine. 'And you and Matt, hey? Still together after twenty years.'

'Twenty years,' I agreed. 'Twenty years and two months, to be precise.'

'Twenty years and two months!' Chloe echoed. 'Wow.'

'I was eligible for parole after ten,' I joked, 'but he wouldn't let me out.'

We stood in silence for a second, the awkwardness between us almost palpable. One of Chloe's children came over and tugged at her hand and asked her something, and she responded as if relieved to have a break from talking to me.

'But no kids yet?' she asked, once her son had been supplied with the required cereal bar from her handbag.

'Not yet.' I smiled as widely as I could.

'Enjoy it while you can.' She gave a rather forced laugh. 'They're a blessing, but my God they're hard work.'

'I'm sure they are,' I agreed, leaving her to guess which part of her statement I was agreeing with.

Then she leaned in towards me, her face suddenly serious, the bright social smile slipping away.

'Did you and Matt always know?' she asked. 'Like, from the moment you met? That you'd be together forever?'

'Not exactly. I mean, you remember how I agonised over whether he was even going to ask me out?'

'Did you? You always seemed so sure of him.'

I tried to remember what it had been like. There must have been times when I mooned over the phone in my parents' hallway, wondering when he would call. Moments when he'd seemed aloof or distracted or grumpy, and I'd wondered if it was all about to go wrong. But I couldn't remember them. In my mind, those first months, when we were seventeen and falling madly in love, had been calm, uninterrupted happiness, like a holiday when the sun shines every day.

I said, 'I guess it kind of happened one day at a time. You know how it is. You start going out and then you just... don't stop, and the next thing you know you're married and it's your twenty-year high school reunion.'

Chloe smiled. It seemed more genuine now, although still uncertain. 'Do you mind me asking... Did Matt ever...'

She tailed off, her eyes slipping away from mine like marbles on a glass tabletop.

'Sorry to interrupt you two.' Matt appeared next to me, holding a fresh glass of wine for me.

Then Chloe's son approached her again, announcing in a loud whisper that he needed the toilet.

'Sorry, Abbie. Let me sort this guy out. It's been lovely talking to you.'

Clearly she didn't expect me to wait and find out what she'd been about to ask me next about my relationship.

I took the glass from my husband and sipped the wine. He'd

managed to get hold of something better than the lukewarm, insipid stuff I'd been drinking earlier.

'Thanks. Are you having fun?'

He shrugged. 'It's okay. On a scale of one to ten, one being a root canal and ten a holiday in the Maldives, about a five, I guess.'

'Want to head home?'

'Yeah, I guess. But there's something we should do first.'

'Finish our drinks?'

'Yeah, obviously that. I had to lie to the guy behind the bar and say I supported Manchester United to get that chablis.'

'You're a true hero of our time. Right up there with Nelson Mandela.'

'Aren't I just? And modest about it, too.'

To my relief, the coldness that had been there between us had thawed; it was as if the argument on the train had never happened.

I finished my drink. 'Come on then, let's do this thing. So long as it's not having a shag behind the science lab, like we did at our leavers' ball.'

Matt laughed. 'I'd forgotten about that. Maybe not the smartest move ever.'

'Why not? If we'd been caught we could've said we were working on a practical Biology assignment.' I took his hand and he led me out of the hall and down a corridor. 'Where are we going? Is this where the library is? Or used to be – I guess they might have moved things around a bit.'

'I reckon it might still be there. That's what I wanted us to go and see.'

We kept walking, and I noticed a strange thing. Although – obviously – I'd never, ever worn high heels to school and I was wearing them now, my footsteps on the paved walkway sounded familiar. The air smelled familiar, too, as if years and years of school lunches, mown grass, disinfectant and girls' floral deodorant had permeated the very fabric of the building.

And something in my heart seemed to have travelled back in time, too – like I was seventeen again, walking to the library with Matt, my feelings for him still fresh and unchartered. We'd spent so many afternoons there, across from each other at one of the wooden tables, the smells of dusty books and the ink from our ballpoint pens all around us, our feet brushing against each other occasionally.

Whenever they did, we'd look up, our eyes would meet, and we'd smile.

Now, I found myself smiling too, relishing the warmth of Matt's hand in mine, feeling the familiar rhythm of his body next to mine as we walked in unison.

But Matt stopped suddenly and said, 'Oh. Bloody hell. Look at that.'

Where the library had been, there was a whole new building. A sign above the door said 'Learning Resources Centre'. Where the old wooden tables had been, there were now new, white-topped melamine ones. I remembered the room being in permanent semi-darkness, so we'd had to squint down at the pages of our books; now, expanses of plate-glass windows illuminated it. There were books, still, tidily arranged in shelves along the walls, but there were computer monitors on the desks now, wireless mouses and keyboards and cables snaking down to plug points under the floor.

I blinked, as if I could somehow conjure back the place I'd expected to see. But I couldn't – any more than I could make myself seventeen again, or fall in love for the first time again.

CHAPTER THREE

'So how did your school reunion thing go, Abs?' Kate asked, splashing wine into our four glasses with her usual careless abandon.

'Oh God. It was okay, I guess. I mean, it was interesting to see people, meet their kids and their other halves, stuff like that.' I took a huge gulp of icy sauvignon blanc. 'But Matt and I had a fight on the way, so that made it all a bit awks. Actually, a lot awks.'

Seeing the identical expressions of concerned sadness on my friends' faces made me want to cry, but I swallowed the lump in my throat with more wine.

'Things have been... not great... for a while now, right?' Rowan queried cautiously.

'But you'll get through it, won't you?' said Naomi. 'I mean, it's you and Matt we're talking about here. *You and Matt!*'

'If things don't work out between the two of you, what hope is there for the rest of us?' Kate demanded.

'I don't know.' Miserably, I sank some more wine. I'd considered fronting it out, had even stored up some hilarious anecdotes from the reunion to regale the Girlfriends' Club with (like

Matt's story of the moment when Rosie's five-year-old had asked in ringing tones why Lisa Adams had been nicknamed Death-grip, and the room fell silent as everyone remembered it was because of her alleged hand-job technique). But now I was here, I found I wanted to confide rather than entertain.

These three women were, after all, my closest friends in the world. Seeing Chloe at the reunion the previous Saturday and realising what a huge chasm had opened up between us had reminded me how much I valued Kate, Naomi and Rowan – even though, in the beginning, we hadn't expected to become properly close friends.

It was Kate who'd suggested it, on one of the rare occasions when we'd turned up to watch our boyfriends' Wednesday night five-a-side footie match. She'd been going out with Ryan, Matt's brother, at that stage; Naomi's then-boyfriend, whose name I could barely recall now, had been the goalie; Rowan was engaged to Paul and Zara had been dating Patch. There were a few other guys who'd sometimes turn up for a game, or a few games, or stick around for weeks or months, too, but if they had girlfriends they evidently had better things to do with their mid-week evenings.

Anyway, we'd perched on the sidelines, half-watching our menfolk charging around the floodlit pitch, our hands buried in our pockets and our scarves wound so high we could barely see each other's faces. We'd been introduced to one another, but it was too cold to talk.

A few minutes before half-time, Kate had turned to me and said, 'You know what? This is rubbish, isn't it?'

'Absolute pants,' I agreed through chattering teeth.

'I wouldn't mind the boredom if it wasn't so freezing,' chipped in Naomi.

'And I wouldn't mind being freezing if I wasn't bored shit-less,' agreed Rowan.

Zara must have said something, too – Zara always did.

'You know what? Why don't we sack it off and go to the pub?' Kate suggested.

'That wouldn't be very supportive, would it?' said Rowan, but her grin gave her away.

'They don't need us to support them – they seem to be managing perfectly well out there on their own,' said Naomi.

'Actually, they're four–one down,' I pointed out. 'Ryan just scored an own goal and Patch looks like he's been mud-wrestling.'

'All the more reason to avoid the recriminations afterwards,' said Kate. 'Come on – the Fox and Hounds over the road is meant to be decent.'

'It's got an open fire,' said Rowan.

'And mulled wine,' said Naomi.

That decided us. We hurried away from the pitch and crossed the street, firing off texts to our boyfriends as we walked, giggling like schoolgirls bunking off double maths.

The pub had the advertised open fire, and the mulled wine. Kate bought a jug of it and a few packets of crisps and pork scratchings, and we sat together round a shiny-topped wooden table, carefully ignoring the next-door table of rowdy blokes who looked like estate agents on a lads' night out.

Rowan filled our glasses. I ripped open the bags of snacks. And then silence fell. I realised, looking around the table, that I barely knew these women. Zara, with her brutally short fringe and huge cat-like green eyes, worked in fashion, I remembered Matt saying. Pretty, dark-haired Rowan had mentioned something about being a make-up artist. Kate had said she'd come straight from work, and given she was wearing a seriously gorgeous, expensive-looking suit, work was clearly high-powered.

'So.' Naomi picked a leaf out of her wavy red hair, inspected it briefly, then put it on the table next to the wine. 'You're locked in a shop overnight. What shop would you choose, and why?'

Kate laughed. 'This is like one of those icebreakers at corporate training days. "If you were a chocolate bar…"'

'No, it's way easier than that,' I said. 'I'd pick a bookshop. One with comfy chairs and a café. I'd need loads of coffee because I'd want to get through at least three novels overnight. And there'd be those dome things with cakes under them, and I'd try a bit of each of them, the way you always want to in cafés but can't because they'll think you're a greedy bastard.'

'God, I haven't read a book in ages,' Rowan said. 'I'd pick Selfridges, all the way. Or maybe Harvey Nicks. I'd try on all the designer clothes I could never, ever afford in a million years and then I'd put on a silk nightie, spray on a load of Flowerbomb and go to sleep on one of those squashy sofas they have in the personal shopping bit.'

'I'd pick a luxury car showroom.' Zara sounded as if she wasn't considering this for the first time. 'Okay, it wouldn't be the most comfortable night ever. But in the morning when they opened up I'd be in floods of tears and they'd give me the keys to a Porsche in return for not suing the pants off them.'

'Am I allowed to pick a bed shop or is that cheating?' Kate asked. 'I have the most horrible insomnia and I'd basically spend the night trying out all the beds until I found one that worked, and then in the morning I'd buy it and sleep brilliantly for the rest of my life.'

We all looked expectantly at Naomi.

'I can't believe no one's said IKEA!' she said. 'I mean, how could you not want to spend the night in there, in one of the tiny apartments they've got set up, imagining your life being all perfect and scaled-down and Swedish? I'm not sure I can be friends with you guys.'

We all dissolved into laughter, and I realised that the magic had happened – we were friends already.

After that, we began meeting up on occasional Wednesdays while the men were playing, then for a while it was every Wednesday, then eventually we'd settled on the first Wednesday of the month, and that had stuck. Over the years, the other relationships had ended and shifted, until Matt and I were the only one of the original couples still together. The guys who played in the team came and went. For a while, Andy, who Matt had introduced to his footie mate Grant, had joined the group, declaring himself an honorary girlfriend. But, as was usually the case with Andy, neither the romance with Grant nor the honorary membership of the Girlfriends' Club had lasted. There was only one relationship in his life Andy took truly seriously, and it wasn't with a person.

We didn't really see Zara any more; she'd moved to Paris a few years back and we all kind of lost touch. But otherwise, here we were, with more than ten years' worth of water under the bridge, closer than ever. When Rowan's daughter Clara had broken her wrist in a school gymnastics competition, it was Naomi who'd driven her to the hospital. When Naomi's twins were born, we'd descended en masse to see them. When Kate got her latest shiny new job, we sent her flowers and champagne to celebrate. It felt like we'd shared each significant moment of the intervening years with each other.

And now, I found myself wondering, with a lurching feeling in my stomach like descending thirty floors in a lift, whether the end of my marriage was going to be the latest in the series.

'You really love each other, though, don't you?' Rowan's eyes were full of concern. Of all of us, she believed most fervently in the idea of fairy-tale romance, even though she'd been single for the longest. Or perhaps, now I thought about it, *because* she'd been single for the longest.

'All relationships go through rough patches,' Naomi said. 'Patches – ha, see what I did there? Patch and I could hardly bear to look at each other for about a year after Toby and

Meredith were born. We were both just so knackered, I think it sent us a bit loopy. I honestly didn't think we'd get through it.'

'What is it with you and Matt, anyway, Abs?' Kate asked. 'I mean, I know you've had issues, but you were working through them, right?'

'It's not just that.' My words came out slowly, as if I was thinking aloud, which I suppose I was. Often, being with the Girlfriends' Club made me feel like I was conducting an internal dialogue with a wiser, funnier, kinder version of myself. 'It's like... we can't talk to each other any more, or not like we used to. We argue way more than we ever did before. I almost feel like I don't want to talk to him, because it'll end up in an argument.'

'Both of you working from home can't help,' Naomi said. 'Being around each other all the time. You need space from each other, otherwise there's no mystery left.'

'Once Paul had seen me push a baby out of my chuff, I think that was game over for our mystery,' Rowan interjected.

'Yet another reason to be glad I had a C-section,' remarked Naomi. 'My vagina's honeymoon-fresh. At least that's what the obstetrician said.'

'Honeymoon-what?' Kate demanded. 'That's the most misogynistic thing I ever— but anyway, we're talking about Abbie here.'

'Believe me, after twenty years there wasn't a whole lot of mystery anyway. But yes, being together twenty-four-seven isn't helping.'

I thought of telling them about my epiphany over the coffee spoon, but hesitated. The strength of feeling it had unleashed in me still scared me when I looked back on it.

'What happens when you think back on what first attracted you to him?' Rowan pushed a wing of dark brown hair behind her ear. 'What made you fall in love with him in the first place? Is that stuff still there?'

'Yeeesss, I guess so. He's still the kindest man I've ever known. I mean, he's inconsiderate sometimes, but isn't everyone?'

Again, I thought of the spoon, and my reaction.

As if she'd read my mind, Naomi said, 'Patch leaves his clothes on the bathroom floor every. Single. Day. Honestly, the white-hot rage it gives me is scary. I'm like, "Patrick, I have two children to look after in this house and they are more than I can handle. I really don't need a third. Just use the damn laundry basket." And he looks like a little kicked puppy and says he's sorry and then I spend the next hour feeling guilty, because he's an amazing dad and he does do loads, and then I feel cross with myself for feeling guilty because, seriously, how long does it take to pick up your clothes?'

'And then the next day he does it again?' Kate said, gesturing to the waitress for a bottle of wine. It was our third, I reckoned, although it might have been our fourth.

'Rinse and repeat,' Naomi confirmed.

'Honestly, it makes me feel so ecstatically happy to be single,' Kate said. 'Doesn't it you, Ro?'

Rowan nodded, but she didn't look convinced. 'Maybe you need to do something to, like, rekindle the spark, Abs.'

'Like what?' I asked. 'Weekly date nights, that kind of thing? We tried that a while back, but it just ended up being the same as every other night, only in a restaurant instead of at home.'

'What do you actually enjoy doing together?' Rowan pressed. 'Do more of that.'

'We like going for walks,' I said. 'I know, rock and roll. But we do. Get our Zimmer frames out and off we totter together.'

Kate laughed. 'Give over, you're only thirty-seven.'

I sighed, tipped the last of the wine in my glass into my mouth and splashed the rest of the bottle into our four glasses.

'It'll be okay, I think. I hope so, anyway. I'm sure it's just a phase. Just – you know – one of those things.'

'I'm sure it is.' Rowan reached over and gave my hand a little squeeze. 'You two – you're like the ultimate love story.'

'Romeo and Juliet, only without the poison and the dagger and the hapless priest,' said Naomi.

'I mean, didn't you say that right from the moment you met, you knew he was the guy for you?' said Kate.

'How did you meet, anyway?' asked Rowan. 'I know it was at school, but did he copy your French translations from the next-door desk or pull up your skirt with his hockey stick or poke you with a compass or what? Go on, indulge me – I love a good meet-cute.'

'I can't believe Abbie hasn't told you this story. How did you miss it?' Kate asked.

'It's not that romantic really,' I said. 'He saved me from a pigeon.'

SPRING 2001
WHOLE AGAIN

Starting at a new sixth-form college halfway through the year wasn't ideal. Even Abbie's mum had acknowledged that. 'Not ideal' – that was the phrase she used. Shortly followed by, 'But you'll cope. You'll thrive. You always do.'

Abbie wasn't so sure. At her school in Manchester, she'd had a small but close group of friends, the drama club that she enjoyed without excelling at, and a few boys she fancied without any of them threatening the special place David Beckham had in her heart. It was all familiar and safe and she'd imagined it wouldn't change until the inevitable, massive upheaval of leaving school for university happened.

But now, her dad had got a new job in That London, and her mum had found a house in an area that was in a catchment for a Very Good School, one that had a reputation for small class sizes and individualised teaching. Abbie didn't give a monkey's about all that. She just wanted to fade into the background – but clearly, as a new girl in a small year group, backgrounds weren't for the likes of her.

On her first day, she'd hovered in front of the mirror on the landing at home, trying to convince herself that her knee-length skirt, her neatly tied-back hair and her tidily pulled-up socks would render her if not invisible, at least unnoticeable.

But as soon as she arrived at the bus stop, she realised the extent of her error.

Plugged into Sony Walkmans, their skirts rolled up almost to crotch level, their sheets of hair held back from their faces by only a couple of insecurely placed grips, the other girls weren't playing it safe. Not one bit.

And the boys, lounging against the walls of the bus shelter (why did it never seem to rain here?), were more intimidating still. One fair-haired lad was positively peacocking around, surrounded by a cluster of admirers, all laughing uproariously at some joke he'd just cracked, which Abbie had heard but not understood.

Desperately trying to disappear, Abbie perched on the bench in the bus shelter and rummaged in her school bag. She definitely wasn't watching the group of her soon-to-be school-mates – not the blond boy, whose tie was loosened to half-mast and who was talking loudly about Carrie's shoes on *Sex and the City*; not the girl with glossy red hair and a perfect smattering of freckles, who was handing her friend a tampon like it was the most normal thing to do, even right there in the street; not the tall, gangly boy with floppy almost-black hair who was hovering on the outskirts of the group, watching them with wry amusement. She was looking in her bag for something very important.

But what?

She couldn't just rummage and then stop rummaging. That would look weird. She also couldn't carry on rummaging indefinitely – that would look even weirder.

'Frigging bus, why is it always late on a Wednesday when I've got chemistry with Mr Lucas?' complained the red-haired girl.

'Chemistry with Mr Lucas?' echoed the blond boy. 'We never knew you felt that way, Rosie.'

'He meets her eyes over the graduated cylinder and her ovaries do the cha-cha slide,' said Rosie's friend, and they all dissolved into gales of laughter.

Even though, objectively, Abbie knew no one was looking at her – no one even cared; they were all too busy showing off to one another to pay her any attention – she felt as if a spotlight was arcing through the sky above them, and might at any moment settle on her, making her the focus of the banter. If that happened, she might literally die.

She kept her eyes focused rigidly on her bag and the ground between her feet, and a pigeon came into view, strutting along the pavement, its head bobbing and its eyes bright, with dusty grey feathers and a slightly deformed left foot.

In her bag, her hand found the plastic box with her lunch in it – a peanut butter sandwich, which she'd hastily slapped together that morning, knowing she wouldn't be able to face lunch in the canteen. She prised open the box, tore off a corner of crust and offered it to the bird, wondering too late whether feeding a feral London pigeon might mark her out as the weirdest person ever. It snapped the morsel up into its beak, retreated to a safe distance and pecked away contentedly until the food was gone – and the bus arrived without anyone commenting on her, her sandwich or the pigeon.

The day improved after that. In English Literature, she sat next to a girl called Chloe, who seemed friendly. She wasn't behind in any of her lessons. She ate her lunch alone, but that was expected – a relief, even. She noticed the tall dark boy looking at her and exchanged a smile with him. She found out his name was Matt – but then, half the school seemed to be called Matt, as if it was another in-joke she didn't understand.

At home that night, she stood in front of the mirror again and experimented with rolling her skirt up to mid-thigh, until her mother spotted her and said, 'Not on my watch you don't, missy.'

So the next day Abbie waited until she'd left the house to hitch it up to almost knicker-exposing levels.

At the bus stop, the same crowd was waiting. Rosie was there, and her friend, who was called Amber, and blond Andy with his endless stream of obscure in-jokes, and tall Matt, or Tall Matt, as Abbie had learned to think of him.

And the pigeon.

As she had the previous day, Abbie perched silently on the bench, letting the flood of chatter wash over her. She felt less like disappearing than she had the day before, but still nowhere nearly confident enough to join in. She didn't have a Walkman of her own – it had been that or hair straighteners for her last birthday, and the GHDs had won the day – so she couldn't lose herself in Hear'Say. Instead, she found herself digging through her school bag again, and again breaking off a crust of her sandwich to give to the bird with the deformed claw.

Abbie wondered if it knew that it looked different from the other birds – if it was glad its feathers were such a nondescript grey, so its gnarled claw would be less likely to be noticed. And then she told herself not to be ridiculous – what was she even doing, inventing some absurd co-dependent relationship in her head with a bloody pigeon?

But the following day, even though Rosie looked at her when she arrived at the bus stop and said, 'Oh, hi,' and Tall Matt gave her another of those smiles that seemed almost too wide for his thin face, she was relieved to see the pigeon there again, and happy to give it what she'd come to think of as its share of her lunch.

She'd never much liked eating crusts, anyway.

But this time, the bird didn't carry its treasure off to devour at a safe distance. It stayed there by her feet, pecking happily away, and Abbie watched it, enchanted. Maybe she had some mysterious power over animals. Maybe she'd become a vet. Or maybe pigs would fly – she'd only just passed her Biology

GCSE and immediately given up the subject, relieved she'd never again have to think about the anatomy of the earthworm or the role of the vas deferens in human reproduction (which frankly was enough to put anyone off the idea for life).

Still though, it was nice to improve the tough life of a city pigeon in some small way. Maybe she could volunteer at an animal shelter and meet a man with kind eyes who'd fall in love with her, and eventually they'd buy a cottage in the countryside and keep rescued ex-battery chickens in the back garden.

She was still lost in her dream when the bus pulled up, and she barely noticed Andy, Rosie and the rest of them jostling their way on board. Just in time, she sprang to her feet and jumped through the doors, which snapped closed behind her.

She was halfway up the stairs before she realised the pigeon had followed her. It half-jumped, half-flew up each step, close on her heels, looking perfectly at home, as if it rode the bus every day of its life.

But Abbie was mortified. Feeding a pigeon was one thing – it was only mildly eccentric behaviour – but having a pigeon literally stalk her was something else entirely.

The top deck of the bus was full – there was only one seat left, right at the back, next to Tall Matt. Feeling her face flame, Abbie made her way down the aisle towards it, the pigeon following closely at her heels.

'Well, look who's here,' Andy observed. 'If it isn't our own Doctor Dolittle.'

Rosie and Amber stopped singing Atomic Kitten (except they changed the lyric to 'You can lick my hole again', which they thought was the most hilarious thing ever) and started singing the song from *Mary Poppins* about the old lady who fed the birds on the steps of St Paul's.

Abbie knew that this was a crisis point. Either she needed to find some way to style it out – and fast – or it would be social death. These people would laugh at her *every day* for the next year and a half. No boy would ever ask her out. Even Chloe wouldn't want to be friends with someone whose nickname was Tuppence.

But she had no idea what styling it out would look like. She stood there, looking down at Tall Matt, gripping the back of the next-door seat, paralysed with awkwardness.

And then the pigeon crapped all over the floor of the bus.

'Oh my God!' Amber snatched up her bag.

'That is so gross.' Rosie tucked her feet up on the seat, her slender legs bending at an acute angle and her skirt slipping so Abbie could have seen her knickers if she'd wanted to look.

'You know, they're riddled with parasites,' Andy remarked. 'Ticks, lice, red blood mites.'

At least someone had been concentrating in Biology, Abbie thought fleetingly.

'Oh my God!' Rosie snatched her blazer from around her waist and flapped it at the pigeon. 'Get away from us! Disgusting thing.'

Panicked, the pigeon took off, flapped briefly against the roof of the bus, and then descended again, a few feet away from Abbie. It stared at her, and she was sure she could see fear in its beady eyes, as if it was thinking, *This is all your fault.*

This is all your *fault*, Abbie thought back fiercely.

'We'd better get rid of it then.' Matt stood up, so tall he had to duck his head.

For a second Abbie imagined that he might be about to make a grab for the bird and wring its neck, or something awful like that. If that happened she would never, ever be able to show her face on the bus again. She'd have to move schools, or bunk off every day and sit in a park, or run away and join the circus.

'Come on.' Impatiently, Matt held out his hand to Abbie. 'Gimme your sandwich. Seems your mate likes peanut butter.'

Abbie fumbled frantically in her bag, found the plastic box and wrestled with its lid.

'Hurry,' Matt said. 'We're almost at the next stop.'

With sweating hands, she handed him the sandwich and flopped bonelessly into the seat he'd vacated.

They watched as Matt made his way back towards the stairs, sprinkling crumbs behind him, the pigeon following. The two of them disappeared out of sight just as the bus jerked to a stop.

A few seconds later, Matt was back, looking smug and brushing crumbs off his hands on his trouser legs. An ironic cheer went up from the bus passengers.

'There,' he said. 'Nothing to it.'

'Did you get him out?' Abbie asked.

'He flew straight out of the door as soon as it opened.'

Abbie breathed a silent prayer of thanks. 'Do you think he'll be okay? I mean, will he find his way back?'

'Abbie.' Matt sat down next to her, as if it was the most natural thing in the world. 'Have you never heard of a homing pigeon?'

Of course she had. Abbie felt her face turn scarlet again, and then noticed that Matt was smiling at her.

'Thanks,' she said.

'You're welcome. Sorry about your lunch.'

Abbie didn't know how she knew, but she was sure that, after that, everything would be all right. Things settled into a rhythm: the pigeon was still there at the bus stop most mornings, and she still fed it crusts of bread, but it never tried to stow away on the bus again. Amber, Rosie and Andy seemed to tolerate her, even though she doubted they'd ever be close friends. Chloe asked her to go for McDonald's and a movie on a Saturday afternoon.

And Matt started walking home with Abbie most days after school, even though the bus was quicker and they didn't really live in the same direction. They chatted, laughed together, developed private jokes of their own. Matt even gave her a mix CD he'd recorded for her.

And one day, he asked, casually as anything, 'You coming to Andy's party tomorrow night?'

'I don't know,' Abbie said. 'Am I?'

'Yeah, I guess you are.'

And again, Abbie didn't know how, but she knew that would be the night they first kissed.

CHAPTER FOUR

'There's no hangover like a Girlfriends' Club hangover,' Kate once remarked darkly, after one particularly epic night when we'd moved from pisco sours to prosecco to espresso martinis, and then still thought it was a good idea to buy cans of gin and tonic to keep us refreshed on the train home.

As I opened my eyes, cautiously so I could gauge whether the morning sun would feel like an axe hitting my brain or just like the light that blinds you in the dentist's chair, her words haunted me. The previous night had been a heavy one, no doubt about it, but the signs were positive so far: my hangover was definitely bad, but it wasn't cripplingly bad. Possibly, for once, the doner kebabs we'd bought and eaten in the street like feral students hadn't been such a terrible idea.

I turned over in bed, relieved to notice that although my stomach lurched a bit, it didn't actively churn like I was on one of those spinning fairground rides.

Matt's side of the bed was empty; I could hear the shower running and his tuneless singing. When he sang in the shower, it meant he was happy. I strained my ears to make out the tune

– it was familiar, but not one he sang often. I could barely make out any words, but one of them, surely, was 'tuppence'.

I listened harder. Yes, it definitely was. I felt a strange twist in my heart that was a mixture of sadness and happiness as I realised he was singing the song from *Mary Poppins* about the old lady who sold breadcrumbs for the pigeons at St Paul's.

How random. Maybe I was singing it when I got home last night. I hoped not – pity the poor Uber driver if so. Or maybe Matt had just coincidentally, even subconsciously, also been recalling that day on the bus all those years ago.

I picked up my phone from the bedside table. I'd remembered to plug it in to charge, so I couldn't have been all that pissed. Positively virtuous, by Girlfriends' Club standards. I rubbed my eye and there was no black smear of mascara on my finger, so I must have taken off my make-up too.

Smashing it, Abbie, I told myself. Top self-preservation skills, right there.

Feeling almost cheery, I swiped my phone to life.

The Girlfriends' Club WhatsApp group was abuzz with new messages.

Naomi: Morning, campers, how are the heads? Kids didn't sleep. Again. I think I got about 45 minutes and I feel like someone's been sandpapering my eyeballs.

Kate: I was feeling like a crock of shit when I woke up, but a legs session with my trainer sorted me right out. I'm in the office already, two coffees and a bacon muffin down.

Rowan: Great thing about teenagers is they don't wake you up. Bad thing is you're expected to wake them. Clara's late for school and she's forgotten her phone and obviously this is all my fault. No work until this afternoon though, thank fuck.

Me: Not too awful actually. I didn't cry last night, did I?

Kate: You didn't cry. You sang, though.

Naomi: That 'Feed the Birds' song, and then 'Yellow' by Coldplay.

Oh God. Sorry, Uber driver.

Me: Shit. Sorry, guys.

Kate: That's okay. You were really sweet actually.

Rowan: You know, I was thinking. This is going to sound completely crazy but hear me out.

There was an expectant pause on the group. We could all see that Rowan was typing. I wondered whether I could quickly get up and have a wee, and maybe persuade Matt to make me a coffee – he'd finished in the bathroom and I could hear him crashing about in the kitchen. I braced myself mentally for the inevitable teaspoon-next-to-the-sink moment that lay in my not-too-distant future.

But before I could lever myself out of bed, Rowan's message popped up on my screen. She must have written it at warp speed.

Rowan: You and Matt. I mean, you and Matt, right? You two are made for each other. You've been so happy together. Just the way you looked last night when you were talking about him, Abs – you didn't cry but I almost did. We all so want you guys to be okay. And I've had an idea.

There was another short pause before her next message appeared.

Rowan: What if you did more stuff like the school reunion? I mean, I know that was crap but you could do other stuff that wouldn't be. Like going on that same bus journey you went on, with the pigeon?

Me: Ro, I think that pigeon's long gone to the big pavement pizza in the sky.

Rowan: Not that pigeon! But you could, like, go and feed the pigeons in Trafalgar Square. You could even make a peanut butter sandwich. It would be so romantic.

Kate: You're not allowed to feed the pigeons in Trafalgar Square any more, babe. There are signs up about it and everything.

Naomi: Because if people feed them they overbreed and then they have to get some dude with a hawk to come and take them out.

Me: I wouldn't want to be responsible for some brutal pigeon genocide.

Rowan: Oh, for God's sake! I've eaten bagels with more sense of romance than you lot. Maybe not the pigeons, then. But other stuff. Like that party you went to at Andy's parents' house – could you go back there? Revisit the scene of your first kiss?

Kate: Andy's mum and dad sold their house when they lost all their money in the financial crash in 2008, remember?

Naomi: I see what you mean, though, Ro. Think about it, Abbie. You must have had a proper first date together, right? First time you shagged? Your first Christmas together? All that stuff – relive the moments and rekindle the spark!

Me: I'm not sure I want to relive the first time we shagged.

Rowan: Come on! I bet it was amazing.

Naomi: Please don't tell us about it now though. After bugger-all sleep and two shitty nappies I never want to think about having sex again.

Me: Ahaha – don't worry, no details. We were on holiday in Cornwall with his mum and dad – cringe!

Kate: Okay, maybe that's a bit ambitious. But how about the other stuff?

Me: I think our first date was probably Burger King or something.

Kate: Maybe not ambitious enough!

Me: We used to go for walks together, when we moved into our first flat. We were so skint we couldn't afford to go out, so that was our thing a couple of nights a week – a walk and a pint in the pub after.

Rowan: Hmmm. Not quite what I had in mind but whatever works for you.

Me: I mean, we're all about the rock 'n' roll lifestyle. When we weren't trashing hotel rooms and drinking tequila out of the bottle, we went for walks.

Naomi: Nothing wrong with walks. When the twins were tiny I used to walk with them in their buggy the whole time because it was the only way to get them to sleep. Shame it doesn't work any more.

Me: Okay, I'll do it. Watch this space.

A selection of emojis (including the dancing lady from Rowan and a Halloween pumpkin from Naomi, although that made no sense and I guessed she must've sent it by mistake) and kisses followed, and I imagined my friends putting down their phones, turning to their laptops and getting on with their days.

I supposed I'd better do the same.

I levered myself out of bed and went to the bathroom. There didn't seem much point in having a shower so I cleaned my teeth, washed my face and pulled my hair back into a ponytail. I remembered when I used to make an effort getting ready for work in the mornings: styling my hair, getting dressed in a carefully chosen outfit that conveyed the right mix of creative and professional, tucking my keys, phone, purse and make-up bag into my beloved Rag & Bone bag, which Matt had saved up for months to buy me for Christmas, kissing him goodbye and leaving the house.

Now, going to work consisted of putting on a clean top over my pyjama bottoms and going downstairs. Sometimes, if I had a client meeting, I'd even wear a bra.

When I got downstairs, my husband was already at his desk – or at least, at the side of our kitchen table that did duty as a desk. It would have made more sense for one of us to work from the second bedroom, but we'd never discussed doing that – it just felt wrong, somehow. That room had never been intended to be a space where people worked. It was meant to be for something altogether different.

So opposite ends of the table it was. Matt glanced up from his screen when he heard me and gave a half-wave, followed by the gesture that meant he was on a call – which in turn meant that I would have to wait to make the coffee and toast that felt like the only thing that would get me through the next hour, so as not to be pottering about in the background of his video meeting.

Stomach grumbling, I pulled out my chair and sat down, feeling the familiar pressure of the wood on my bottom. It was mildly uncomfortable now; by the end of the day I'd feel like I'd been given six of the best by a sadistic headmaster.

It was only a few minutes after nine, and I wasn't due to start work until nine thirty but, my coffee plans on hold for the moment, I opened my email and launched Zoom. Seconds later, my laptop pinged with an incoming call.

'Morning, Marc.' I forced a note of bright efficiency into my voice, slotting my earbuds in as I spoke.

'Jesus Christ, Abbie. You look like shit.' The creative director of Cardew Henderson prided himself on speaking as he found. 'Were you out with your coven last night? Falling out of some dodgy bar at three in the morning and vomiting on the pavement? Leaving your shoes in a taxi? Hmmm?'

'I had a few drinks with the girls, yes,' I admitted frostily.

'Well, you'd better get some slap on before the meeting with the Talon client and their branding agency. I can't have our senior copywriter looking like she's been indulging in the client's product all night.'

I resisted the urge to say that, when a case of Talon, our newest client's hard seltzer, had been delivered to my home a few months back, the first taste had transported me back so vividly to being sick after too much Smirnoff Ice twenty years ago, I'd never opened another one. The remainder of the case was still languishing in the cupboard under the kitchen sink, because it had brought back similar memories in Matt.

And then there was the box of period pants I'd taken delivery of from another new client, which were similarly languishing, this time in the bathroom, because I couldn't quite summon up the confidence to wear them, even when I was sitting at home almost all the time.

It was okay, though. I could write about how they made women feel confident, even if I felt nothing like that myself.

'I'll be prepared for the meeting, don't worry,' I said.

'Well.' Marc sounded only partially mollified. 'I actually wanted to ask you to call Bastian and tell him to get the art guys working on that presentation, stat. Right now it looks like a ten-year-old on glue put it together, and there are typos on every second slide.'

I tried hard not to roll my eyes. 'I'll speak to him – and proofread everything before the meeting.'

Marc gave a grunt that I decided to assume passed as a thank you. Then he said, 'Hold on, Bastian wants a call. Now. You and me.'

'Uh, right, okay. Be there in a second.'

The prospect of toast becoming more distant by the moment, I left my call with Marc and waited for Bastian to invite me to the next one. This was shaping up to be one of those days, I realised.

Well, another of those days, strictly speaking.

When I'd first accepted the job as senior copywriter at Cardew Henderson, a more prestigious advertising agency than the one that had employed me previously, I'd anticipated that my job would require me to be as the person specification had said: someone who was calm under pressure and could produce slick, compelling copy to tight deadlines while being the lead point of contact for clients where necessary. I hadn't expected that the office would be shut for months on end while the company shifted to hybrid working; or that Marc and Bastian would spend as much time squabbling with each other as they spent doing their jobs; or that the hustle of bringing new clients on board for campaigns that needed to be orchestrated on vanishingly tight schedules would leave me so muddle-headed with stress I'd once catch myself describing a cherry-flavoured alcoholic drink as 'revolutionising your period' and reusable sanitary protection as 'the most fun you'll have with your clothes on'.

But I had no time to muse. A notification popped up on my screen, and seconds later so did Marc and Bastian's faces with their almost identical spade-shaped beards and thick-framed glasses. Behind Marc was a series of cubes filled with bottles of wine; behind Bastian a steel-framed door looking out into an elegantly minimalist garden.

Except I knew that in reality, like me and Matt, they were actually at opposite ends of their kitchen table.

'I've got news, kids,' Bastian said. As managing director of the agency, bringing in new business was his main remit, and good news from him meant bad news for me. 'We landed the Quim account!'

'The what now?' Marc asked, although I assumed he must have been privy to the pitch and the subsequent negotiations as Bastian conducted them, from his vantage point in the same room.

'Quim. It's a new sex toy e-tailer,' Bastian explained. 'The website's due to go live in late November, to capture the Christmas and VD market. It's—'

'Wait, what?' Marc cut in. 'VD? Are they selling sex toys or clap medication?'

'Not clap, you idiot. Valentine's Day. You know, when couples express their deep and undying love for each other. Happens on the fourteenth of February, I'm told.'

'What, deep and undying love does? I must have missed it this year. Anyway, what did you say this outfit's called? Cum? Isn't that going to mess with their search-engine optimisation something dreadful?'

'God, you just don't pay attention, do you? Not cum. Quim. It means... I'm sure Abbie will be able to enlighten you.'

It wasn't the first time he'd thrown a curveball like that. Just a few months ago, when we'd first landed the Talon gig, I'd had to mute myself while I frantically googled what the hell yuzu was meant to taste like.

But this time, thanks to a medieval literature module during my long-ago English Literature degree, I was on firmer ground.

'Quim is an archaic term for... well, female genitalia,' I said.

'Oh right,' Marc said. 'Gotcha.'

'Their logo is a stylised apple slice,' Bastian went on. 'The pip's meant to represent the clit. They had to explain that to me, too, on account of my never having seen a clit.'

'Me neither,' said Marc. 'I mean, seriously. Eeeuuw.'

Bastian nodded his agreement. 'Which is where you come in, Abbie.'

I didn't point out that I hadn't seen that many clits myself – any, really, because I wasn't in the habit of gazing at my own with the aid of a hand mirror.

'We'll be writing copy for the website?' I asked.

'Correct,' Bastian replied. 'Copy, product descriptions, the lot. They'll be sending some product to your home address to help get you in the zone, and there's a spreadsheet listing everything, which I'll email over.'

'So get your sex goddess on, Abbie.' On my screen, I saw a grin spread across Marc's face. 'You're going to be needing it.'

'Just so's you know,' Bastian said, 'the launch is going to be all about celebrating the new hedonism, while harking back to the glory days of the 2000s. You know, sexual freedom, body positivity, all that.'

If I remember correctly, body positivity back then was about as much of a thing as fat rolls on Kate Moss, I thought.

'Great stuff,' Marc enthused. 'I bet Abbie can't wait to get her head around it. Right, gotta go. We've got another meeting.'

Their faces froze, then flicked into blankness, and I was left staring at my screen, equally blankly.

Then I looked around my kitchen, noticing the crack in the plaster we hadn't been able to find anyone to come out and fix, the cobweb in the corner I forgot about whenever I got the feather duster out, and Matt's teaspoon next to the sink. I wondered if I'd ever buy a bra with lace on it again, or dance in a club until after midnight. I wondered whether eating digestive biscuits in bed counted as hedonism, and whether 'sexual freedom' included the freedom not to be arsed to have sex.

Whatever the new roaring twenties were, I thought gloomily, they had yet to make an appearance in my life, and my own twenties – whether roaring or not – felt like the distant past. When it came to my body, I was about as positive as a pregnancy test with just one, lonely line on it.

And as for my inner sex goddess, she'd been AWOL for a lot longer than I cared to remember.

At five thirty, after spending the afternoon cringing as I researched rival 'adult' online retailers, with offerings ranging from feather ticklers to full-on rubber gimp suits, I logged off, stood up, stretched and looked out of the window. The view of our garden was the same as always: the parched square of lawn, the barbecue that was still full of spent coals from last summer, the apricot-coloured rose bush that bloomed in glorious profusion year after year, despite our neglect.

Shame our marriage doesn't do that, I thought, with a pang of sadness so powerful it squeezed my stomach.

I heard the snap of Matt's laptop closing and the scrape of

his chair, and turned to see him stand and stretch just like I'd done, only higher, his hand sending the pendant light swinging wildly. I imagined the evening progressing as our evenings always did: Matt slouching over to the sofa and flicking on the telly, me messaging my friends on WhatsApp to hear about the progress of their hangovers and the minutiae of their days, me heading upstairs for a shower, one of us throwing together a meal from whatever we could find in the fridge.

And I heard my voice say, loud in the silence now the tapping of our keyboards and the murmur of our voices on calls was stilled, 'Fancy going for a walk?'

SPRING 2001
BREATHLESS

It was the smell of smoke that woke Abbie from a confused dream that the house was on fire and she needed to get her mum and dad out safely, but she couldn't because every time she opened a door or turned down a passageway, Matt was there and his smile distracted her from the urgency of her plight. But all the time, the smell kept getting stronger and stronger, her movements more and more urgent, until at last her eyes pinged open and she realised it was her own hair she was smelling, saturated with the clouds of cigarette smoke that had filled Andy's parents' living room the previous night.

She turned over in bed, the wisps of the dream fading away even as the smell hung around. Her mouth tasted of sour alcopop, and there was another unfamiliar smell clinging to her – something pleasantly sharp and bitter. It reminded her of someone – of Matt.

And then she remembered the kiss. At once her whole body grew still and she lay on her back, eyes closed again, letting every second of the previous night replay in her mind. She could almost feel his lips on hers, his arms around her, the smell of him – that must be the other scent she had noticed: the aftershave he'd been wearing, spicy and a bit fruity, like a sexy Christmas pudding. She could still hear the fountain splashing, Coldplay on the stereo, Matt's breath as he broke off the kiss to smile down at her, before kissing her again, on and on.

Her whole body felt replete with happiness and remembered pleasure. She prayed that she'd be able to recall every detail, every moment of it, as clearly as she could now, forever.

And then she thought, *Maybe there'll be another kiss?*

The idea was enough to make her sit upright, eyes wide. The previous night, she had been so ecstatically in the moment that it hadn't crossed her mind that this might be the beginning of something – or the end, just a one-off snog at a party. Or worse – that Matt might say things about her, that she was easy, that she was a bad kisser, that there was something horribly wrong with her that she'd never known about, but now Matt did and so would everyone at school.

Chilled at the prospect, she jumped out of bed and hurried to the bathroom. Much as she longed for the scent of Matt to cling to her forever, the smell of smoke had to go. She'd never tried a cigarette and the last thing she needed was a lecture from her mum she hadn't even earned.

She cleaned her teeth and showered, then pulled on her dressing gown and padded downstairs to the kitchen, suddenly ravenous. She could smell roasting beef, but she knew lunch wouldn't be ready for hours, so she raided the bread bin and cut four slices of fresh white bread, so thick she had to squash them into the toaster. She spread them with butter and strawberry jam, piled them onto a plate and returned to her bedroom with a mug of strong, milky tea, longing to be alone again with the CD Matt had burned for her and her memories of every moment they'd spent together – but especially the night before – burned as clearly on her memory, destined to be replayed as often.

By the evening, her rapture had faded. She'd gone through

agonies of excitement and doubt every time she heard footsteps outside, wondering if it might be Matt, because he didn't have her parents' phone number and neither of them had mobiles. She'd had a recap call with Chloe, during which she'd been able to reveal almost nothing that had happened because her parents were in the next-door room watching the Grand Prix on television. She'd played Matt's CD and her own Coldplay one so often the lyrics were beginning to lose their potency.

And the next day, she'd come face to face with him and then she'd know.

She walked to the bus stop on Monday morning, avid to see Matt but also braced for the worst: the humiliation of him blanking her, of the other kids mocking her because they knew what had happened. But Matt behaved just the same as always, coming to sit next to her, feeding the pigeon with her, chatting to her about the party and the new band he'd discovered. And that afternoon, he walked home with her, pausing around the corner from her house and giving her the lightest kiss on the lips that meant as much as a promise.

They fell into a routine over those next few weeks. The bus stop in the mornings, the walk home. Often they'd do their homework together in the school library or Abbie or Matt's bedroom, distracted from their studying by yet more kisses. On Sundays they hung out in the park with friends, Matt and his mates kicking a football around, someone playing music on a ghetto blaster, the girls stretching out their bare legs to catch the sun and gossiping idly.

Then, one Friday as they walked home, Matt asked, almost shyly, 'Are you doing anything tomorrow night?'

Delight thrilled through Abbie as she thought, *I am now.*

'I don't think so,' she said.

'Want to come out with me?'

This meant something different – something more than sitting in a room together, having coffee and biscuits in Matt's parents' kitchen or going round to Andy's place to watch movies when his mum and dad were out.

This meant a date. A real-life, actual, proper date.

'Of course.' Abbie miraculously managed to sound casual. 'I'd like that.'

But her mind was already whirring. Where would he take her? Did this mean something? And most importantly, what was she going to wear?

She enlisted help from the latest edition of *Company* magazine as well as from Chloe, who objected at first on the basis that she had an essay about Cordelia to write. But Abbie persuaded her that there was masses of time left to finish it, and the two girls spent Saturday afternoon in Abbie's room, experimenting with different colours of nail enamel, make-up looks and outfits, playing The Corrs at full volume and giggling helplessly at anything and nothing.

At last, Abbie was satisfied with her appearance: a skinny white one-shoulder vest, her beloved low-rise jeans with a chunky belt borrowed from Chloe, her trusty platform trainers, frosted pink lip gloss and painstakingly straightened hair. Chloe headed off to meet friends to go bowling; Abbie waited increasingly nervously for Matt's knock on the door.

He wasn't late. Matt was never late. He knocked at six o'clock exactly and Abbie flew downstairs, flinging open the door before her mother could get to it, tucking her keys in her bag and calling out a goodbye.

'You look nice,' Matt said.

Abbie said, 'So do you.'

They looked at each other and she realised he was just as nervous as she was, which made her nerves almost vanish.

'This feels kind of weird, doesn't it?' she asked.

'Weird? I don't know what you're taking about.'

They both laughed.

'Because you take girls out on dates all the time, right?'

'Course. You're my fourth this week.'

'What happened to the others?'

'They were just practice. I had to make sure I had my A game on.'

'That and figure out how to hold a knife and fork.'

By the time they'd reached the high street, they were laughing together, delighting in their shared silliness, the wittiest people in the world.

'So where are we going?' Abbie asked.

Matt gave her a proud, shy smile. 'I thought Nando's.'

Nando's. Wow. She hadn't set her sights higher than Burger King.

'You like peri-peri chicken, right?' Matt went on.

'Of course. But only if it's really hot.' She'd never had peri-peri chicken before, but liking hot food seemed sophisticated and daring.

Halfway through her meal, though, Abbie had begun to regret her bold choice. The burger was delicious, thick chicken fillets in a soft sesame-seed bun, laden with mayonnaise, lettuce and cheese. And hot sauce. Really hot. That was the problem. The first bite literally took her breath away, and she had to gulp her Diet Coke to ease the burn. But it didn't help that much. As she ate, she felt her lips begin to tingle and then smart. Her nose was running and she could feel tears building in her eyes, threatening to send mascara coursing down her cheeks.

'Are you okay?' Matt asked.

'Of course. It's great. I just need to use the bathroom.'

She fled to the ladies', where she ran her tongue under the cold tap, blew her nose and mopped her eyes, assessing her options. She could say she was full, but it seemed horribly wasteful to not finish food Matt had paid for. She could admit the truth: that it was too spicy for her to eat. But she wasn't going to do that. She had her pride – and, more importantly, she had a boyfriend she was determined to impress.

A fresh coat of lip gloss in place, she returned to Matt, who was waiting patiently in front of his own half-finished meal.

'Want to try some of this?' she asked. 'It's really yum.'

'Go on then.'

She passed her burger over to Matt, and he took a generous bite. She watched as his eyes widened in surprise then filled with tears.

'Oh my God,' he gasped. 'Jesus Christ. That's bloody napalm.'

'Is it?' With all the casualness she could muster, Abbie took another bite, and then another. 'I mean, it's tasty. Full of flavour.'

The worst was over now; her mouth was numbed by the onslaught of chilli. She was going to survive this.

'You have seriously got asbestos tastebuds,' Matt said admiringly.

Abbie glowed with pride. She probably wasn't going to be able to feel his kisses later on, but that didn't matter. They'd had their first date; he still liked her. So what if she had to pretend she liked food hotter than the surface of the sun for the rest of her life?

They finished their meal and debated ordering ice cream, or having another refill of the bottomless soft drink, but Abbie decided she was too full (and adding creamy dessert to the firepit she'd lit in her stomach didn't seem like the cleverest idea ever). And besides, night was falling and the prospect of being alone with Matt in the warm twilit evening was more appealing than any food.

'Shall we go, then?' he asked.

She nodded and they stood up and left the restaurant, veering off the main street to head down towards the park. The night was warm, but heavy clouds hung over the horizon, turning the colours of flame in the setting sun.

This must be what my insides look like after that extra-hot chicken, Abbie thought fleetingly, but then her mind returned to Matt.

They paused by the edge of the duck pond, listening to the honking overhead as a flock of geese returned to land on the water, the distant strains of music and the laughter of a group of teenagers hanging out somewhere close by, the rustle of the breeze stirring the leaves of the chestnut trees overhead.

Together, they moved over to a metal bench and sat down. The residual heat of the day soaked through the seat of Abbie's jeans, and Matt's arm around her shoulders was warm too. She leaned against him, then turned her face up for the kiss she was now confident enough to expect.

Matt's kisses had always been tender but this one was urgent too. Abbie lost herself in it, feeling as if her whole body was melting into Matt's, into the cooling evening air, into the sounds that surrounded them and the breeze caressing her skin.

He hooked his fingers into the metal grommets that studded her belt and pulled her close. She hooked one leg over his and sat on his lap, facing him, their bodies pressed together, their faces smiling into each other.

'Nice belt,' he said.

'It's not mine,' Abbie admitted. 'I borrowed it from Chloe.'

'From Chloe?' Matt's hands shifted, as if the metal studs had suddenly become too hot to touch.

'Mmhmm.' Abbie leaned back in to kiss him, and he hesitated for a second before his lips met hers again and his hands found the warm skin of her waist.

They stayed there until it was fully dark, the black night wrapping around them like a blanket, and then it was time for Matt to walk her home.

CHAPTER FIVE

'A walk?' Matt echoed incredulously, as if I'd suggested we visit a sex dungeon.

'A walk,' I agreed firmly. 'Remember? We used to like going for walks. It'll be good for us. I'm just going to change and put on some trainers.'

I hurried upstairs, pulled off my pyjama bottoms (such a skanky habit; I resolved to get dressed properly the next morning), and put on shorts and flip-flops. When I got back downstairs, Matt was standing by the front door, swinging his keys. He didn't look exactly enthusiastic about our minor adventure, but at least he wasn't on the sofa staring at his phone.

'So where are we going to walk?' he asked.

'I thought just... you know... kind of potter around. Like we used to.'

He swung open the door. 'God, remember that? It was like, what, six years ago?'

'More like seven or eight. When we were saving so hard to buy this place we couldn't afford anything.'

'No holidays.'

'Except that one time we went with your brother to Wales.'

'No meals out.'

'Burgers in the pub once a month, remember? It was our big payday treat.'

'When I dropped my mobile in the sink that time, we had to share one for two whole months until my contract ran out.'

'I didn't buy clothes for the longest time. When I interviewed for my last job I had to borrow a suit from Kate.'

'But we got there in the end.'

'In the end.' I couldn't help a note of resentment creeping into my voice, but I forced a smile onto my face. Now wasn't the time for recriminations. This was about reconnecting with happy memories, not sad ones.

Fortunately, Matt seemed not to notice the dark turn my thoughts had taken. We'd reached the end of our road now. The pavement was hot: I could feel the warmth through the thin soles of my flip-flops. I eased my shirt away from my back to try and circulate some cool air around my body, but the air wasn't cool. Part of me wanted to turn back, return to the shade of our living room and resume normal service for the evening. But a bigger part was enjoying being here with Matt, reminiscing, a feeling of closeness between us that felt both familiar and strange.

'Which way shall we go?' he asked.

'Left? Loop round the park and then back along the high street?'

'Sure.'

We turned and walked further, a long terrace of Victorian houses stretching ahead of us. They looked identical at first – when I walked this way normally, hurrying to the shops or the station, I'd assumed they were all the same. But now, with no purpose other than to stroll through the evening heat with my husband, I began to notice differences. Some had beige pebbledashing obscuring their brickwork, some had elaborate gables, one had a brick wall along its front garden with crenellations like a medieval castle.

And on the wall sat a black cat. When we passed, it let out a brief meow, almost impatient, as if saying, 'Ahem!'

'Hello.' Matt turned and tracked back a few steps, holding out a hand towards the cat. It leaned its head forward and butted its face against his fingers.

'Aren't you friendly?' I reached out too and touched the hot fur of its back. 'Just hanging out there waiting for people to pass by and fuss you, is that the plan?'

The cat stood up, arching its back in a stretch, and started to purr. Clearly, being made much of by random passers-by was exactly the plan. I listened to Matt talking nonsense to it – asking it if it was too hot in that black fur coat, praising its red collar, which was adorned with a diamanté heart, admiring the length and profusion of its whiskers – and felt a smile spread across my face.

'I suppose we'd better get on,' he said at last.

But, a few doors further along, Matt spotted another cat. This one was sprawled on top of a wheelie bin, its ginger fur almost camouflaged against the brown plastic.

'Hey there.' He stopped so suddenly I almost cannoned into his back. 'Do you want some attention too?'

But the cat regarded us suspiciously for a second before standing up, leaping off the bin and disappearing under a bush.

I laughed. 'Can't win them all.'

'I feel so bad,' Matt said. 'There it was, having a lovely time on its bin, and I ruined it.'

'You did,' I confirmed. 'You're basically a cat-disturbing monster.'

'It just needs to learn to trust me,' he said. 'Next time, I'll approach more slowly, possibly armed with prawns.'

'You can't feed prawns to random cats! What if it had a shellfish allergy?'

'A cat with a shellfish allergy? Come on. What next – vegan, paleo, keto cats?'

'Aren't all cats basically keto?'

'Yeah, I guess. But only some of them bang on about it endlessly to their mates.'

We'd reached the end of the road now, but instead of cutting through the park, we stayed on the pavement. Neither of us suggested it – we just did it, because we knew that the chances of seeing more cats were better. And we did. We saw a black-and-white cat sunning itself on a shed roof, which ignored us determinedly when we called it. We saw an elegant fluffy grey cat, which chirruped with satisfaction when Matt stroked it. We met a handsome tabby with a white bib.

And at some point before we reached the high street, I realised we were holding hands.

'No more cats now, I guess,' Matt said as we passed the last of the houses and the first of the shops.

'There might be more on our way home.'

But suddenly, the prospect of returning home to the flat, making a salad and cooking the chicken breasts that were nearing their use-by date, flicking through the TV channels and arguing about what to watch, seemed unbearably bleak.

'I'm starving,' Matt remarked.

'Maybe we could get something to eat while we're out.'

'This isn't exactly the gourmet hub of London.'

We paused, looking around at the fried chicken shop, the takeaway pizza place, the sketchy pub and the slightly less sketchy one, and the Thai place, which had a small queue outside its door.

'We could go to the Nando's round the corner,' I suggested tentatively.

'Nando's? We haven't been there for years.'

'I know. It would be a blast from the past.'

But clearly Matt wasn't going to need persuading; he'd

already headed off down the road in the direction I'd indicated, walking so quickly I had to trot to keep up.

'Scene of our first date, remember?' he asked over his shoulder.

'Really? I thought that was Burger King.'

'Come on! It was totally Nando's. I was a classy kid – I took you to the best places. I had to work two Saturdays at HMV to pay for that date.'

'My God. I remember now. I was too embarrassed to order because I thought I'd have to pay half and it was well expensive.'

We walked into the cool, dimly lit interior of the restaurant, approached the counter together and studied the menu.

'There's loads of new stuff,' Matt said. 'Blimey. Halloumi fries. Fancy AF.'

'And a new flavour marinade. Smokey barbecue, no less. And vegan chicken. What did the vegan option used to be, back in the day?'

'Quarter chicken without the chicken?'

I giggled. 'Fries and coleslaw?'

'Nope. There's mayo in coleslaw.'

'Poor bloody vegans. It took some doing, back then.'

'They're getting their revenge now, though,' Matt said. 'Anyway, you'll have a double chicken burger with cheese, extra hot?'

'I will. And we can have wine.'

'Or beer. On account of being adults now and everything.'

Our eyes met and we beamed at each other, delighted with the people we'd been then and the people we were now.

'A half chicken, lemon and herb, spicy rice, coleslaw and a beer.' Matt placed his order and the girl behind the counter smiled at him like this was the best thing she'd heard all day, that's how infectious his sudden happiness was.

I ordered my own food, receiving a cheery but dialled-down

version of the same smile from the server, and we made our way to a table.

Once again, I remembered that first date all those years ago – sitting there opposite Matt, not sure quite what to do with my face (not least because if I closed my mouth, my lip gloss would stick it together and it would never unstick), but at the same time just wanting to grin and grin at him, and later kiss him and kiss him.

I couldn't remember what we talked about, but I was sure we were never silent, and we laughed a lot, the kind of shrieky, silly laughter teenagers do, when you think you've stopped laughing and then your eyes meet and it sets you off again. I remember thinking we were the two coolest, cleverest, wittiest people in all the world.

Now, all I could find to say was, 'I can't believe how many cats there are in our neighbourhood.'

'Funny, isn't it? We've lived here for six years already, you'd think we'd have noticed.'

'That tabby one was so cute. I wonder if it hangs out there all day, waiting for its humans to get back from work.'

'It would be kind of cool to come home and get that enthusiastic a welcome.'

I remembered Matt getting back from the gym earlier, and how all I'd said when he walked in the door had been, 'Did you remember to get dishwasher tablets?' and how I'd had to suppress my irritation when he said, 'Nah. I'll go out later.'

Fortunately, our food arrived and we both dived into the chicken, fries, rice and all the rest, and I found myself returning to that comforting memory from the past.

'I spent the whole afternoon getting ready for that date,' I remembered.

'I was worried you'd want something really pricey and I wouldn't have enough cash, and end up washing dishes because I couldn't pay the bill,' Matt said.

I hesitated for a second, then admitted: 'You know, I'd never ordered extra-hot anything in my life before that. I only did it to impress you and I legit thought my mouth was on fire.'

'You what? You totally had me fooled. I can't believe you've hidden that from me all this time.'

That's not the only thing I've hidden from you, I thought, my sense of unease returning and casting a shadow over our happiness. It felt so fleeting these days, so fragile, as if I couldn't take refuge in happy memories without sad ones rushing in to overwhelm them.

But Matt seemed oblivious of the dark turn my thoughts had taken.

'Maybe we should get a cat, after all,' he said. 'They're cute. It would have company with us both at home.'

His words felt like a punch in the gut – the last thing I needed after inhaling a double chicken burger with extra cheese and two glasses of chenin blanc.

'What do you mean? We talked about this.'

'Yeah, I know, but we just kind of said we weren't going to get a pet for now. In case – you know.'

My lips, stinging from the hot sauce, felt oddly numb and immobile. 'Are you saying that's changed?'

'No, but... It might do. I just think we can't keep putting stuff on hold forever. Like us both working at the kitchen table, in case.'

All the ease and happy companionability between us seemed to have evaporated, leaving only a cold knot of dread inside of me. Dread of – what, exactly? Naming the thing that had been there between us for what felt like forever – although really it had only been a few years – growing bigger and bigger and harder and harder to talk about? Returning to the hope and disappointment, the anticipation and misery, that had been paused for us for over a year now?

I wasn't sure whether Matt could feel it too, but I guessed

he did, because his face had changed quite suddenly from relaxed and smiling to almost fearful.

'Abbie? Have I upset you? We don't have to talk about it.'

'We're already talking about it,' I said.

And, now that we were, it felt like there was nothing else we could talk about. So we finished our meal in silence, walked home and got into bed, the stretch of sheet between us feeling as wide as an ocean.

CHAPTER SIX

At my desk the next day, despite having put on a bra, a skirt and even some make-up (and a top, obviously; I wasn't doing *that* kind of video call for work – although given Bastian's insistence that I 'really get my hands dirty' on the Quim copywriting, I wouldn't have been surprised if such a thing lay in my future), I found it impossible to concentrate. I kept casting furtive glances at Matt opposite me, searching for signs that he, too, felt wounded by what we'd said the previous night. But his face was focused and still; only his hands moved, tapping on his keyboard and occasionally pushing his glasses higher up his face.

I tried to apply my brain to an introductory paragraph setting out how the array of products sold by quim.com would give them vaginas toned as an Olympic weightlifter's arms, drive their partners wild with desire and make their orgasms worthy of an interview on *The Goop Lab*, but I couldn't do it – I might as well have been trying to come up with instructions on how to fly to the moon without the aid of a rocket-launcher.

Fortunately, I was rescued – kind of – by a summons to the all-team meeting to discuss our imminent return to the office. At least, it would be imminent as soon as Bastian, Marc and Vishni, the office manager, had managed to secure a new premises that Marc thought was worthy of the agency's cutting-edge image, Bastian thought was affordable and Vishni could figure out a way of fitting the requisite number of desks into.

'We'll be hot-desking, of course,' Vishni told the assembled faces on my screen.

'Which will mean a strict clean-desk policy,' Bastian said. 'There will be lockers for you to secure your belongings at the end of the day.'

Marc unmuted himself. 'What? But what about my Dionaeas?'

'They'll have to go,' Bastian said. 'It's disgusting, anyway, having a bunch of carnivorous plants on your desk. There was a dead insect in that Venus whatsit for days last year. It turned my stomach to see it.'

'The trouble with you,' Marc snapped, 'at least, one of the troubles with you, is you don't appreciate the wonders of nature.'

'I appreciate nature just fine when it's not sucking the guts out of a housefly.'

I tuned out their bickering, and when at last the meeting was over I changed my status to busy, picked up my phone and went out into the garden. It was almost too hot to endure being outside – the plans we'd had for a shady tree we could sit under in the evenings with a glass of wine, a flagstone path leading under a pergola, perhaps even a water feature or at least a bird bath, had come to nothing.

I pulled one of the battered plastic chairs into the patch of shade offered by the neighbour's wall and perched on it, taking out my phone. I'd only briefly been a smoker, back at university when it had still been cool, before dire health warnings and the spiralling costs of those lethal, addictive, blissful sticks of nicotine had put me off.

But suddenly, I found myself longing for a cigarette more than anything.

I took out my phone and opened WhatsApp. Rowan had sent a message the previous night, which I'd seen flash up as a notification but not been able to bring myself to read properly.

Rowan: @Abbie, how's it going? Been thinking about you. Any progress on Operation Memory Lane?

Then there was a bunch of chat between her, Kate and Naomi about how their days were going. Evidently Kate's new boss was an incompetent mansplainer, Rowan couldn't decide between Charlotte Tilbury nail polish and an Apple Music voucher for Clara's birthday, and Naomi had actually slept for seven hours and felt like a new woman.

Their messages lifted my gloom for a moment. Just seeing the words on that tiny screen, it was easy to imagine that we were all together, pulling each other close into a group hug.

Abbie: Ugh, not so good. You won't believe what happened. We accidentally did recreate our first date – same food and everything. It wasn't Burger King after all – it was Nando's.

I waited a second to see whether anyone was online to read my message. Sometimes replies came instantly; sometimes they could take hours. I imagined Kate at a boardroom table in the shiny City tower where she worked, the icy air conditioning allowing her to wear her severe grey suit and tights without breaking a sweat. Naomi would probably be in the park with the kids, trying to get them to toddle off some energy in the hope that they'd sleep through again tonight. Rowan would be working, though, same as me, sitting at her laptop at home.

I pinned my hopes on Rowan. If she didn't reply, I'd have to go back inside and catch up on the latest slew of emails.

Sure enough, Rowan had read my message and was replying.

> *Rowan: That's so sweet and so random! I can't believe Matt did that without even knowing about my idea! So why wasn't it good?*

> *Abbie: It was at first.*

Rapidly, I summed up the walk, the cats, the spontaneous decision to eat out, the memories that had come rushing back.

> *Abbie: So it's a good idea, in theory.*

> *Rowan: But what went wrong?*

> *Abbie: We had a row.*

> *Rowan: Oh no! What about?*

> *Abbie: The usual.*

And I added a sad-face emoji, twin to the one Rowan had posted.

> *Naomi: Just catching up, on way home with kids. How are things this morning?*

> *Abbie: We're not talking. But he put his spoon in the dishwasher so he knows I'm upset.*

> *Rowan: Do you think if you tried again, and really, really made sure not to talk about the difficult stuff, it might be better?*

Through the window, I could see Matt's back, his shoulders stooped as he bent over his laptop, his hair still mussed at the back from sleep. Sadness and anger fought inside me against the wave of tenderness I felt for him.

Abbie: I just don't know.

Rowan: But you'll try?

Abbie: I guess. Gotta go, love you both.

I made my way back inside, my phone hanging loosely from my hand. I needed to focus – the series of social-media tiles I needed to write about the five different flavours of Talon and the blog post about 'How to feel proud of your period' weren't going to research themselves, and there was only so much I could delegate to Craig, the junior copywriter. But I kept looking up from my screen at Matt, and occasionally I'd catch him looking at me. Then our eyes slid away, our faces unsmiling.

At last, I couldn't bear it any more.

'Fancy a sandwich?'

He started as if I'd slammed his computer closed on his fingers. 'Sure. Thanks.'

'Ham and cheese toastie?'

'That would be great.'

'Mustard or pickle?'

He hesitated. 'Both. Go on – go crazy.'

We looked at each other properly now, and we both managed to smile, although I knew our faces were just masks hiding the hurt beneath.

I assembled the sandwiches and cooked them one at a time in a pan on the stove, a plate and the heavy cast-iron skillet we'd had for a wedding present – which I hardly ever used because lifting it hurt my wrists – weighing them down. First Matt's, then mine. By the time mine was finished, his would have been cooling, but he hadn't started to eat.

'Is that okay?' I asked.

'I'm sure it's delicious. I was just waiting for you. Can't go stuffing my face while you're slaving over a hot stove.'

He could have, of course. I wouldn't have minded. But still, his thoughtfulness made my heart melt just like the cheese oozing out from between the slices of bread in the pan.

I cut my sandwich in half and sat down, and we ate together, strings of cheese stretching from our mouths, our fingers greasy with butter. When we'd finished, Matt cleared away the plates and pans.

'Fancy going for a walk again this evening?' I asked. 'See if we can find any new cats?'

Matt's face relaxed into a proper smile. 'Sounds like a plan.'

The next evening, Matt had a rare, hastily organised night out with friends at a bar in town. Andy had suggested it; Matt's brother Ryan was in London for a work meeting and a few of their other old mates had been roped in too. Matt asked me cautiously if I wanted to go along.

'No! God, no. It's fine. You go. It'll do you good.'

He looked at me beadily. 'Is it because Andy's going to be there?'

Yes. A night out with Andy, trying to ignore his too-frequent toilet breaks and pretending there wasn't an elephant the size of, well, an elephant in the room all night wasn't my idea of fun. Matt clearly thought catching up with his old mate was worth the potential aggro, but I didn't.

'Of course not,' I lied. 'It's just – it's a boys' night. Come on. You don't want me there, cramping your style when you want to talk about who's going to win the Euros and Emilia Clarke's tits.'

'I'm not sure Emilia's tits are on offer as a prize for anything right now,' Matt quipped.

'Well, if that changes, let me know and I'll get myself in the draw.'

He laughed and went off to get ready, crashing out of the house half an hour later smelling of my rose and geranium shower gel, wearing a shirt with little cartoon robots on it that I'd bought him for Christmas.

I stood in the hallway for a moment, at once relishing the quiet and the prospect of having the flat to myself for a few hours, and feeling strangely at a loose end. If I'd had more notice, I could have bought in a load of food that I liked and Matt didn't: chicken livers to have on toast with hot sauce, or a three-bean chilli ready meal, or even just a massive pack of salt and vinegar crisps to eat all to myself.

But I hadn't had time to lay in supplies, and I hadn't the inclination to go out, even if our local supermarket did stretch to chicken livers, which it didn't. I could have a long, scented bath with candles, even though it was still light, I decided. With a glass of wine. And watch something on my tablet that Matt would take the piss out of me for if he was there. And I could WhatsApp the Girlfriends' Club from the bath, and hopefully one of them would have a free evening too and fancy a chat.

But as it turned out, Kate was out at a client dinner, Patch was one of the friends who'd responded to Matt's last-minute invitation so Naomi was wrangling the twins on her own, and Rowan had taken her mum to the cinema because Clara was at a sleepover.

So I was truly on my own. It was okay, though. I enjoyed my bath and my wine, and watched a couple of episodes of *Glow Up* in the cooling water, then devoured several slices of toast and marmalade in my dressing gown before realising that the marmalade was making my wine taste funny.

I returned to the bathroom and looked despondently at my face in the mirror. I remembered asking Rowan a while ago when the best time was to start using retinol on your skin, and her saying, 'Ten years ago.' I'd well and truly missed that boat: I could see fine lines around my eyes and deeper ones between my eyebrows and on either side of my mouth. There were violet shadows under my eyes and my hair looked dry and lifeless.

God. I remembered how I used to spend hours getting ready to go out, how straightening my hair and fake-tanning my legs and painting my nails and doing my make-up, then taking it all off and doing it again because I fancied trying a different look, then trying on outfit after outfit until my bedroom floor was littered with clothes, had seemed a worthwhile way of spending time.

More than worthwhile – fun even.

I remembered how, even when Matt and I were at our skin-test, saving furiously for our house deposit, the money I spent at the hairdresser and the beautician had been sacrosanct.

'You've got to feel good about yourself, Abs,' he'd said. 'I mean, I think you'd look gorgeous no matter what, but I have to admit I'm kind of invested in the wax thing.'

How long had it been since I'd bothered putting on make-up regularly, or had a manicure, or asked the hairdresser to do anything more complicated with my hair than cut off the split ends? How long had it been since I'd gone into Boots or Super-drug and emerged laden with new eyeshadow colours, fancy emollients for my face and body, serums that promised to trans-form my hair, tubing mascaras and felt-tip eyeliners? How long since I'd had a beauty therapist rip my pubic hair out by the roots and paid her for the privilege? How long since I'd felt like the archetypal Quim customer ('experimental, erotic, empow-ered') allegedly felt all the time?

'You've let yourself go, Abbie,' I told my reflection, and my reflection nodded gloomily back.

I pulled open the top drawer of the rickety IKEA cabinet next to the basin, where my make-up lived. There it all was, a jumble of bottles and tubes, pencils and crayons, pots and wands. Wands – ha, I'd need some serious magic to help me right now, I thought.

Well, help was at hand. My face was already moisturised and, apart from a rogue toast crumb in the corner of my mouth, ready to go. I switched on the light and got started.

Half an hour later, I'd applied a full face of slap and, after digging out my trusty GHDs, transformed my hair from a wavy, frizzy mess to something almost like the smooth, silken sheets I'd been so proud of back in the noughties.

I unplugged the straighteners and wandered into our bedroom, shrugging off my dressing gown, then turned back and checked that I had actually unplugged them. I opened my wardrobe and surveyed the contents.

One good thing about being too skint to buy many new clothes was that I had kept most of my old ones, so looking at them was like turning the pages of a photo album. Each garment, each pair of shoes, had a store of memories – possibly memories I could recreate.

There was the first pair of skinny jeans I'd ever bought, which I'd worn with trepidation at first, thinking they made my legs look like parsnips, then got used to and worn over and over, until the stretch had gone and they weren't skinny any more. I'd been wearing them the day we moved in here, kneeling on the floor in them while Matt and I assembled flat-pack furniture together.

There was the floaty kaftan I'd bought for our last beach holiday together – almost five years ago, it must have been. Looking at it, I could almost taste the ocean breeze as Matt and I watched the sun set from our hotel balcony, pina coladas in our hands. As soon as darkness fell, we'd pulled each other back inside, shedding our clothes and ending up intertwined on the bed, perspiration drying on our skin, almost too late for our dinner reservation.

There was the cashmere jumper Matt had bought me as a congratulations present the day I started my new job, which I'd never worn because it made me itch but couldn't bear to part with because it had been a gift from him.

And there was the jumpsuit I'd bought for Matt's and my engagement party.

I eased its hanger off the rail and looked at it. It hadn't cost much – none of my clothes had – but oh my God, I loved it. It was hot pink, with spaghetti straps, a draped front and tapered legs. I remembered trying it on in the fitting room, twirling with delight, before handing over my credit card with barely a tremor and swishing out of the shop, the glossy rope-handled bag swinging by my side.

I remembered it being impossible to wear any underwear with it, because bra straps would show and even the most allegedly invisible pants would ruin the line.

I remembered Matt being almost unable to keep his hands off me when I wore it. Maybe, if I wore it now, with my hair and make-up all done, and I was wearing it when he got home after his night out, he'd remember how much he'd fancied me back then and fancy me again.

I'd been pretty skinny back then, and I was less skinny now. But it had never been tight – I could at least try it, and if the zip didn't do up, that didn't matter. I held the fabric up to my face, sure I could detect an echo of the DKNY Woman perfume I used to wear. The garment slid off the hanger as easily as water from a glass, and I stepped carefully into it, easing the thin straps up over my shoulders.

It was going to fit – I was sure of it. I reached behind to the base of my spine, gripped the small metal tab and eased it up.

There was a brief moment of resistance before it slid easily up to between my shoulder blades. I did a little twirl in front of the mirror, smiling.

A pretty pointless way to spend the evening, but it had made me feel good. And there were still a few inches of wine left in the bottle. Matt had said he wouldn't be back late – I might as well have another drink and surprise him in my finery when he got back.

But first, I needed a wee. I returned to the bathroom, unzipping the jumpsuit as I walked. Only the brief resistance I'd encountered getting the zip up was more stubborn now I was trying to get it down. *It must be the seam around the waist*, I thought, tugging gently at the metal tab. The fabric must be slightly thicker there – I just needed to ease it past.

But it wouldn't ease.

I pulled the zip up and tried again, with zero success. My hands had started to sweat and it was harder to grip the tab of the zip, and I could feel the fabric encasing my upper body more tightly than I'd realised.

I was trapped. Trapped inside a bloody jumpsuit, with a face full of make-up, great hair and a bladder I was becoming more conscious of by the minute.

I had no idea what time Matt would be home. He'd said, 'Not late,' but that could mean anything from ten thirty to two thirty. It was almost ten thirty now. If he was home by eleven I'd probably be all right – just. But if he wasn't? I pictured myself waiting and waiting, getting increasingly desperate, vainly attempting to pee down one leg of the jumpsuit and it ending in disaster.

No. I needed help – and fast.

I grabbed my phone, tapped on to WhatsApp and explained the situation as quickly as I could to the Girlfriends' Club.

Naomi: I'd come over and help but I've just got the kids to sleep and I swear if I even move they'll wake up. I'm sat here in agony with a cramp in my foot so you have all my sympathy.

Rowan: Oh balls, I just got home. I'd come but it would take over an hour and by then Matt might be back, right?

Naomi: Have you tried running a pencil up and down the zip? That's meant to loosen them. Or Vaseline?

Rowan: Olive oil?

Abbie: Wouldn't that stain it horribly?

Naomi: Or you could order a Deliveroo and ask the driver to help you?

Rowan: That's a genius idea! Do that.

Abbie: I am not doing that!

Rowan: Why not?

Abbie: Because it'd be like the beginning of the cheesiest porno ever, is why not.

Kate: Could you unpick a seam?

Abbie: Not really. No unpicker for a start. I could cut myself out of it but I just tried it on for the first time in years and I realised I really like it.

Clearly, with the best will in the world, my friends weren't going to be able to come to my rescue. There was only one person left who could.

I tapped the green receiver icon on my phone and scrolled down until I found Matt's number, realising how long it had been since I'd needed to call him, because he'd always been there, right opposite me at the kitchen table. I pressed the button and heard the buzzing trill in my ear – and then, like an echo or a stereo system whose speakers weren't quite in synch, an answering ring from outside the open window.

Could it be? I looked out and, sure enough, there was Matt's dark head approaching our front door.

As I watched, he fumbled in his pocket for his keys, then changed his mind and fumbled in the other pocket for his phone, then fumbled both of them and dropped them, the phone skidding one way on the pavement and the keys rattling in the opposite direction.

Great. A drunk man – just the help I needed in this delicate situation.

But he was here and, tipsy or not, he was a whole heap better than the nothing I'd had before.

I rushed downstairs and flung open the front door just as Matt scrambled up from his hands and knees, keys and phone back in his hands.

'Wow,' he said. 'You look absolutely gorgeous. That trouser thing is lethal.'

'It's a jumpsuit,' I corrected him, as I always did when he paid me the same compliment. 'Only right now it's basically a straitjacket. The zip's stuck and I can't get out of it.'

'Oh no. Well, the cavalry's arrived. Hold on, I just need to have a piss.'

'So do I!' I followed him up the stairs. 'Seriously, Matt, this is urgent. I've been bursting for a wee for ages.'

'I'm being as quick as I can,' he promised, his voice muffled by the bathroom door. 'Just as well we had to put Andy in an Uber and call it a night early.'

'Was he...?'

'Yep.' Matt emerged, wiping his still-soapy hands on his jeans. 'Right. Turn round and let me take a look.'

I obeyed, and seconds later felt his warm hands and warmer breath on my shoulders. He smelled of bourbon – they must have been drinking old-fashioneds. The jumpsuit's straps pressed on my collarbones as Matt tugged gently at the zip, but, just as it had when I tried, it stuck fast at the waist.

'Lubrication,' he said. 'That's what we need. Have we any...?'

'Nope.' I felt myself involuntarily shifting from foot to foot. It didn't help. 'There's some of that dry oil stuff I use on my legs. We could try that.'

'Dry oil? Isn't that a whatchamacallit?'

'An oxymoron. You know, like action cricket.'

'Microsoft Works?' Matt suggested.

'Marital bliss? Come on, Matt, there's a time and a place to have a stimulating chat about figures of speech and this is. Not. It.'

'Sorry, sorry. I'm on it.' He flung open the bathroom cabinet. 'Is it this stuff?'

'No, that's micellar oil for taking off make-up. Hold on.' I pushed past him and found the bottle, hidden behind a tube of hair serum. 'Here. Got to be worth a try.'

'Right.' I turned around again and heard a rattle as he dropped the cap of the bottle, then felt a trickle of oil running down my back. 'Shit, it's gone everywhere. The floor's going to be like an ice rink.'

'Never mind that. Has it worked?'

'Let me just... Fuck. It's made the slip all zippery. I mean the—'

'I know what you mean! Has it worked?'

'I don't know, I can't grip the thingamajig. Wait here.'

I heard the thunder of his feet on the stairs as he ran down them two at a time and willed him to take care – the last thing this night needed was Matt with a broken ankle *and* me stuck in a jumpsuit.

But he reappeared safely, bright yellow washing-up gloves on his hands.

'Purchase.' He waggled his rubber-encased fingers at me. Then his face fell. 'Oh my God. Purchase. That reminds me. I bought you a bottle of that perfume you always used to wear. DIY?'

'DKNY?'

'That's the badger. Only I must've left it on the Tube. Or in the bar. I'm so sorry, Abs.'

'Matt, that's lovely. It really is. Thank you for thinking of it. Only now, please help me get out of this thing.'

'Hold on. I've just got to get a zip on the grip, see? I mean—'

I felt giggles rising in my throat, threatening to spill over, but I suppressed them. That would be more than my bladder could handle right now.

'Maybe wash the zip pull first?' I suggested.

'On it. Basic science, right?'

Now, I felt the chill of shower gel on my back as Matt squirted it everywhere except, as far as I could tell, on the area where it was needed. But I wasn't about to start picking holes in his technique.

He tugged at the zip again. Again, I felt it resist when it reached my waist. Matt tugged harder.

'Don't break it,' I begged.

'I'm trying. It's just— There!'

'Oh my God.' I shrugged the straps off my shoulders and the jumpsuit slid down all the way to the floor. I stepped out of it, hopping frantically on one leg for a second when my right foot caught in the fabric. 'Thank you! I'm free! Free to wee!'

A minute or so later, I came out of the bathroom, almost light-headed with relief. Matt was sitting on the bed, cradling the jumpsuit on his lap.

'That oil stuff went everywhere,' he said mournfully. 'I hope I haven't ruined it.'

'Matt, if you hadn't got home when you did I'd have had to take a breadknife to the damn thing and that would've ruined it for sure.'

'I'll take it to the dry cleaner tomorrow.'

I sat down next to him. 'I won't be able to wear it again unless there's someone who can accompany me to the loo every time.'

'That would be an honour and a privilege.'

Now, the giggles that I'd quashed earlier came bubbling out of me, and Matt started to laugh too. Every time one of us got ourselves under control, we'd meet the other's eyes and that would set us off again. We ended up lying next to each other on the bed, weak and hiccupping, our eyes wet with tears.

We hadn't laughed like that for ages. Not for months. If a ruined garment was the price to pay for that, I thought, I'd pay it gladly, every time.

'Okay?' Abbie asked.

'Just a second. You read too fast.'

'You read too slowly.'

'Okay, I'm done,' Matt said, and Abbie turned the page.

They were lying on Matt's bed in his parents' house, Abbie's hips between Matt's thighs, her head resting on his shoulder, reading *Monstrous Regiment* together. Matt had introduced her to Terry Pratchett soon after they met, and it had become a tradition for them to buy his latest novel as soon as it came out, but only one copy, and read it together.

It was a pleasure they looked forward to eagerly, but it was also, on this grim January afternoon, about the only thing there was to do. Christmas was over and soon they'd both be heading back to university and the months of separation that entailed. Although she was enjoying her English Literature course and liked her friends, the prospect of being separated from Matt always gave her a sick feeling of impending loss that was worse than the reality of being apart.

She wanted these last few days with him to last forever, like her Christmas tub of Body Shop avocado body butter – but at the same time she wanted to devour them, like she had the box of seashell-shaped chocolate truffles her mum gave her every year.

'What are you waiting for?' Matt asked.

'Oh. Sorry.' Abbie turned the next page, even though she'd barely been reading – the thought of saying goodbye to Matt had torn her concentration away from the book. She wiggled her bum higher up the bed and nestled her back more closely against Matt's chest, wishing she could somehow bottle the feeling of his arms around her, the smell of his threadbare cotton jumper, the way his hands looked resting on her thighs.

'Are you two decent?' Ryan's voice called from the other side of the closed door, followed by a thunderous knock, and Matt's brother bursting in. 'You've got a visitor.'

'Afternoon, kids.' Andy strolled in and perched on the end of the bed. 'Hope I'm not interrupting anything. You look ever so cosy.'

'We were just reading,' Abbie said.

'I thought you were skiing with your parents,' Matt said.

Andy gave an exaggerated shudder. 'I came home early. Ghastly activity. Even the après-ski, which ought to be delightful – all those lush men in their tans and jumpers getting sloshed on schnapps – isn't any fun.'

'Why not?' Abbie asked.

'Because all they want to do is talk about fucking skiing,' Andy intoned mournfully. 'I'm like, "Come on, darling, let's get you out of those wet epaulettes" – or whatever they're called – and he'll be all, "Yes, sweetie, but first let me finish telling you how I almost wiped out on a black run." Too tedious for words.'

Abbie and Matt laughed.

'We're pretty tedious too, I have to admit,' Matt said. 'We've hardly left the house since New Year's Eve.'

'And that's where I come in,' Andy said. 'Come on, my pretties – you shall go to the ball!'

Abbie looked up, startled. It was unusual for Andy to just rock up like this, without texting first or anything. And, more unusually still, she realised he was wearing a suit. She vaguely remembered him saying that his dad had had one tailor-made for him to wear to work-experience interviews, and she supposed this was it. Not that Andy had ever mentioned actually going to any interviews.

'Ball? What ball?' she asked.

'A mere figure of speech. But you'll need to get some decent threads on. We're going to The Ritz.'

'The Ritz?' Matt asked. 'Why?'

'As the man said, because it's there.'

'But we can't—' Matt began, and Abbie knew what he was about to say: *We can't afford it.* And he was right – of course they couldn't.

But Andy wasn't listening. He'd pulled open Matt's wardrobe and was rifling through the contents, pulling out a grape-coloured corduroy shirt and throwing it over to them, so it landed on Abbie's head.

'Get that on, and put on some decent trousers instead of those dreadful trackie bottoms. And then we'll need to get madam here home and changed.'

There was no arguing. Matt sat up, levering Abbie off his chest, and she watched as he hastily changed his clothes.

'I haven't shaved,' he said.

'Designer stubble. Very Hugh Jackman.' Andy nodded approvingly as Matt buttoned his shirt. 'You'll do. Come on now – part two of my fairy godmother act is about to commence.'

Abbie thrust her feet into her Ugg boots and the three of them hurried downstairs and out into the cold street. The walk to Abbie's house took only a few minutes, and Andy kept up a constant stream of chatter so she didn't have a chance to ask what on earth had brought this on.

The two boys stationed themselves outside her bedroom door while she put on some make-up and pulled her not-very-clean hair up with a claw clip. Then Andy made her parade up and down the landing in a succession of different outfits, before giving his seal of approval to a midnight-blue satin shift dress.

'Are you sure?' she asked. 'It looks a bit like a nightie.'

'Sure does,' Matt said. 'Smoking hot.'

'Freezing cold, more like,' said Abbie's mum, passing the foot of the stairs on her way to the kitchen. 'Mind you wear a coat.'

Abbie rolled her eyes, but pulled on her battered parka. There was no chance of her being allowed to wear her warm, comfortable sheepskin boots, however – Andy insisted on high, strappy silver sandals.

'We'll get a cab,' he said. 'It'll turn into a pumpkin at midnight, but for now, we're all good.'

Abbie and Matt met each other's eyes, horror mirrored in their faces. Getting a taxi home was unavoidable sometimes, if they missed the last Tube and there were no night buses and they were in a group who could all chip in for it. But a taxi to go out? It was an unthinkable indulgence.

Andy insisted, however – and insisted on paying. When they walked into the bar, Abbie's unease faded for a second, swept away by the sheer glamour of the room. The vast, glittering chandelier; the even vaster Christmas tree, laden with silver and gold baubles and twinkling with what looked like thousands of tiny lights; the richly patterned carpet under their feet, so thick and plushy her heels sank deep into it with every step.

They were escorted to a table, and Andy said, 'Must pop to the boys' room,' leaving them alone.

Tentatively, knowing what she would find between its stiff covers but almost too frightened to look, Abbie opened the menu.

'Fifteen pounds for a cocktail, are you fucking kidding me?' she whispered to Matt.

'I've got that cash I was saving for our summer holiday in Ibiza,' Matt said. 'We'll dip into that. It'll be okay.'

'Do you think I can order a lemonade?'

'We'll just have a couple of rounds and then go on somewhere cheaper,' Matt promised. 'Enjoy it while we're here.'

'I never knew places this posh even existed,' Abbie breathed. 'Look, the waiters are all wearing white gloves.'

'And that bloke playing the piano's in an actual tailcoat.'

'He's playing the Black Eyed Peas,' Abbie realised, and the two of them dissolved into giggles, more out of nerves than because it was actually funny.

Then Andy reappeared, followed by a waiter with a tray bearing three pink cocktails. Andy lit a cigarette, raised his glass and said, 'Cheers. To us – to you two – to friendship.'

They clinked glasses and sipped. The drink was at once sweet and tart, with a powerful hit of vodka. It was the most delicious thing Abbie had ever tasted – or possibly the seaweed-flavoured rice crackers, which the waiter had served in a little cut-glass dish, were more delicious still.

Abbie was barely halfway through her drink when Andy drained his glass and stood up.

'Now,' he said, 'I'm going to love and leave you, my pretties.'

'Why?' Matt asked. 'What's up?'

'I've a date,' Andy said. 'But I won't be far away. Room 216, to be precise. And I'll only be a couple of hours.'

Abbie took another gulp of her drink. The alcohol had taken some of the edge off her unease, but not all.

'You're got a date? Here? Who with?' she asked.

'I couldn't possibly name names. Let's just say that although milkshakes are my first love, I don't mind an oil sheik either. The drinks are on his room tab, so keep ordering whatever you want. He's not short of a few quid.'

Andy stood, slinging his suit jacket over one shoulder, and strolled off. They watched as he paused to have a word with the waiter, then disappeared into the lobby.

Moments later, two more drinks arrived, and another bowl of rice crackers.

'Is he...' she began. 'I mean, is Andy going upstairs to...'

'Shag a sheik?' Matt finished. 'I shouldn't think they'll be playing backgammon up there.'

'But is it okay? I mean, is it safe?'

'Andy's a big boy, Abs. He can look after himself. He'll have a great time.'

Suppressing her doubts, Abbie took a sip of her drink and reached across the table for Matt's hand. She wished she had a fraction of Andy's confidence – the casual indifference with which he'd placed his order with the waiter, the easy assumption that the bill would be picked up without a second glance, the way he'd gone off to have sex with a stranger in a hotel bedroom like it was something he did all the time.

Not that she ever wanted to have sex with anyone other than Matt.

'Hey.' Matt squeezed her hand. 'Stop worrying. He'll be fine. I expect he brought us here so he'd have backup, just in case it gets hairy. If he's not back by eleven we'll sound the alarm. Okay?'

'Okay, I guess,' Abbie agreed.

After another drink, she felt herself begin to relax and allowed herself to enjoy the experience: the glamour of this place she'd never have been able to come to normally, her handsome boyfriend next to her, the Christmas tree and music.

And the Japanese rice crackers, obviously.

Still, when Andy returned, just after ten thirty, she felt a flood of relief. He was smiling, his eyes bright, cracking jokes even more frenetically than usual – although he didn't tell them anything about what had gone on in room 216.

They stayed until midnight, then got a taxi home, dropping Andy off first and then returning to the humble safety of Matt's bedroom.

'See?' he said, as they lay in the narrow bed, slotting together like spoons. 'There was nothing to worry about.'

It was only much, much later that Abbie recalled that night and realised she was right to have worried – but that, perhaps, she'd been worrying about the wrong thing.

CHAPTER SEVEN

'Hey,' I said to Matt when he got in from the gym and sank onto the sofa, sipping from his water bottle and scrolling through stuff on his phone, 'I think we should go out.'

'What? You mean *out* out?'

'Yep. I thought we could go into town and have cocktails at The Ritz.'

Matt looked at me like I'd just suggested spending four months in Outer Mongolia immersing ourselves in the lifestyle of a nomadic tribe.

'But why?'

'Because we can. Well, we can if we have, like, one cocktail each and then the cheapest beer they offer and then get the Tube home.'

'The Ritz, though, Abs? Seriously?'

'Seriously,' I said firmly. Then I sat down on the sofa next to Matt and went on, 'Remember, we went there once with Andy. We thought it was off-the-scale fabulous. We'd never been anywhere that glam before.'

'We've never been anywhere that glam again,' Matt pointed out.

'Well, yes, there is that. But you see, I've been thinking.'

'Is that what that burning smell is?'

'Oi!' I dug an elbow into his ribs. 'Less backchat and more listening. I've been thinking it would be a good idea to, like, try and revisit some of the amazing times we've had together.'

'Like the time we went to Paris and you ate a dodgy oyster and spent three days spewing?'

'Not the spewing, doofus. But yes, maybe we could go to Paris. Maybe next year. But in the meantime, there are so many other cool things we could do. You know how all those smug wankers post "hashtag making memories" on Insta? Like that, only kind of remaking memories.'

'And not being smug wankers?'

'Ideally not. Although of course there's always a risk we might tip over the edge occasionally. But I think it would be fun. And good for us. Like the school reunion was – and going to Nando's.'

Matt winced, and I wished I hadn't mentioned that night, which had ended in the very opposite of smugness. But I could see I'd swayed him.

'A trip down memory lane, you say?' he asked.

I remembered what Rowan had called it: Operation Memory Lane. It might be a bit too soon to mention to Matt just how invested my mates were in my plan.

'Something like that,' I said.

'I'm up for that,' Matt agreed. 'Do I need to put on proper clothes?'

'As opposed to what? Pyjamas? Yes. Jeans? Probably.'

'Right. On it.'

He hurried upstairs, peeling off his sweaty kit. I heard the damp thud as he dropped it in the washing basket then the hiss of the shower starting up. He hadn't noticed, but I'd already showered myself and put on a bronze-coloured midi skirt I'd bought a few years back for a party, which I hoped would still pass muster, a fitted black T-shirt and trainers. It was okay to wear trainers with everything now, wasn't it?

A few minutes later Matt reappeared, smelling of soap and steam and wearing black jeans and the stripy shirt his mum had given him for Christmas, which still bore the creases from its packaging.

'This is okay, right? I don't need to iron it or anything?'

I imagined him getting out the ironing board, faffing around for twenty minutes and ending up with a result worse than what he was currently wearing.

'Nah,' I said. 'We'll wing it. You look fine.'

We walked to the station, not holding hands but feeling as if we might be about to, our shoulders making brief contact as we strolled through the darkening evening. The train wasn't busy; few people were venturing the wrong way, into central London rather than back home, on this nothing kind of Tuesday, so we were able to sit next to each other, exchanging recollections of that long-ago evening.

'I wonder if Andy ever wore that suit again,' I mused.

'I bet not. Remember, he dropped out of uni right after and tried to be a conceptual artist?'

'Remember those pink drinks we had. What were they, porn star martinis? Something incredibly naff like that.'

'They'd never put a porn star martini on the menu at The Ritz,' Matt said. 'Far too indelicate. We had cosmopolitans, dahling.'

'Oh my God! Of course we did! We thought they were the most sophisticated thing ever. I haven't had a cosmo for years. Might give it a go next time I get cystitis.'

'You can give it a go in about five minutes,' Matt said. 'It's this stop, right?'

We stepped off the train and joined the straggle of people making their way to the exit. As we inched upwards on the escalator, I could feel excitement mounting inside me, just as slowly and steadily. And when we emerged onto the street and saw the sparkling lights of The Ritz gleaming ahead of us, I grabbed Matt's hand and squeezed it as eagerly as if I was a child off to see Santa Claus.

We stepped into the lobby. I could feel the glow of glamour from that long-ago night hanging over my shoulders still. I could almost see us there, at the corner table where we'd spent the night, Andy's golden head and Matt's dark one and my curtain of sleek hair glowing in the light from the chandelier. I could practically taste the pink cocktails, remembering how exotic and sophisticated they'd seemed to me then, and hear the piano music over the endless waves of our laughter.

But something had changed. The room, which had glittered back then like something out of a fairy tale – like stepping inside a Christmas tree – seemed smaller, somehow, now. The carpet under our feet, which I remembered having to walk over tentatively as a newborn foal lest my high heels sank inextricably into it, seemed flat now, its colours muted under my trainers. The people, who I remembered seeming like beings so sophisticated they might have arrived from another world, now looked commonplace, the women overly made-up and bored, the men decades older than their partners.

Even the smell, which I remembered as redolent with fresh flowers, cigars and expensive perfume, now only seemed to be that of air freshener and a whiff of cigarette smoke from the street outside.

Matt and I paused together for barely a second, but I could see doubt in his face that must have mirrored mine.

'It's... different,' I murmured.

'I think it's the same,' he said softly. 'We're different.'

But there wasn't time for us to analyse the situation. A suited doorman approached us, not the suave, polished, all-powerful host of my memory but a young man in a suit that didn't quite fit, a smile on his face but a smattering of acne on his chin.

'Sir, madam,' he said. 'How may I help you this evening?'

'We were hoping to have a drink in the bar,' Matt said. I wondered if what he was thinking was, *We were hoping it would be different.*

The man looked us up and down. I wondered how much the staff here were paid: probably not much over minimum wage, if that. I wondered if he had a boss who shouted at him, and how long he'd been on his shift. I wondered whether he lived in the kind of place you read about where people sleep three to a room and there's a tiny kitchen with nowhere to sit and no living room.

'No jeans,' the man said, the polite smile still on his face. 'No trainers. Sorry.'

'But we—' Matt began, but I cut him off.

'No problem,' I said. 'We'll go somewhere else.'

We turned and left, emerging into the street again feeling not like we'd conquered the world, as we had back on that night with Andy, but like naughty teenagers sent packing after trying to get into a club without ID.

'Well,' Matt said. 'That's us told.'

We stood together on the pavement, silent and unmoving. I felt a bit sick, almost ashamed. Like I'd done something far stupider than trying to get into a fancy venue wearing the wrong shoes – like I'd failed myself, somehow, and failed Matt, too. Like the whole idea of recreating magical moments from our past was just a stupid game that would earn me nothing more than stupid prizes.

What if other things that had made me giddy with happiness back then would seem as faded and tarnished as this had when I tried to relive them?

'I'm sorry,' I said, blinking hard against the tears that were threatening to fall.

'Why be sorry? That's crazy talk. It's not your fault they've got a stick-up-the-arse dress code.'

'But I should have—'

'You should have what? Let me spend another night on the sofa watching *Taskmaster*?'

I managed a half-laugh. 'You could squeeze in a couple of episodes before bed if we head home now.'

'Home? Bollocks to that. We couldn't recreate an old memory, so let's make a new one.'

'Steady on, Matt. You're heading dangerously close to smug wanker territory.'

'Maybe. But we're also dangerously close to this new place that does lobster rolls for a tenner.'

'Lobster rolls for a tenner? What a time to be alive.'

'I know, right? I think it's just across the road and down one of those side streets. Hold on.'

Matt produced his phone from his pocket and tapped the screen, then set off at a purposeful speed, getting sworn at by a Deliveroo rider and almost mown down by a black cab. I followed more cautiously, hurrying to catch him up once I'd crossed Piccadilly in one piece.

'Here we are.' Matt stopped outside an unassuming wooden door, a neon-pink lobster above it the only indication we'd arrived at the right place. He pushed open the door and I almost fell down a steep flight of stairs.

'Are you sure this is a restaurant, not a dodgy swingers' club?'

'We'll soon find out. And if it is...'

'Hashtag making memories?'

We were both giggling like teenagers when we reached the bottom of the stairs. A beaming girl with a spectacular Afro showed us to a tiny table, set with knives, forks and napkins in a wooden box and laminated menus.

'Not a cosmopolitan to be seen,' I said, glancing at the brief cocktail list.

'There's a dirty martini, though. You like those.'

My mouth watered at the thought of cold gin, sour with olive brine.

'That settles that, then. And an old-fashioned for the gentleman?'

'For sure.' Matt relayed our drinks order to the waitress, and we leaned over the food menu, our heads almost touching across the bare wooden tabletop.

'Lobster rolls and all the sides?' he suggested.

'Maybe not the green salad?'

'But definitely the deep-fried jalapeños.'

'And the mac and cheese.'

I wasn't crazy about mac and cheese, but Matt loved it; I knew he couldn't care less about jalapeños, but I adored them.

This is how it feels to be kind to each other, I thought. *This is how it ought to be all the time.*

Then our cocktails arrived, and the first hit of icy, savoury alcohol banished all deep thoughts from my mind. Perched on our hard, high stools, we demolished our drinks and then ordered more, and then devoured a lobster roll each, plus the extra one Matt had ordered for luck, plus all the side dishes. Matt even had a deep-fried pepper and pretended to enjoy it; I enthused about the mac and cheese. He didn't complain that I put too much salt on the fries, and I pretended I didn't mind when he squirted mayo all over them.

Even though I wasn't hungry afterwards, I ordered a peanut butter cheesecake because I knew Matt wanted to try it as well as the key lime pie he'd ordered for himself.

While we ate, we talked about some of the amazing things we'd done together over the years and wondered whether we could recreate the experiences: the romantic weekend in Paris, of course, but also the times we used to smuggle a flask of brandy-laced hot chocolate into the cinema and watch the longest film that was on, because it was warm and our flat was freezing. The Valentine's Day when we were too skint to buy each other anything but Matt came home with a bunch of witch hazel he'd picked on the common on his walk home and presented it to me tied with a red ribbon saved from a Christmas present. The time when I'd cooked him steak and chips for his birthday wearing nothing but an apron over my bra, pants and high heels.

I found myself remembering other times too. When Matt's mum had had a cancer scare and I'd come home to find him on the sofa, white-faced, clutching his phone, and held him while he cried. When I'd had to pull an all-nighter at work and Matt had turned up at the office at midnight with bacon sandwiches and a hot-water bottle, because he knew the heating went off overnight. When I'd made his thirtieth birthday present: thirty hand-drawn pictures of us, even though I couldn't draw for toffee, and he'd insisted on framing each one and displaying them in our living room.

We were the last to leave the restaurant, stumbling tipsy and stuffed full as pythons into the still-warm evening, holding hands as we walked to the Tube.

'See?' Matt said as we passed The Ritz. 'We didn't need to go there.'

And I realised that he was right.

CHAPTER EIGHT

As summer wore on, daily walks became part of Matt's and my routine. Each evening at about half past five (or six, or six thirty, if Marc and Bastian were being particularly difficult or Matt had been out doing a workshop that had run on), we'd leave the house together and spend an hour or so walking together in the sunshine.

It was a relief, after spending the day indoors, to be outside, surrounded by the smells of summer: rainy pavements one day, a neighbour's barbecue the next, the semen-like smell of sweet chestnut trees for a full couple of weeks. After spending yet another day scouring my online thesaurus for words to use as alternatives to 'orgasm' (and realising that the phrase 'blow his lump' wasn't going to sell a product to anyone, ever), or enduring another internal team meeting during which Bastian bemoaned his failure to find a suitable premises for our new office, being alone with Matt made me feel like I could breathe deeply for the first time in hours.

We didn't talk about very much, apart from the cats we saw. It felt to me as if, in the minefield of possible topics of conversations, cats were the one safe option. Sometimes we retraced the route we'd taken that first day, passing the houses where the black cat with the red collar lived, and the ginger one that liked to sit on the wheelie bin and the one with the fluffy grey cat.

It wasn't like a fondness for strolling the streets and petting cats was going to transport us back in time and make everything perfect between Matt and me – I knew that full well. But it did allow me to connect with my husband again, however briefly, for us to suspend hostilities while we discussed whether the cat we'd spotted stalking geese by the pond in the park had a chance of ever catching one, or whether it was just planning to post with a lifegoals hashtag on cat social media.

One evening, we returned from our walk and I went upstairs to have a relaxing bath, leaving Matt kneeling in front of the open freezer door, gazing into its depths in the hope that somehow a ready-meal lasagne would have materialised and he wouldn't have to cobble together a makeshift pasta sauce from the tins in the cupboard and jars in the fridge.

He'd left the towel he'd used after his shower that morning on the bathroom floor in a damp, festering pile, I noticed. Or more likely it was not his towel but mine. No matter how many times I asked, Matt never seemed to get the message that although we were married, although we shared a bed every night, although I often nicked his T-shirts to wear on weekends because they were somehow more comfortable than my own, towels were sacred.

'But why?' he'd ask when I complained about it. 'There's a dry towel there for you to use – why does it matter if I used it last? I was clean.'

'Because...' I'd wrack my brains, trying to come up with a reason for something that, if I actually thought about it, defied logic. 'Because now you've manned all over it!'

Heaving an exaggerated sigh, even though Matt was on the other side of the flat and wouldn't be able to hear, I hung up the wet towel and sniffed the dry one, trying to detect a hint of man.

But there was only the faint odour of laundry detergent. Either way, it didn't matter – Matt had either used both towels or he hadn't, and there was only one dry one available.

I turned on the taps, squeezed the last of my special rose and geranium body wash – Matt had been at that again, too – under the running water, and pulled off my clothes. These were small things, I told myself; I wasn't going to rescue my marriage by flying off the handle over a damp towel or a four-pound bottle of shower gel. I needed to keep a sense of perspective.

Then, just as I was about to step into the warm, fragrant, bubbly water, I heard the doorbell ring. I hesitated. Matt was downstairs, but Matt liked to listen to music loudly through headphones while he was cooking. I called his name, but he didn't hear.

Cursing silently, I wrapped myself in a towel and raced downstairs. I opened the door a crack, hoping that whoever it was wouldn't notice my state of undress and could be quickly fobbed off.

'Delivery for Abbie Mitchell?' The man's face was barely visible between his logoed red-and-yellow baseball cap and the enormous cardboard carton he was holding.

'That's me. Can you just leave it there? I'll get my husband to bring it in in a second.'

He shook his head. 'No can do, love. I need a signature.'

'I... Okay. Hold on.'

I checked that the towel was secure and opened the door. I was as decently covered as if I was wearing shorts and a strapless top, I tried to reassure myself, and anyway, thanks to the box, he could probably see as little of me as I could of him.

'Careful, it's a bit heavy.' He passed the box over to me and I took it. He was right – it weighed a ton. I backed into the hallway, bent over and put it down. Then, as I stood, I felt the towel come adrift, grabbing at it just too late to spare him an eyeful of my nipples.

'Sorry.' I felt my face flame. 'I'll just sign for this.'

But he took his time finding his electronic device and making a note of my name and address before passing it over with a grin that was just a bit too enthusiastic. I scrawled something that didn't remotely resemble my signature, returned the device and closed the door, wishing him a good evening, although I suspected that, for him at any rate, the day had just peaked.

Then, my bath temporarily forgotten, I knelt down to investigate the parcel. Oh God – there was the familiar Quim logo. Once you knew what it was supposed to represent, it was impossible to unsee it. Barely covered by a bath towel, I'd just taken delivery of a box with a fanny printed on it.

Bastian had mentioned something about a delivery of some samples, but that had been over a week ago and I'd completely forgotten about it. I unpeeled a corner of the tape and ripped it off, lifting the flaps – oh God, *flaps* – and removing a layer of crumpled brown paper.

'Jesus Christ,' I said aloud.

The box was full of stuff. Stuff I'd seen listed on the spreadsheet I'd slowly been working my way through, trying to write alluring descriptions of the items on it. (You try writing alluringly about a fleshlight. Go on, I dare you.) Presumably this was intended to spark my creativity. I reached inside and removed the first thing I saw, raising it up to the light to read the label.

'Holy shit, Abs.' Matt appeared in the hallway, holding a wooden spoon. 'What have you got there?'

'Apparently, it's a vibrating anal probe for prostate pleasure.'

My husband recoiled. 'It's *what?*'

'Don't panic, it's for work.'

'Right. Got you. I mean, for a second there I thought...' His eyes strayed to the spoon in his hand, and I knew where his thoughts were straying, too.

'I mean, if you really wanted...' I began.

'Abs, cheers for offering. I appreciate the thought. If I change my mind about the whole, you know, probe thing, you'll be the first to find out.'

'Sure? It would be really helpful for my research.'

'You know I'm always happy to support you in any way I can,' he said. 'But in this case I'm afraid I'm going to have to— Is that your phone?'

He was right – I could hear insistent trilling from the living room. I dodged past the box and Matt, my towel giving up the struggle and falling to the floor. It was too late for it to be work – even Bastian at his most demanding wouldn't call me at seven thirty in the evening. It could be my mum or dad, which might mean that the other of them was ill. Most likely, it would be a junk call telling me I'd been involved in a car accident that wasn't my fault, or that my tax return was overdue and I'd be fined thousands of pounds if I didn't disclose all my bank details to the caller.

It never crossed my mind that it would be Kate.

Although the Girlfriends' Club chatted all the time, we always did so online. If Kate was ringing me, it must be about something important.

I snatched up my phone and answered, slightly breathlessly.

'Hey, Abs. I thought you weren't going to pick up.'

'I was about to get in the bath. I'm standing here in the living room absolutely starkers.' Realising that the curtains were open and any random passer-by would be able to see me standing there with no clothes on, I ducked back into the hallway.

Kate laughed. She had a great laugh, loud and full-throated, almost a guffaw. 'Lucky neighbours. Give them a twirl.'

'Oh God, I just gave a delivery guy an eyeful. I think I'm all done with flashing for the day.'

Kate cackled again, then her voice became serious. 'Listen, was it Devon you said you and Matt went to the first time you had a holiday together?'

'No, Cornwall.'

'Fantastic! I hoped it was.'

'Why?'

'Because— Now, I need you to hear me out and not just say no right away. Okay?'

I leaned against the wall, aware of Matt listening curiously to our conversation.

Kate paused, and then started to talk very quickly, as if delivering instructions to a brighter-than-usual new recruit in risk management.

'So I had a seaside break booked. Just me – I was really looking forward to getting away on my own for a couple of days. But there's been a massive crisis and I'm going to have to work all weekend. I mean, I could work from there but what would be the point? I'd just be glued to my laptop.'

'Ah, no, that sucks. Can't you go anyway? Change of scene?'

'It just won't work. I might be called into the office at short notice. But you could go! You and Matt. It's such an amazing opportunity, the place is stunning apparently and you know how extortionately overpriced UK holidays are at the moment. I'll send you a link to the website – you won't believe it. It's got sea views and a hot tub and a swimming pool and everything. And it's where you and Matt went for your first holiday. It's basically fate intervening.'

I knew perfectly well that Kate didn't believe in fate any more than she believed in the tooth fairy. Her story was as full of holes as the colander I could see Matt searching for in the kitchen, even though it had lived in the exact same drawer next to the cooker for the past six years.

'But since places are in such high demand, surely you could just ask the holiday company to relet it and get a refund?'

'For God's sake, Abbie, stop second-guessing! The holiday's yours if you want it – so take it!'

'But we're both really busy,' I said, but my mind was whirring. Maybe we could make it happen? I could work while we were there, if I had to. It was the summer holidays now so Matt didn't have any school workshops on the go. 'We can't just disappear to Cornwall for a week.'

'You could just go for a long weekend,' Kate said. 'If you left on the Friday morning early you'd have all Saturday and Sunday and the bank holiday Monday and you could get the sleeper train back.'

'And the train tickets will cost a fortune,' I objected.

'Abbie, listen to me. When was the last time you and Matt had a holiday? Ages ago. And were you planning one this year? No. So take a hit of a couple of hundred quid for train tickets and just. Go.'

I hesitated. I think Kate and I both already knew that she'd persuaded me.

'Let me talk to Matt,' I said. 'And thanks.'

As I put my phone down, I noticed Matt standing in the kitchen, his face full of hope, the colander in his hand.

SUMMER 2001

HOT IN HERRE

It was the third day of Abbie's longed-for holiday with Matt. She'd spent so long dreaming about what it would be like, imagining moonlit walks on the beach, lying with him under a snow-white duvet snogging and touching each other in the ways they'd become more and more expert at – and even doing more. Maybe even going the whole way.

She'd imagined eating fish and chips on a pier with him, sharing the headphones of Matt's new iPod. She'd imagined sunsets and starlight and – somehow – it to be just them all the time.

It hadn't quite turned out that way. Of course it hadn't – if she'd thought about it properly, Abbie would have realised that a holiday with Matt and his family was going to be just that. She liked them – she really did. Julia and Tony, his parents, were perfectly friendly and welcoming to her, had quizzed Matt beforehand on the foods Abbie liked to eat and the things she liked to do, so that the holiday would be as enjoyable for her as it was for them. She even liked Matt's little brother, Ryan, when he wasn't giggling every time Matt and Abbie held hands and emitting endless pinging sounds from his handheld games console.

But still, waking up for the third time in the little attic bedroom of the rented cottage, under the rose-printed duvet with identical roses bordering the window, their scent filling the room, Abbie found herself hoping that today would be different. That it wouldn't involve another visit to an art gallery ('So lovely to have someone who's as fascinated by culture as I am,' Julia said. 'These boys wouldn't care about art unless you put it on a plate in front of them and gave them a knife and fork'), drive to a local beauty spot (which made Abbie so motion sick she was worried she'd throw up all over Matt's parents' car or – worse – over Matt), or evening barbecue ('Come over here and give me a hand with these sausages,' Tony said, just as Matt had sat down next to Abbie, his hand resting on her bare, tanned thigh).

It wasn't that she wasn't having fun – she was. And it wasn't like she wasn't grateful – she honestly did appreciate the kindness and generosity they'd shown to her. She just wished they could, like, leave her and Matt alone. Just for a bit.

They'd had moments together, of course. A stolen half-hour in the sitting room after everyone had gone to bed, on the sofa together with the lights turned off and a patchwork throw pulled over them. But it had felt too exposed, too risky – and then they'd heard Matt's dad thumping across the landing to the bathroom upstairs, and that had killed the moment and they'd stolen back up to their separate bedrooms, Abbie alone and Matt in with Ryan.

There was the walk up the hill behind the house, where they'd paused hand in hand and gazed down over the ever-lasting blue of the sea and up at the dome of the sky and out to the deeper blue line where the two met, only it seemed about a thousand dog-walkers had chosen the same afternoon to go for the same walk, and there was no way they could do anything more than hold hands.

There'd been a few seconds in the garden when Matt's mum had sent them out to pick some mint for the lamb chops, when they'd sneaked a kiss under the magnolia tree, and it was just getting passionate when Ryan appeared on the path from the beach and said, 'Oh God, you two! Get a room!'

If only they could do just that, Abbie thought.

She got out of bed, dressed in shorts and the faded Nirvana T-shirt of Matt's, which she'd put on in a panic the night they thought they were going to be surprised on the sofa, and went downstairs. The cottage was silent. Normally, at half past eight, Matt's mum would be bustling about in the kitchen preparing breakfast, refusing Abbie's offers of help. But today no one seemed to be up. Matt and Ryan might have gone for a run, she guessed – Matt had mentioned that he was feeling bad about wanting to spend time with her at his little brother's expense.

She could make herself useful, anyway. She'd watched Matt's mum's breakfast preparations for the past two days and knew what needed to be done, so she flicked on the kettle, scooped coffee into the cafetiere, put boxes of cereal, jars of jam, marmalade and peanut butter, the fruit bowl and some plates on the table.

Just as she was finishing this task, Tony came downstairs. But there was no sign of Julia.

'You're up bright and early,' he said. 'The boys not awake yet?'

'I think they've gone out somewhere. Shall I make the coffee?'

'Bless you. Julia's got one of her migraines. They normally pass after a few hours, but she won't be up to the Barbara Hepworth museum like we planned.'

'Oh no! Can I get anything for her? Fruit tea? Iced water?'

Tony shook his head. He had the same way of pushing his

hair back from his face as Matt did, Abbie noticed fondly, although his was greying instead of raven black.

'She just needs to lie down. I could murder a coffee, though.'

'What's that?' Matt asked, crashing through the door with his brother, sweating from their early run along the beach.

'Has Mother got one of her heads?' Ryan asked. 'Poor Mum. Still, at least it means we can do something fun, instead of looking at art all morning.'

'We could go for a walk,' Tony said. 'It looks like a gorgeous day. There's that eight-mile circular route over the cliffs we did last year.'

'And practically got sunstroke to show for it,' Matt said.

'Come on, Dad,' Ryan complained. 'I haven't had a chance to surf all holiday. The waves are meant to be ace today.'

He wiggled his hips and broke into a few lines of rap about how it was the right time to shoot his steam and he felt like busting moves.

'And the cricket's on, you know,' Matt said.

Abbie noticed Tony's longing glance towards the television.

'Well, if you boys want to surf...' he began.

'Of course we do,' Matt said. 'And we can teach Abbie, or she can just watch.'

Abbie couldn't think of anything worse than attempting to surf – except possibly feigning interest as Matt and Ryan did their boy stuff. She could lie on the beach and work on her tan, she supposed. But then she caught Matt's eye, and he winked.

'I'd love that,' she said.

'I suppose it's best I stay here in case your mum needs me.' Tony poured coffee into a mug, bending his head to inhale the fragrant steam, and settled down, not at the kitchen table but on the sofa, flicking on the television.

'Right, then.' Matt exchanged a high five with his brother.

'Refuel and head out in fifteen?' Ryan suggested.

It was more like half an hour, but soon they were break-fasted and ready. Matt had packed a rucksack that looked as if it could have contained just about anything apart from a surf-board, and Abbie had put on her bikini under her shorts and T-shirt and packed a bag of her own with sunblock, lip balm and – after a brief hesitation – a condom from the box that had been buried at the bottom of her suitcase all holiday.

She remembered the excruciating embarrassment of going into Boots to buy them, filling her shopping basket with shampoo and nail polish and deodorant as well, as if somehow that would make the motherly lady who worked on the checkout not see the condoms.

If she didn't get to use them, it would all have been for nothing.

She'd wondered how Matt would negotiate abandoning his brother – or if it would even be possible. Maybe she'd have to spend the morning lying on her beach towel reading her book and pretending to be interested in swells and cutback.

But as soon as the three of them were out of sight of the house, Ryan said, 'Off you trot then, kids.'

'You sure?' Matt asked.

'Course. Abbie doesn't give a shit about surfing and you haven't even got your board with you. Rookie error – you're lucky Dad wasn't concentrating.'

Matt grinned ruefully. 'True. Right then, we'll catch you later. Don't drown.'

Ryan jogged off towards the beach and Matt and Abbie waited until he was out of sight, his arm around her shoulders.

'So,' he said.

'So.' Abbie smiled up at him.

'There's a place we used to go when we were kids, about an hour's walk from here. It's a little cove – no one ever goes there. Want to see it?'

Abbie felt like a whole kaleidoscope of butterflies had been let loose inside her stomach. 'Sure.'

They stopped at the shop in the village and bought pasties, crisps, cans of cider and sour sweets, which Matt stuffed into his backpack, and headed off along the path following the coastline. The morning was hot already, but a fresh breeze dried the sweat on Abbie's skin. She could taste salt spray on her lips and hear the shrieks of gulls wheeling over the water.

Her heart was pounding far harder than the gentle incline they were walking up should have made it.

The walk seemed to take forever, but also no time at all: Abbie both longed to reach their destination and feared it. This was a turning point not only in their relationship but in her life, she thought – after today, surely nothing would ever feel the same again.

At last, Matt said, 'Here we are, just over these rocks.'

He held out his hand and Abbie clambered carefully over the outcrop of barnacled boulders, unsteady in her flip-flops.

'Should have worn my hiking boots,' she joked.

'Mmm, and a cagoule maybe. Sexy.'

She giggled. 'Or not so much.'

'Seriously,' Matt said, 'you could wear a black bin liner and you'd still be the sexiest girl on the planet.'

The cove was as secluded as he'd promised, sheltered from the wind and from view by the curve of the cliff face and the rocky barrier they'd just negotiated. In front of them, the sea stretched away to the horizon, its surface broken by lines of foam as the waves washed in and out in a rhythm as regular as Abbie's heartbeat. Matt unzipped his backpack and spread out a blanket on the fine sand. Abbie sat down, stretching her legs out in front of her, and Matt handed her a can of cider.

'Five-star service you get round here,' she said.

'Dunno about that. It's not that cold any more and these are a bit squashed. I'll put the other cans in the water to cool down.'

Matt handed her a pasty and Abbie eased it out of its paper bag and took a bite. He was right, it was a bit squashed, and lukewarm like the cider, but she didn't really care. She was hungry and thirsty and the sharpness of the cider and salty richness of the meat pie tasted like heaven.

When they'd finished eating, Matt lay back on the blanket and Abbie settled next to him, her head nestled on his shoulder. She could feel his hair tickling her cheek and smell his body, a mixture of soap and shampoo and deodorant and just him.

He reached out a hand and stroked the damp hair back from Abbie's face, lightly caressing her cheek and her arm. She felt goosebumps rising on her skin at his touch, and a liquid warmth spreading through her body. He raised himself up on his elbow and leaned over to kiss her. His mouth tasted of cider, as Abbie supposed hers must, too.

They'd done this so often before, knew each other's bodies so well already. Yet still, knowing that this was the time when they'd do the one thing they hadn't yet, the thing they'd both been waiting for, made every touch of Matt's fingers and mouth feel new and almost momentous.

They kissed each other on and on, the heat of the sand under Abbie's back and the heat of the sun on her bare legs and the heat of Matt's body and her own all becoming one, the sun drawing bright squiggles on her eyelids when they were shut and Matt's face right there, so close, smiling down at her, when they were open.

It turned out she wasn't the only one who'd brought condoms. She'd never seen a guy put one on before, and only done it herself on a cucumber in sex ed at school, so she was relieved that Matt seemed to know what he was doing.

'Did you practise on a cucumber, too?' she teased.

'Don't know what you mean – this is much bigger than any cucumber.'

And the two of them dissolved into giggles.

Abbie closed her eyes again, her arms and legs wrapped around Matt, holding him close, a mixture of relief, triumph and tenderness washing over her. Then something else washed over her – a shower of sand that was as sudden and startling as a tidal wave.

'What the...?' Matt gasped, pulling away abruptly. 'Get off of my...'

He rolled off her, and his face was replaced with that of a panting, grinning golden Labrador. It leaned in, gave Abbie's nose a slobbery lick, then veered over to the remains of their picnic, grabbed Abbie's discarded pasty wrapper and bounded off, looking like a dog that had finally found the Holy Grail.

'Oh my God.' Abbie was torn between shock and laughter, but laughter won.

'Holy shit, that gave me the fright of my life,' Matt said. 'I'm really sorry.'

'It's not your fault. But I'm covered in sand. My flip-flops are full of it, and my bikini.'

'My pants too.' Matt lay back next to her, laughing helplessly. 'Next time we're going to have to find a more secluded spot.'

'Who says there'll be a next time?' Abbie teased. 'For all you know, that put me off for life.'

'Oi! Behave yourself.' Gently, he wrestled her down onto the blanket and kissed her, sand now somehow on their lips as well as everywhere else. But she could feel his mouth smiling against hers, and she knew for sure that there would be a next time, and it would be all right.

CHAPTER NINE

We almost missed the train because Matt was looking for his phone charger, and then when we arrived at the holiday cottage he realised that, after all that fuss, he'd still ended up leaving it on the bed.

That pretty much set the tone for our romantic back-in-time trip to Cornwall.

It's not like we didn't try. I'd arranged for a supermarket delivery to the property with all Matt's favourite food and three bottles of champagne far superior to the cava we normally drank when we had something to celebrate, which to be honest had been a while ago now. I packed some slinky satin palazzo pants and a flowery dress so I'd have something nice to change into in the evenings, rather than just mooching around in shorts. I even packed make-up and hair straighteners.

If this holiday didn't get things back on track, I told myself, it wasn't going to be because of lack of effort on my part.

And Matt, once we'd got over the train stress, seemed to be in the same mindset. He'd made a playlist of songs from that summer when we went to Cornwall with his family, and surprised me with it on the train. He produced a bar of my favourite mint chocolate and a copy of *Cosmopolitan* for me to read on the journey, and I dissolved laughing and handed over the *Wired* magazine and tube of Pringles I'd bought as a surprise for him.

When we arrived at the house, I honestly thought everything was going to be perfect. It was just as Kate and the website had described – a sweep of emerald lawn leading down to a narrow, quiet road with the beach just beyond; a king-size bed in our room with a fluffy white duvet like a cloud on it; a marble bathroom with a power shower and a fancy freestanding bath like something in a luxury hotel. Not that we'd stayed in one of those since our honeymoon.

We unpacked our bags, our clothes looking shabby and humble in the sleek fitted wardrobes. Our grocery delivery arrived right on schedule and we unpacked that too, which didn't take long because it was only enough for three days and the kitchen was set up for a group of ten to stay a week. I put a bottle of champagne in the fridge to chill.

'What would you like to do now?' Matt asked.

'Walk on the beach? I'd like to say we could watch the sunset but that won't be for hours yet.'

'Walk on the beach and then a go in the hot tub?'

'And then dinner? Apparently there's a pub down the road that does really good food.'

'Perfect.'

We strolled down to the beach and walked along the tide-line for a while, letting the waves lap over our feet. The sun was shining, a gentle breeze was ruffling my hair, and I could feel my whole body relaxing, as if the warm sunshine was melting something hard and cold that had been there inside me for so long I barely even noticed it was there any more.

'What's that up there?' Matt pointed, shielding his eyes from the sun.

'Where? There at the top of the cliff? Looks like a house. Maybe a farmhouse?'

'The view from up there must be incredible. Want to walk up and take a look?'

'Really?' I looked doubtfully at my flip-flops and more doubtfully still at the narrow, crumbling path leading up from the beach.

'Sure. It's not that steep. We'll get to the top in twenty minutes max.'

I didn't share his confidence, but I said, 'Okay, let's give it a go.'

Matt led the way, scrambling easily up the path on his long legs, his sturdy trainers effortlessly finding footholds. I panted after him, my feet slipping against the plastic of my shoes, my hair beginning to stick to my neck in damp tendrils.

Every so often Matt turned, asked me if I was okay, offered me a handhold over the roughest bits, and I resisted the urge to suggest that we abandon our plan, head back down and watch the sunset from the flat safety of the beach.

Not least because, when I looked behind me at the route back, I suspected that there was no way I'd get back down there unless I slid all the way on my arse.

'Made it!' Matt heaved himself up the final step and extended a hand to help me, which I gratefully took. 'My God, look at that view.'

We turned and gazed out over the expanse of water and sky. From this height, the waves looked more like wrinkles, the sea under the lowering sun like a sheet of aluminium foil that had been crumpled and smoothed out to use again, the beach a narrow ribbon of gold. Behind us, tussocky grass spread up a gentle slope.

I sat down, my legs aching from the climb, my outspread hands digging into the warm, dry grass. After a second, Matt joined me.

'It's breathtaking,' I said. 'We should have brought a picnic.'

'Warm cider, squashed pasties and sour sweets?' He grinned sideways at me, and I felt an answering smile spread over my face.

'And condoms?'

'Don't get ideas, missus. Al-fresco sex is too much risk and not enough reward.'

'I wasn't talking about sex! Eeeuuw. I was thinking about blowing them up and making balloon animals.'

'Not sure I've got the breath left to blow up anything,' Matt admitted.

'Anyway, do you know where we are? That path must've gone sideways – I can't see the cottage we were heading for at all.'

'Not sure. I'll just check my phone.'

There was a pause while Matt stared at the screen, a frown wrinkling his forehead.

'What's wrong?'

'No reception. I should have guessed – we are kind of in the middle of nowhere. Check yours.'

'I left it back at the cottage.'

He gave me a look that quite clearly meant, *What the hell did you do that for?* but said nothing.

I said, 'Look, it can't be that hard to find our way back. If we just follow the line of the cliff, we should come to the road in a bit and then we can walk back down to the village and we'll be able to find our way from there. And probably get a signal too.'

The prospect of walking even another mile in my flip-flops, which I could feel had already shredded the skin between my toes, was hardly appealing, but I was determined to put a brave face on it.

We set off, following a path that was little more than a faint ribbon of flattened grass, but before long we came to a stone wall, ending abruptly at the cliff edge but stretching away inland as far as we could see.

'There must be a stile somewhere,' Matt said. 'We can climb over there.'

'Wouldn't that be trespassing?' I imagined an irate farmer brandishing a pitchfork – or more likely a shotgun – and bellowing, 'Get orf my land!'

'It's the countryside. Right to roam, innit?'

'Are you sure?'

'Not really.'

'God, we are such townies. Come on then, let's look for a stile.'

We followed the wall over the gentle rise of the hill. Beyond, we could see nothing except more hills undulating serenely into the distance, dotted with daisies and the black-and-white figures of grazing cattle. The road must be there somewhere, hidden between the slopes, but we couldn't see it.

My feet were starting to hurt seriously now, and I realised I was getting hungry – and I knew from experience that meant that hangry would follow as certainly as night followed day. Speaking of which, the sunset that had seemed ages away didn't seem so distant any more, and the idea of spending the night in the middle of nowhere wasn't exactly appealing. Sleeping under the stars – a romantic notion until you're faced with the prospect of doing it.

'Should we go back?' Matt suggested.

I thought of that long, treacherous path back down to the beach, and shook my head. 'Look, let's just climb over the wall and cut through this field. It's not great, I know, but we'll be walking forever at this rate, and at least then we'll know we're going in more or less the right direction.'

Matt looked at me. His cheekbones and the bridge of his nose were turning pink and I knew I must have caught the sun, too.

'Right,' he said. 'I'm going over. Once more unto the breach!'

'If there was a breach, we wouldn't have to climb over,' I pointed out.

'Whatever. Stop with your superior knowledge of Shakespeare.'

He swung one of his long legs onto the top of the wall and vaulted easily over. I scrambled up after him, finding footholds in the stones with my flip-flops, grazing my knee, breaking a fingernail and almost losing my footing altogether as I landed heavily on the other side, feeling my ankle twist painfully.

'There isn't really a path through here,' I said. 'Are you sure it's okay?'

'Got a better idea?'

I hadn't. We made our way over the uneven grass, patched with nettles that stung my bare calves agonisingly. I looked enviously at Matt's jeans-clad legs and said nothing.

We crested another gentle rise, and Matt stopped abruptly. In front of us was a herd of cows. At least, I hoped they were cows and not bulls. There must have been a couple of dozen of them, all grazing peacefully. But they looked a hell of a lot bigger than the ones we'd seen a few minutes before, safely in the distance.

'What do we do now?' I asked.

'Stage a rodeo?'

'Not without our Stetson hats. Seriously, though?'

'We walk around them, I guess. Unless you've got—'

'A better idea? No, I have not got a better idea.'

I followed Matt towards the cows. One by one, as we approached, they lifted their heads from the grass and looked at us. Then, one by one, they started to walk towards us. Matt veered slightly away from them; the cows followed.

'Shit. Are they going to – I don't know, stampede or something?' I panted.

'Do I look like Buffalo Bill to you, Abbie? I have no idea. Maybe they think we're going to feed them, or milk them, or whatever.'

Matt increased his pace and I hurried in his wake, struggling to keep up on the rough terrain. The cows had no such difficulty; one or two of the more enthusiastic ones even broke into a trot, keeping pace with him easily. We were about halfway across the field now; I could see the wall on the other side inching closer, but the cows weren't so much inching as striding.

'Come on, Abbie, get a move on,' Matt called over his shoulder.

'I'm trying!' I replied, but I was so out of breath, and he was so far ahead of me, I don't think he heard.

The cow in front of the group – the ringleader, I expect she thought of herself as, the Regina George of the cow world – tossed her head and increased her pace, closing the gap between Matt and the herd.

'I'm making a run for it,' he called over his shoulder, and sprinted for the wall.

I followed – at least, I tried to. I managed about ten yards before, entirely predictably, I stepped on a cowpat, my foot skidded from under me, and that was it. Woman down. Cows one, Matt and me nil.

'Well, that certainly got the holiday off to a good start.' Matt reached over and put a glass brimming with gin and tonic on the edge of the bathtub in which I was lying. The warm water stung my nettle rash and the raw skin on my feet, but I didn't care – at least I was no longer trespassing in a field, being pursued by cows with murderous intent.

'Care to join me?' I asked.

Matt shook his head. 'There's not enough room in there for two. We'll have a go in the hot tub tomorrow.'

'And tonight?'

'We could try the pub? Or make something if you're not up to walking any further.'

I wasn't sure I was – but at the same time, the prospect of a massive steak and ale pie, or possibly mussels and chips, was more than tempting.

'I can't believe you chased those cows away,' I said. 'That was seriously impressive.'

'Well, I couldn't risk my wife being trampled to death on my watch. What would I have told your friends?'

'That I'd deliberately provoked them and you had no choice but to run for your life?'

'Yeah, they'd have believed that, for sure. Everyone knows you've got form for cow provocation.'

'That's me. Let me out of the city and there I am, taunting farm animals right, left and centre.'

We laughed, and I felt myself relax in the hot water. A large gulp of gin and tonic soothed me further. For a second, back there in the field, I really had felt like I was in serious danger. I can't say my whole life had flashed before my eyes, but it had been close – I was pretty sure I'd read in the paper a while back about a woman being trampled by cattle so badly she'd ended up in hospital, and I really, really didn't want that to be me.

Apart from anything else, Marc and Bastian would have hit the roof if their senior copywriter was laid up in a high-dependency unit covered in hoof-shaped bruises, and they had to find someone else to write about clit stimulators and uplift waspies for the Quim website.

'I really, really didn't want you to get trampled by cows,' Matt said, echoing my thoughts. 'You know, I've grown quite fond of you over the years.'

'You're not so bad yourself. Even if you do cheat at Monopoly.'

'I do not cheat at Monopoly!'

'Yes, you do. Last time we played, you hid a five-hundred-pound note under the board and produced it just when I thought I'd won.'

'That's not cheating, that's tactics.'

'It's blatant cheating. Will you wash my back? The water's getting cold.'

I leaned forward and felt Matt's strong, gentle hands rubbing soap into my skin. His touch was tender, especially on the sunburned bits around my neck. I remembered how it used to be, when he had only to brush my hand or look at me a certain way to send a frisson of longing through me that was as potent as the gin I'd almost finished.

I didn't feel that now, although I wanted to. But I felt something else I hadn't in a long time – the sense that, maybe, we had a future together and not just a past.

He rinsed the soap off my back and I stood up, stepping carefully out of the bathtub. Matt pressed a fluffy towel around my shoulders and pulled me close. I wrapped my arms around him, too, and we looked at each other for a long moment, before he bent down to kiss me.

CHAPTER TEN

'Oh my God.' Naomi blotted her eyes with a paper napkin. 'I shouldn't laugh. You poor things, it must have been awful. But still. Exit, pursued by cows.'

'They've evil fuckers,' Kate said darkly, splashing more rosé into our glasses, and I remembered that her uncle was a farmer in Somerset so she knew all about bovine malice. Not that I could imagine her ever going near a cow in her sleek suits and designer shoes.

'It's okay,' I said. 'I can see the funny side of it myself now. Kind of.'

'What happened after that?' Rowan asked, snapping a cheese straw in half and putting both bits in her mouth at once. 'I can't wait to tell Clara this story – she might actually crack a smile for once.'

'Well, first thing was, I sat up – after a bit; I'd literally knocked the wind out of myself, which I didn't know was even a thing – and I was surrounded by cows, all looking at me like, "What the hell is wrong with you?" And then Matt came back and shooed them away, and we realised the road was just the other side of the field and we got back to the cottage.'

'Happy ending, then?' Kate asked hopefully.

'Well, in the sense that we weren't stampeded to death, I guess so. And the rest of the weekend was lovely, although that night it started to rain and basically it didn't stop.'

'Cue lots of romantic afternoons beneath the fluffy white duvet?' suggested Rowan.

'Sadly not. The backs of my thighs were so sunburned I could barely sit down, which ruled out any bedroom shenanigans.'

'You could have gone on top, surely?' Naomi suggested.

'Or given him a—' Rowan began.

But Kate saw my face and interrupted. 'So what did you do instead?'

I took a long swallow of wine. 'We played Monopoly. And Matt let me win for once, which was nice of him.'

'I'm sorry it wasn't perfect,' Kate said. 'I honestly imagined the two of you strolling on the beach and having loads of sex.'

'Maybe that was a bit ambitious,' I admitted. 'But we did have a great time. And we felt – you know, closer.'

'So you're not giving up?' Rowan asked. 'On the whole recapturing-the-romance thing, I mean?'

I shook my head. 'The weird thing is, I think it's kind of working. Like the other day, I was remembering when Matt gave me make-up brushes for my birthday.'

'He did what?' Naomi asked. 'Seriously? That's next level. Patch bought me an electric toothbrush once like it was this grand romantic gesture.'

'Not just any make-up brushes,' I went on. 'He actually went to a specialist shop in town that sells the fancy ones make-up artists use and spent about half an hour in there interrogating the saleswomen about which were the best ones.'

'I knew that,' Rowan said. 'Because he asked me where he should go to buy them and I told him. I'd have gone with him but I was working.'

'He's done loads of that sort of thing over the years,' I said. 'Like, bought me my favourite tomato soup when I've been ill and run me baths after I've had a rubbish day at work – little things like that. And remembering them has made me feel like I really want to make things work.'

'I'm so glad you do,' Rowan said. 'If I had someone who did that stuff for me, you'd have to prise him out of my cold, dead hands.'

'I know, right? But anyway, I was just thinking about the make-up brushes, when I was meant to be working, and Matt walked in with a special cushion he'd bought to give me better back support, because our kitchen chairs are murder when you're sat in them for eight hours a day.'

'He really is a keeper,' said Naomi.

'That's what I thought, after the cushion thing. Then I went upstairs and saw he'd left crusty dried toothpaste all over the basin in the bathroom, and I thought maybe I should go down and hack him into tiny pieces with his safety razor. But I didn't.'

'That's true love, right there,' Naomi said. 'Patch would be six feet deep under the patio if he pulled shit like that toothpaste thing.'

'So what's next on the memory-lane itinerary?' Kate asked.

'I was thinking,' I said, 'about a picnic I prepared for Matt and me one time. We were home from uni after our first year and we went up to Hampstead Heath. I did the whole posh thing – smoked salmon and strawberries and champagne and everything.'

'Hampstead Heath,' Naomi said. 'That's where we were when Patch first told me he loved me. You know what it's like – you spend months and months pussyfooting around and saying stuff like, "I love the way you laugh," or, "I love the way your face looks when you orgasm," or—'

'Stop!' Rowan said. 'God. We have to see Patch sometimes,

remember? The last thing we want is to keep picturing his O face.'

'Actually,' Naomi said, a bit smugly, 'it was my O face. But anyway. My point was that once you do finally properly drop the L bomb, it's like you can't stop. Patch and I used to text each other back and forth for hours saying it.'

'So did Matt and I,' I agreed, and the realisation made me feel suddenly sad again. I couldn't remember the last time I'd texted my husband just to tell him I loved him. So when Naomi went to the loo and Kate went to the bar to get another bottle, I gave Rowan a discreet wink, took out my phone and did just that.

Hey. I'm not sure if I've told you this recently, but I love you very much xxxxx

But by the time I got home, tipsy from too much rosé and with my cheeks aching from laughing, Matt still hadn't replied. Glancing at my phone as I left the Tube station and turned down the road that led to our flat, I felt briefly pissed off – he'd read the message, I could see, but he hadn't even acknowledged it.

But I pushed my annoyance aside. Perhaps he was waiting for me to get home before telling me that he loved me too. Perhaps he'd already been asleep and surfaced just enough to see the text, but not enough to respond.

But I could see as I approached the building that Matt was awake – a light was shining in our living room, obscured by the curtains but sending slices of gold onto the pavement, damp from the earlier rain.

I unlocked the door and pushed it open, calling out my husband's name. But he didn't answer.

'Matt?' I said again, turning into the living room. 'Are you okay?'

He was sitting on the sofa, the lamp on the side table next to him lit but the TV switched off. He didn't have his phone in his hand; he was just staring, apparently at nothing.

He turned his head towards me, a smile on his face so forced I might as well have been looking at a bare skull. The brightness of the lamp highlighted the threads of silver in his dark hair, and I felt my heart swell with sudden sadness – or just the anticipation of sadness.

We're going to grow old together. That was the plan all along. But it meant that every day we spent together was one less day we'd have in our future – so how could we bear to waste any of them in unhappiness?

'Good evening?' he asked.

'Lovely. Girlfriends' Club always is.'

He smiled again, a bit more normally this time, then stood up. 'Can I make you a cup of tea?'

Tea? I'd been planning to go straight to bed, so I wouldn't have to face my morning call with Bastian crippled by lack of sleep as well as a hangover. But Matt didn't want me to drink tea; he must want to talk to me.

'Just a glass of water would be great, thanks.'

He disappeared into the kitchen and I heard the tap running, and sat down on the sofa to wait for him. Then I noticed the folded sheet of paper on the coffee table, its colour a drab yet distinctive not-quite-white-and-not-quite-grey, with the familiar blue logo at its top.

I knew then. I knew right away what that terrible un-smile of Matt's had meant.

He came back with two glasses of water and sat down next to me. I knew he could see from my face that I was aware something was wrong, if not exactly what.

'So we got a letter,' he began.

I nodded. 'And you opened it.'

'That's okay, isn't it? You were out, and it was addressed to both of us. I thought...'

You thought it would be good news. You thought I'd walk in the door, drunk and giddy after my night out, and you'd be able to give it to me and we'd dance round the living room together and maybe open a bottle of fizz and get even drunker.

'It's fine that you opened it. Honestly. I'm not upset about that.'

But I'm about to be upset about something else.

'Okay,' Matt said. 'That's good. I was worried there for a second. Do you want to read it?'

I reached out my hand, but although I could just see, in the top third of the A4 sheet, below the logo and our address, the salutation 'Dear Mr and Mrs Mitchell', I knew I couldn't bear to read any further. I would eventually. I'd read it over and over. Just not tonight.

I shook my head. 'Just tell me what it says.'

Matt took a breath. I could hear the air going into his lungs and knew that when it came out again, it would be carrying the words I could hardly bear to hear.

'It says they apologise once again for the delay in getting our fertility treatment under way, but that services across the trust have been disrupted due to circumstances beyond their control. And then it says that regrettably...'

'They won't do it now?' My lips felt like they were made of stone; I could hardly get the words out.

'They won't do it now. They say that when we began the process and got put on the waiting list, you were thirty-five and within the allowable age for treatment, but that by the time we'd be seen, owing to the aforementioned delays, you'll be almost thirty-eight and, unfortunately, owing to funding constraints...'

'We'll have to fuck off?'

'Basically. They say there are private providers that have

different criteria and that there's information on their website, and we can approach our GP for a referral or go direct.'

'Like we did four years ago. Because we didn't want to wait.'

'And it didn't work.'

'Ten grand we saved and saved to scrape together and it didn't work.'

'And the time after didn't work either.'

'The one we borrowed against the house to pay for.'

'Abbie, I'm really sorry.'

'It's not your fault, Matt.'

'It's at least half my fault.'

We looked at each other, the foot or so of space between us seeming like miles. Our sadness was shared, so why did it make us feel so separate?

I said, 'We could go private again. We could give it one last try.'

'Abs, we're both older now.'

I couldn't help noticing that even in his shattering disappointment, he was kind to me. He didn't point out that it was me getting older that mattered, with my ovaries shrivelling or my hormones declining or whatever they do, more and more every day, whereas he'd still have viable sperm when he was seventy.

'And it didn't work before, so why would it work now?' I asked pointlessly, because there wasn't an answer.

'And besides, we can't afford it.'

'We could sell the flat. Or remortgage, like we did before.' The words tumbled out without me even knowing they were there in my head, waiting to be said.

'We don't have enough equity to remortgage. And we couldn't sell it. Abbie, you know that.'

Of course I knew that. I knew perfectly well that our home was our refuge, our security, the place we'd moved to hoping that this was the beginning of us as a family. And our finances, precarious for years, were just starting to get back on an even keel. We couldn't throw all that under a bus, not for anything. Not even for this.

Part of me wanted to rant at Matt, to blame him for this, tell him that if he hadn't invited Andy to come and live with us, all this would never have been a problem. We'd be in a different place now – in the house we'd dreamed of with the children we'd expected to be able to have.

But I knew that would be not only cruel and unfair, but also fundamentally untrue. I knew that whatever harsh words I said wouldn't change a thing: I'd still have the knowledge inside me that this was all my fault, not Matt's and not Andy's.

'I'm knackered,' I said. 'I can't talk about this now. It's too much. I'm going to bed.'

And I stood up and left him there alone on the sofa, still staring at the piece of paper in his hand.

AUTUMN 2008

LIES

Abbie and Matt had lived in a succession of rented apartments, with a succession of different housemates. There was the place in South West London with the rising damp and the silver birch tree in the garden. There were Simon and Lucia, who cooked incredible pasta and had noisy sex at three in the morning, which was hilarious at first, but after about the tenth time of being jerked from sleep by Simon exhorting his girlfriend to tell him how much she wanted it, dirty girl, became too high a price to pay even for the pasta. There was the flat in East London, just when Hackney was becoming fashionable, with the amazing cocktail bar down the road and the crack dealers on the corner. There were Cathy, David and Lawrence, who according to Facebook were now living together in a polyamorous relationship. There was the next place in Hackney, where the ceiling collapsed thanks to the weight of the landlord's belongings in the loft. There was Federico, the ideal flatmate because he spent almost every night at his boyfriend's place.

And then, finally, there was the place in Tottenham in North London, where they persuaded each other to move because it was way cheaper than Hackney and they were saving up and up for a deposit on a flat of their own. In the first two years they lived there, there seemed to be a dizzying succession of flatmates. Sometimes it seemed like just weeks between someone moving in, plastic CD cases slithering from their backpack, and them moving out again, leaving behind a half-dead cactus in a pot, a dog-eared array of Waterstones three-for-two paperbacks and a mysterious patch of mould on their bedroom wall.

It was fine – it was standard twenty-something living. But at the same time, for a couple as settled as Abbie and Matt already were, it was disruptive.

Then, one Sunday when they were perched on the brick wall surrounding the flowerbed in the back garden, drinking cans of Stella Artois and watching sausages smoke and sizzle on the barbecue, Matt said, 'You know Andy's looking for a place to stay.'

'Is he? What happened to the swanky flat in Islington he had with William?'

'It was his parents' buy-to-let investment. They had to sell it. And William dumped him – possibly because there was no more free rent.'

Their eyes met. They'd had numerous conversations about the financial crash, and whether it would mean that property prices would fall, finally, to within their reach or that no one who wasn't a millionaire would be able to get a mortgage again, ever.

'Poor Andy,' Abbie said.

'Yeah, he's had a shit time of it. Hitting the coke a bit hard too, I think.'

Abbie rolled her eyes. She was all too familiar with Andy's party lifestyle – there'd been plenty of times when they'd met up for Sunday lunch or what was meant to be a chilled couple of pints somewhere, only for Andy to turn up jittery and wild-eyed, not having been to bed since Friday night.

'Anyway, he's after a room,' Matt went on. 'It would be nice to have someone we know living here, don't you think?'

Abbie thought. Part of her could imagine life with Andy as a housemate being fun – his never-ending fund of toe-curling but hilarious stories about his one-night stands, his ebullience and energy, his ability to whip up delicious meals from the *River Café Cookbook* without turning a hair.

But there'd be downsides, too. Andy and Matt were friends – closer almost than Matt and his own brother. Would she feel excluded, like a third wheel? Andy could be moody too, retreating into dark and morose states that could last for days, during which he cancelled any arrangements he'd made and chucked sickies from work. And his good moods might not be easy to live with, either – more than once, he'd woken Matt up at three in the morning calling because he wanted to chat, or wanted Matt to hear a new dance track he'd discovered, or was in the late-night newsagent and couldn't remember whether he liked grape or raspberry Fanta best.

'It could be fun, I guess,' Abbie said. 'But aren't you worried if something went wrong, what it might do to your friendship?'

'Andy and I are like this.' Matt held up two fingers pressed together. 'I reckon it'd take more than a dust-up over whose turn it is to do the dusting to change that. And what kind of a mate would I be if I didn't help him out when he was in a tight spot?'

Somewhere in Abbie's head, an alarm bell rang faintly. 'He'll pay his share of the rent, right? Same as Melissa did?'

'Of course he will. God, I'm a nice person, but I'm not that nice. We need to keep building up our deposit fund, right?'

'Eyes on the prize,' Abbie said, and they tapped the rims of their beer cans together and toasted the decision.

A week later, Andy moved in. He arrived in a taxi with a case of Moët and his clothes in bin liners, and as far as Abbie could tell he never actually unpacked them. But those first few weeks were uproarious fun.

The first night they got to bed at five in the morning, and Abbie struggled through the next day at work mainlining coffee and wishing she had matchsticks to prop her eyes open with. The first weekend Andy invited Naomi, Patch, Zara, Ryan, Kate, Rowan and Paul over for dinner (his own ex, Will, would have been conspicuously NFI had he not inconveniently been in Glasgow with work). He made little pillows of pasta stuffed with spinach and ricotta, rack of lamb, chocolate nemesis and a cheeseboard that made the fridge smell like rancid socks for days, and Abbie had never seen anything like the kitchen the next day. She and Matt did the clearing up because Andy was prostrated in bed with 'a weapons-grade hangover', which was only fair, really, since he'd done all the hard work the previous day.

On his first payday, Andy came home with a glassine bag of what he called 'ching', even though as far as Abbie knew he'd never been to Scotland in his life, and she and Matt had to awkwardly decline his invitation to partake, and then try not to let their shock and disapproval show as Andy chopped up fat white lines on the coffee table and had a few bumps before heading out and returning at dawn with a strange man in tow.

'I'm sure it was just a one-off,' Matt said. 'He's stressed, that's all. And his freelance contract is ending in a couple of weeks, so he won't be able to afford coke for a bit.'

'He'll get another job,' Abbie fretted. 'He'll have to. And what then? I mean, I'm not a prude, you know I'm not, but in our own home it's a bit...'

'Stop worrying,' Matt said. 'I'll have a word with him.'

Abbie never knew whether Matt had had a word or not. Andy announced that he was going to take a couple of months' sabbatical because he needed some headspace, and spent them lying on the sofa eating crisps, smoking weed and watching back-to-back reruns of *Buffy the Vampire Slayer* or listening to McFly with the volume turned up so loud the neighbours started posting angry notes through the letterbox. There were no more gourmet dinners: in the evenings Andy would say, 'You lovebirds need your space,' and leave the flat, returning long after midnight, or sometimes even when Abbie and Matt were already up for work.

One afternoon he decided to make a cheese toastie on the ironing board and forgot to switch off the iron, and if the neighbours hadn't heard the smoke alarm God knew what would have happened.

Abbie wished she could pretend none of this mattered. But she drew the line at pretending Andy not paying the rent didn't matter.

'It's just a few days late,' Matt said. 'He's just started a new job. Give him a chance.'

Abbie bit her tongue. But when she walked into the bathroom one morning to find Andy doing a line off the toilet lid, she felt a deep sense of foreboding: if this was the way he was behaving, the new job wasn't going to last either.

And it didn't.

Another period of 'sabbatical' ensued, only this time it wasn't just *Buffy* and toasted sandwiches. Abbie was sure Andy's drug use was escalating, and she started to worry not only about where the rent was coming from, but increasingly about Andy's health. He'd lost an alarming amount of weight; he was gaunt and hollow-eyed and rarely seemed to eat or sleep. He still went out at night, but he didn't stay out and he returned alone to spend the nights alternately pacing from the front window to the kitchen door, and sitting on the floor biting his nails until his cuticles were ragged and bleeding.

This time, Abbie took it upon herself to talk to Andy. She picked a Tuesday night, when Matt was working late – not because she wanted to go behind his back, but because, if her actions caused a rift, at least it would only be between her and Andy, not between Andy and Matt.

'I was going to make a risotto,' was her opening gambit. 'Fancy some?'

Andy looked at her with a ghost of the dazzling smile that could light up a room. 'Yeah, thanks. That would be great.'

'Better still,' Abbie continued, 'fancy helping me make it? You know I'm shit at cooking and you're basically the Naked Chef.'

'You should be so lucky,' Andy quipped. 'Unless you want me to get my kit off in the kitchen?'

'I think you're fine as you are, thanks.'

Abbie chopped onion, celery and garlic, and Andy dissolved a chicken stock cube in hot water, bemoaning the fact there was no time and no chicken carcass to make the real thing.

'Don't blame me if it comes out crap, that's all,' he said.

'I won't.' Abbie hesitated, her knife hammering furiously on the chopping board, and then she said, 'Andy, is everything okay with you? I mean, I know it's stressful looking for work and everything. I've been worried. I can't help noticing...'

'That I've been going a bit hard on the old marching powder? Babe, you're not wrong. I know. Like you said, it's been stressful. The last job – I really wanted that to work out and they let me go after two weeks. It knocks your confidence, you know.'

Andy's confidence had never seemed anything other than pure Teflon to Abbie, but she knew appearances could be deceptive. If she listened – if he opened up to her – maybe she could help him.

'I'm sorry,' she said. 'And I know splitting up with William must have hurt, too. But if you're not getting enough sleep and not eating properly, that's going to make you feel worse, not better.'

Andy dropped the stock-cube wrapper on the floor and sat down, his hands over his eyes.

'I'm sorry.' His words were muffled. 'I've been a rubbish

housemate and a rubbish friend. I've been using too much, I know I have. It's a crutch. I oughtn't to need it but sometimes it's felt like I do.'

'You don't really.' Abbie slid into the chair next to his and put her arm round his shoulder. 'You've got us. You've got so many friends. You're amazing and talented and so many people love you and want you to succeed. If you want to stop taking what you've been taking, we'll help you.'

'Really?' Andy turned to face her, his eyes bright with tears and what Abbie thought might be hope.

In bed that night, she whispered an account of their conversation to Matt.

'I think he genuinely wants to stop,' she said. 'I think we properly connected. I think he just feels really alone sometimes.'

But her hopes were unfounded. The heart-to-heart with Andy resulted in him taking to his bed for two days, emerging rested and remorseful and spending a further two days applying for jobs. Then on Friday night he went out and didn't return all weekend, and the following week he was back to watching *Buffy* on the sofa and heading out on unspecified errands in the evening.

Abbie knew he was using drugs again. She just had no idea what, or how serious it was, or what on earth she and Matt were meant to do about it.

Sometimes Andy seemed almost like his old self, animated and giggly, cooking meals but not eating them, making them stay up late while he played his favourite albums from the 1970s. Mostly, though, he was morose, silent, often unwashed.

And then things started to go missing. One lunchtime, the day before payday, Abbie had to let a colleague buy her sandwich because the twenty-pound note she was sure – absolutely positive – was in her purse, wasn't. The TAG Heuer watch Matt's parents had given him for his twenty-first birthday vanished, and although he said he must have left it in the locker room at the gym, Abbie could see a shadow of doubt in his face. And then Abbie's work Blackberry, her pride and joy, acquired after a recent promotion from junior copywriter to copywriter, disappeared too.

'I left it in the living room on charge last night,' she told Matt, having insisted they go to the pub for a drink and a chat. 'I know I did. And it's gone. I had to tell my line manager and – well, it's covered by the company insurance. But she wasn't happy.'

'Have you looked everywhere for it?'

'I've looked absolutely everywhere.' Abbie's voice rose. 'But you don't seem to want to look anywhere – especially under your own damn nose. Come on, Matt. You know what's going on.'

'Andy's my mate. He'd never do stuff like that.'

Abbie softened. 'Look, I know he's your mate. He's my friend, too. But I'm really worried about him – I think he's in trouble. I think he must owe money to people, otherwise – you're right – he'd never take stuff from us. And we're not helping him by pretending nothing's wrong when it is.'

Again, Matt promised to speak to Andy. And one night, Abbie lay in bed alone, tense under the duvet, listening to their voices. The bedroom door was closed so she couldn't make out any words, only Matt's calm tone and Andy's increasingly agitated one.

At last, she heard Andy, his voice high with distress, say, 'I'll pay it all back! I don't know why the fuck you thought I wouldn't.'

Then the front door slammed and a few minutes later Matt joined her in bed, taking her into his arms in the darkness. She didn't need to ask him what had happened.

The next day, Andy presented Matt with a crisp new fifty-pound note. Matt showed it to Abbie with pride, saying it represented a first instalment. But it was also a last instalment.

A week later, Abbie got in from work to find Matt sitting at his recently acquired laptop, his face almost grey with shock. She hurried over to him.

'What's going on? What's wrong? Has something happened at work?'

Matt shook his head. 'I left the computer here this morning – I didn't need it at work today. And I'd logged on to the online banking earlier to check our savings account balance.'

Abbie felt as if she'd swallowed something huge and ice cold. 'There was almost eight grand in there, last time we checked.'

Matt said nothing, but turned the screen slightly so Abbie could see it. She didn't want to look – she didn't need to.

'He's taken it, hasn't he?'

'It might not have been Andy,' Matt said desperately. 'It might have been some kind of mistake at the bank. I'll call them first thing tomorrow.'

But they both knew there'd been no mistake at the bank.

CHAPTER ELEVEN

I woke up in bed alone, with a horrible, sick sense that something was wrong. Matt wasn't there next to me, but that wasn't particularly unusual – quite often he got up early to go for a run or to the gym, or just to sit and drink coffee, looking out at the morning and – I hoped – planning his day or – I feared – mulling over the state of our marriage and how and when it had all gone so wrong.

Which was definitely not projection on my part, as I definitely never did the latter.

Except – oh, wait – that was exactly what I was doing now, as the full awfulness of the news we'd received the previous night, and the way I'd responded to it, descended on my hungover head with a weight of smothering dread and guilt.

I thought that row – the one we had after Andy transferred our savings to his own bank account, then withdrew it all in cash to pay the debts he'd accrued – was the worst we'd ever have. I thought it could mean the end of everything for us, and it might have, only I was so devastated for Matt, and he was so blindsided by Andy's betrayal, I couldn't help wanting to comfort him. He comforted me back, and we clung to each other, promising that somehow we would get through this.

And we did, in a sense. But we never recovered the money – that was gone for good. And what troubled me even more was how much it had eroded my trust in Matt's judgement. There'd been red flags all over the place, even before Andy had moved in. Streams of them, like bunting at a fair for disaster capitalists, but Matt had given his old friend the benefit of the doubt. I'd been complicit, too; loving Andy (although not as much as Matt did), enjoying his company, relishing the way the gleam of his glamour reflected off me, making me feel different, special, singled out.

Neither of us had expected to be used so cruelly. Both of us – all of us, really, all Andy's friends – had loved him and been hurt by him. Some of us – Matt, Kate, Rowan, but not me – had been able to forgive if not forget.

Back then – before we were married, before the years of trying for a baby, before the unsuccessful infertility treatment – I'd at least felt we were able to salvage something from the carnage Andy had wrought.

Now, I wasn't so sure.

I realised that, all these years, I'd been carrying a weight of anger and disappointment, which last night's realisation that our chance of having a family had been scuppered once and for all had brought to the surface. I remembered how I'd felt back then, looking forward so happily and confidently to my future family with Matt.

I'd imagined a little house with a garden. I'd imagined Matt and me swinging our child between us by the hands as we walked up the path towards the front door. I'd imagined birthday cakes with candles on them – first one, then two, then three, and on and on until whatever age children stopped wanting candles on their cakes. I'd imagined coming home from work, picking my baby up from nursery, popping to the park to play on the swings before going home for tea and bath and bedtime.

The pictures in my mind were so vivid I could practically feel the sticky fingers in mine, hear the splashing of bathwater, smell sausages sizzling in a pan.

First, the dream of the house had been snatched from me by Andy. He'd never have been able to pay us back – he didn't have the money and so neither did we. We'd redoubled our efforts to save, of course, but it had taken far longer than we'd expected, with property prices rising and rising around us far faster than our bank balance could inch upwards.

And then having a baby hadn't happened either. There'd been the first tentative year of trying, when I'd just stopped taking the pill and we'd said we would see what happened. Then, when nothing did, we'd started paying a bit more attention to the time of the month, my temperature, not just how often we had sex but when and how many nights had passed since the last time and even how long I lay on my back afterwards, my feet on a pillow.

And when that hadn't worked, we'd started the treadmill of investigations into whether something might be wrong, and if so what. We never used the words, but the questions hovered over us: whose fault was it? Whose body wasn't working? Could it be fixed?

As it turned out, the answers were both of us, and maybe.

We'd embarked on a 'fertility journey', borrowing against the flat to pay for private treatment because I was already over thirty and the waiting time on the NHS was so long just thinking about it made me panic. And it hadn't worked. The first time, there'd been no viable embryos. The second time, two had been transferred into my body, and neither one had stuck around long enough to live and grow. And two were all we'd had.

So it was back to our GP and on to the waiting list for our

one free go at treatment, in the hope that this time it would be different.

And now, here we were. Too old, too late, too skint.

Last night, in my shock and devastation (and, okay, more than a little tipsiness), I'd blamed Matt for it all. Thinking about that now made me feel sick with guilt. It wasn't his fault our stupid bodies didn't work the way they were meant to. It wasn't his fault there were thousands of other couples like us all wanting the same thing, many with a better chance of success than we had. It wasn't his fault Andy had been in a terrible, dark place when he lived with us and done things he would never normally have dreamed of doing.

Was it Matt's fault that he'd trusted his friend and believed the best of him? Probably. But if he hadn't been that kind of person, would I have fallen in love with him and stayed in love with him for so long? Almost certainly not.

Was I still in love with him? It was hard to know. I knew I wanted to be. I knew I wanted the man who'd held me close all those years back and comforted me when I cried tears that seemed like they'd never stop, and told me he was sorry and we'd make it all right somehow, to hold me and comfort me now. I wanted to make things right, to rediscover all the ways we made each other feel: secure, giddy with happiness, sexy, loved.

I forced myself to get up and dress for work. Matt was already at the kitchen table, his laptop open in front of him, his fingers busy on the keys. He looked up when I came in and half-smiled, but his face was full of wariness and hurt.

'Morning,' I said.

'Morning. You okay?'

'Been better. Listen, I'm sorry about last night. I was upset, but you were too. I shouldn't have left you on your own.'

He shrugged, giving that twisted half-smile again. 'Happens to the best of us.'

Right then, I didn't feel like the best of anyone. But my apology had been as accepted as it was going to get.

I opened my own computer and logged on to my email and the workplace collaboration platform.

The first thing I saw was a message from Bastian.

Guys, see the below from Kendra at Quim. Action ASAP please.

Doom settling on me even more heavily, I scrolled down.

Hi Bas,

There's some great work here on the copy. But I feel it's lacking something – the sassiness, the vavavoom we know is the essence of our Quim lady. She's hot! She's empowered! She digs her body and her sex life – whether it's with one person, or lots, or just herself. This really needs to come through in the form of words we use, and right now lots of it is feeling a bit flat. Can you get the guys/gals on the wordsmithing side to take a look please and zhuzh it up a bit? Hopefully the product samples I pinged over by courier will help get the synapses firing ;)

Visual WiP looks ace. Speak soon.

K

My shoulders already tensing, I got up and switched on the kettle. Matt's teaspoon was next to the sink, but it barely impinged on my sense of gloom. How could I zhuzh anything when I was so unzhuzhed myself? How could I channel empowerment when I felt so helpless? How could I put myself in the shoes (thigh-high leather boots or feathery kitten-heeled mules, no doubt) of a sassy, sexy woman who loved her body when mine had betrayed me over and over?

Fighting back tears, I made myself coffee, and one for Matt too, and sat down again to try to remember what it was like to have sex for fun.

Fortunately, work kept me busy that day – too busy to do more than check in briefly on the Girlfriends' Club WhatsApp and compare notes on our hangovers. Every time I looked up from my screen, it seemed Matt was looking up from his, and our eyes would meet then slither away again.

The aftermath of the previous night hung in the air like toxic smog, more debilitating than any hangover. It wasn't like if we talked to each other the argument would reignite and before we knew it we'd be raging at each other again; it was more that we were both too bruised, too tender, to risk saying anything that would reopen the still-raw wounds from last night.

But at last, five thirty came and we couldn't pretend to be too busy to communicate any longer.

Matt stood up, snapped his laptop closed, stretched, filled a glass of water from the tap and drank it. I logged out of everything, checked my phone and pushed back my chair.

'Fancy a walk?' Matt asked tentatively.

'Sure. I'll just get some trainers on.'

I perched on the stairs to lace up my shoes, trying not to think about the empty second bedroom upstairs. Perhaps it would make sense, now, for us to buy a desk and one of us to claim that as our workspace. But it felt too soon – my dreams of the room becoming a nursery, green and white bunting on the walls, later on maybe bunk beds where children's voices would whisper long into the night – were still too fresh to be extinguished with such final practicality.

'Where do you want to walk?' I asked, getting to my feet and pocketing my keys.

'Go and see whether the grey cat with the blue collar's there?' Matt suggested. 'We didn't see him last time.'

'Okay. Then back round the park and look for the shouty tortoiseshell?'

'Gotcha.' Matt opened the front door and the golden light of late afternoon streamed in.

Then I said, 'Actually, you know what I'd like to do?'

'What?'

'Walk over to the old flat. Where we used to live. You know, when Andy...'

Matt looked startled. 'Are you sure?'

'Yes,' I said firmly. 'I think that's what we should do.'

WINTER 2001
SOMETHIN' STUPID

Having a birthday three days before Christmas sucked, there was no question about that. As Abbie complained to Chloe on the last day of term, it sucked massive hairy balls.

Even though her parents delayed putting up the Christmas tree until her birthday celebrations were over; even though they'd never, ever given her a joint present; even though it had meant that in primary school she got to be Mary in the nativity play more often than was strictly fair, it still sucked.

It felt as if the whole of December was this massive build-up to the main event of Christmas, and her birthday was an annoying blip in the mounting excitement. It meant that it was almost always impossible for her to have a birthday party with her friends, because they'd already left for their nan's up in Yorkshire or that was the night their neighbours always had their drinks thing and they had to go to that, or their big sister was getting back from uni that night. It meant that the two land-mark days of the year were crowded into far too short a space of time, with nothing to get excited about the whole rest of the year – except for Valentine's Day, and what kind of tragic loser got excited about that?

Still, this year, before the start of her final few months of school, Abbie found herself feeling giddy with excitement about her birthday. Everything felt different this year, because this year she had Matt. She didn't have to worry about arranging a party that no one would come to, because she and Matt were going to see Slade II at the Roundhouse – not a band either of them were particularly enthusiastic about, but they were playing on the day and they could just about afford the tickets.

And Matt would buy her a birthday present. Not that she particularly cared what it was – she wasn't some grabby gold-digger. But he'd give her a parcel, with a card he'd written in, and she'd open it and, whatever it was, she'd treasure it forever, like she already did the mix CD he'd burned for her and the wire cage from the bottle of supermarket sparkling wine they'd shared on Matt's own eighteenth birthday, which he'd bent into the shape of a tiny chair, and the jumper he'd lent her to wear once when they'd been in the park and it had suddenly turned cold, which she hoped he'd never want back.

After the gig, they made their way back to the Tube station, slowed by the choking mass of people. Everyone was festive: there were Christmas jumpers and Santa hats and one girl even had a string of LED fairy lights wound through her hair, a miracle of technology Abbie had never seen before. So far, so annoyingly Christmassy – but Abbie was too happy to be annoyed. A busker was murdering the Robbie Williams and Nicole Kidman song that Abbie had heard approximately one billion times already that week – not that she cared, because she knew there would be nothing at all stupid about saying 'I love you'.

'Want to come back to mine?' Matt asked. 'There's pizza in the freezer, and I've got your birthday present there.'

'You didn't have to get me a present.'

'Fine. I won't give it to you then.'

She elbowed him in the ribs and they both laughed, then

grabbed each other's hands and made a death-defying leap onto the train just as the doors were closing. The carriage was crowded, the crush of people pushed them close together, and they'd both had a couple of beers at the gig. So when the rocking of the train sent Abbie staggering on her platform shoes, it felt like the most natural thing in the world for Matt to fold his arm (the one that wasn't holding the high-up handrail, which Abbie resentfully felt was only possible for properly tall people to use without cutting off the blood supply to their hand) around her and pull her close.

She leaned gratefully against him, feeling the warmth of his body through their thick coats, and tilted her face up for a kiss. His lips against hers mouthed, *Happy birthday*, and hers answered, *Thank you.*

Fifteen minutes and a train change later, they walked along the familiar street to Matt's parents' house. Abbie had got to know Julia and Tony over the past few months, at first cringing with embarrassment when his mum and dad had come home from work to find her there, ostensibly studying with their son but actually mostly snogging. But it seemed she was pretty much accepted now as part of the furniture.

Even the unspoken rule about them not being in Matt's bedroom together without the door being left open appeared to have been relaxed – not that it made much difference, because Matt's fifteen-year-old brother could be relied upon to come crashing in if they ever closed it, offering every excuse in the book from, 'I was just looking for my headphones – I thought I left them on your bed,' through, 'Hey, bro, what was that thing you did to beat the Triads in Grand Theft Auto?' to a more forthright, 'What the fuck are you two up to in there?'

Now, though, Abbie felt quite comfortable walking through the front door behind her boyfriend and beamed with pleasure when Julia, festive in a red velour tracksuit, greeted her with a hug and a kiss, wished her happy birthday and said that she'd be up icing the Christmas cake for another forty-five minutes if Abbie wanted a lift home, and that Matt must be sure to walk back with her if she didn't.

'Abbie might need a lift, Mum,' Matt said mysteriously.

Julia gave him a look that was half baffled and half affectionate, and said, 'Oh right. Of course. Well, don't be too long up there.'

Puzzled, Abbie followed Matt up the dimly lit stairs to his bedroom. The stair rails were festooned with tinsel and twinkling lights, and the smells of baking gradually gave way to the less pleasant scent that always emanated from Ryan's bedroom: a subtle blend of strong toiletries, used socks and, well, boy.

Matt's room had smelled that way the first time Abbie had entered it a few months before. Now – possibly following a quiet word from his mother – it smelled of fabric softener and incense, with an unmistakeable hint of Matt underlining it all.

But today there was a new odour – something Abbie had never smelled before. It wasn't unpleasant, just different. If anything, it reminded her of the time she'd been to the circus with her mum and dad when she was little. A dusty yet fresh smell, overlaid with something that was definitely animal rather than human.

She didn't have time to analyse it, though – not the smell, nor the unfamiliar, bulky shape in the corner underneath Matt's desk – because he pulled her into his arms and they kissed, and for a few minutes nothing in the world existed apart from Matt's lips on hers and his warm hands caressing her back underneath her jumper.

'So, birthday girl,' Matt said at last, moving away from her. 'Would you like your present?'

'I don't mind,' Abbie said, although privately she couldn't wait, even if it was only another mix CD or a box of Thorntons chocolates or the belly chain she'd admired the other day when she'd persuaded Matt to go into Claire's Accessories for a browse.

'Card first,' he said. 'That's the rule, right?'

'Of course.' Abbie didn't mind opening her card first, not one bit – she wanted to see what Matt had written in it more than she wanted any present.

Matt handed her a square white envelope and she carefully eased open the flap without tearing the paper. Unless the card had nothing at all written in it, or something so naff she'd never be able to bring herself to read it ever again, which she was fairly confident it wouldn't, she'd be opening it and gazing at it and analysing it multiple times, starting as soon as she was in bed at home that night, running her fingers over the writing to see if she could feel the impression of Matt's pen.

The card had a picture of the galaxy on the front – an infinity of stars arcing away into the darkness of the universe. Abbie smiled – space was the kind of thing Matt was fascinated by but she found bewildering and, if she thought about it too hard, a bit frightening too.

The message on the front was, *Hope your birthday goes with a Big Bang*.

'Nice,' Abbie said. 'So you're saying you want the universe to explode in clouds of space dust and humankind as we know it to be obliterated.'

'You didn't listen in Physics, did you?' Matt said. 'The Big Bang theory means that the universe is expanding the whole time.'

'Ah, so you're saying I'm expanding the whole time?' Abbie teased. 'That makes it okay then.'

'Don't be daft.' Matt grinned, then he hung his head and muttered, 'But... uh... the way I feel about you is.'

Abbie felt a flood of warmth that started in her face and spread through her whole body. She met his eyes and they both beamed.

'Me too,' she murmured, then ducked her face again and opened the card. Inside, in his messy, spidery writing, he'd written, 'Happiest of birthdays to my amazing, beautiful girlfriend Abbie.' And under that was a quote from the Coldplay song that had been playing the night they first kissed.

Abbie thrilled with happiness. He'd remembered. He'd bought her a card that was – kind of – themed around that moment.

'Thank you,' she said, serious now.

'Wait until you see your present.'

Abbie realised that Matt had been hovering, slightly nervously, over the large object in the corner. She felt a sudden jolt of apprehension – what if she hated it? What if it was – she didn't know – a Christmas jumper or a biography of Bill Gates, or something else that she'd have to pretend to like?

It wasn't. Matt pulled away the covering – an old sheet, she noticed, with a hole in the middle where someone must have stuck their toe through. The smell in the room grew slightly stronger. The object was a cage – a cage lined with fresh wood shavings. And in the shavings—

Abbie let out an involuntary squeak of alarm, which was answered by a squeak from within the cage. She caught a glimpse of Matt's delighted face and tried not to recoil.

'Are those...?' she began faintly.

'Rats,' Matt said proudly.

Rats? Did my boyfriend really, seriously, think I'd want a pair of rats? Was the card some kind of portal to a parallel universe in which Abbie's normal boyfriend had been replaced with an actual insane person?

'Look how cute they are.' Oblivious of Abbie's horror, Matt knelt down and unfastened the cage. He reached in and gently lifted out a small grey-and-white furry body.

Nonononono. Don't try and make me touch it! She'd scream or puke or run away, or possibly all three at the same time.

'They make great pets,' he went on. 'They're super clean and so intelligent, and when you go away to uni you can take them with you to keep you company.'

If this was some kind of elaborate strategy to make sure no other bloke would go near Abbie for the three years of her degree course, Matt had totally nailed it, she thought.

'This is Woyzeck,' Matt said, cradling the rat tenderly. 'He's tamer than the other one, Stanik – you can just see him in there under the shavings. He's all white.'

Abbie found her voice. 'Woyzeck and Stanik? Why?'

'Woyzeck after that play we read in English Lit, remember? It was your first week at school and I couldn't concentrate on it because I kept staring at you. And Stanik because – well, it kind of goes with Woyzeck.'

In spite of herself, Abbie felt her heart thaw. Matt meant well. He'd thought carefully about this gift and wanted to give her something special – way more special than cheap jewellery from Claire's. She leaned a bit closer – just a bit – and peered at the small animal in Matt's hand.

And the weirdest thing happened. In the space of a second, the rat stopped being a disgusting, terrifying creature that would bite her and give her some horrendous disease and possibly even touch her with its gross scaly tail. Its nose was pink and tiny, surrounded by a fan of the finest white whiskers. Its eyes were bright and curious. Its ears were perfect little almost-complete circles, like a baby's fingernails or two not-quite-full moons. Its fur looked softer than the softest thing.

She reached out and gently touched it with a fingertip. Its fur was as soft as it looked – softer, even; so soft she could hardly tell where the warm air of the room ended and the rat's coat began.

'He's beautiful,' she breathed, astonishing herself by leaning in and stroking the top of Woyzeck's head, then kissing Matt's hand. 'Oh my God, Matt, I love him! They're the best present ever.'

Tenderly, Matt placed the rat back in the cage and closed the door. Then they pulled each other close and kissed and kissed, shedding their clothes and letting their bodies move together in the now-familiar rhythm, barely hearing Ryan yelling out to his mother to ask where she'd hidden the Sellotape, the soft rustling of Abbie's new pets in their wood-shaving bed, or Matt's dad singing loudly along to 'It's the Most Wonderful Time of the Year'.

And then Julia called from downstairs that if Matt expected her to play taxi to a pair of rodents at gone midnight, he'd better let Abbie get dressed, because she, Julia, had to be up in the morning even if he had nothing to do but lie around reading in bed. And the two of them scuttled downstairs, Matt carrying the cage, warmed with happiness. Already, for Abbie, just as the smell of brandy and pine needles and spice would always mean Christmas, she knew the smell of wood shavings would always remind her of that birthday.

CHAPTER TWELVE

It had been a long time since we visited our old neighbourhood, even though it was only around four miles from where we lived now. I couldn't remember ever having been back to the flat since we moved out, although for a while I'd continued to use the hairdresser there, and there was a place Matt used to go sometimes to buy freshly ground coffee.

Gradually, though, we'd felt our ties to the old place loosen and give way. I found a new hair salon; Matt found a new coffee supplier. We didn't miss the flat at all; our memories of it had become too tarnished. Still, as we approached the familiar streets, I felt a growing sense of regret.

For what, exactly? Not for the decisions we'd taken, which had been sensible, rational, the only ones we could have made at the time. Not for the area itself, which was just another hub in the sprawl of North London, with slightly different but similar corner shops, supermarkets, pizza restaurants and charity shops to our local ones now.

It was me I missed, I realised – us. The Matt and Abbie who'd moved into the flat not knowing what would happen there, and who'd moved out years older, somewhat wiser, but still full of hope.

'Remember the pub on the corner?' I said. 'We used to do the quiz there every Tuesday.'

'We even won that one time. Forty quid and our burgers on the house. What was the place called again?'

'The Something Arms? Isn't it coming up on the corner here?'

But the pub was closed now, boarded up, graffiti tags sprayed on the metal shutters that covered its windows.

As we walked down the high street, I felt a tightness underneath my ribcage – a feeling of tension that was almost but not quite fear. What if the building itself was gone, or changed beyond recognition? What if coming here with Matt, today of all days, with last night's argument still souring the mood between us, had been a terrible idea? What if returning wouldn't lay the ghosts of the past but bring them back to haunt us even more than they already did?

'Here we are,' Matt said. 'Victoria Road.'

'The Polish deli's there,' I noticed. 'Remember those mushroom-flavour crisps we always used to buy when we were hungover?'

'God, just thinking about them makes me feel a bit sick.' Matt shuddered. 'But we used to trough bags and bags of them.'

'It'll be the association. Your body hears "mushroom crisps" and it thinks "hangover from hell".'

'That would be it. Just thinking about those last rounds of Jägerbombs makes my liver cringe.'

We laughed, and I felt our mood lift a bit. We strolled past the familiar houses, most sub-divided into flats, as ours had been. Lots had cars parked out front, but some still had lovingly tended front gardens. More, though, were neglected, waist-high weeds flourishing in the late summer heat.

'At least we can't accuse it of having got gentrified,' Matt said.

'True. If it had, there'd have been a florist outside the station and that pub would have been serving Yorkshire pudding burritos.'

'It's on this corner here, isn't it?'

We walked a little further, getting closer and closer to the house where we used to live. But as we strolled, I felt the sense of companionship that had been keeping my hand in Matt's, keeping our chat flowing, keeping the memories alive, fade a little, replaced with something a bit like apprehension.

What were we actually doing here? What was the point of it? Although we'd been happy in that shabby two-bedroom flat at first, in spite of the cooker that went from cold to cremate as soon as you turned your back and the shower that did the same, in spite of the fact that it was too far to walk to the station and you had to get a bus which was always late and often too full to get on, it had never been the same after Andy moved out.

It had stopped feeling like a home and begun to seem more like a prison.

But that was the point, I told myself firmly – by coming here with Matt, I could lay those ghosts to rest, gain a new appreciation for the home we had now, take another small step forward.

Maybe.

I sensed that Matt was having similar misgivings. His normal purposeful strides had slowed so that I didn't have to hurry to keep up with him as I usually did. The grip of his hand around mine had loosened. Instead of talking about our memories of living here, he began making banal remarks about the peeling plaster on the front of one house, the bright floral curtains in the window of another, the overgrown wisteria cascading over the wall of a third.

He even passed a particularly handsome tuxedo cat without even noticing it.

At last, our footsteps slowed completely and we stopped.

'This is it,' Matt said. 'Number eighty-five.'

'Eighty-five C,' I said. 'That was us. The second-floor flat.'

We approached the front door tentatively and peered at the bells. I remembered fitting a label with our names on it into the plastic slot soon after we moved in; there were new names there now.

'Musa and Goodhew,' Matt read. 'I wonder what they're like.'

'I hope they're happy,' I murmured.

'I hope the landlord's sorted out the cooker,' Matt joked feebly.

'We could buzz. Say we used to live here.'

'That would be weird.'

'Yeah, it would.'

Together, we stepped back, turning away from the door and retreating to the pavement. We looked up to the window that had been our bedroom. I remembered waking up there, morning after morning, to rain spattering the glass or sunshine flooding through it; in winter darkness and midsummer light.

I remembered waking up there after Andy's betrayal, and the feeling that everything had changed.

As we watched, the curtains in the upstairs room parted. Although it was barely dusk, the light was switched on and we could clearly see inside. A young man, shirtless, stood looking out at the evening, his arms stretched wide. Then a girl came up behind him and hugged him, her arms white against the dark skin of his chest.

He threw back his head in laughter we couldn't hear, then turned and embraced her, and they pulled each other into a passionate kiss.

'Time to go,' Matt said.

I nodded. Knocking now was out of the question.

'They've just had a shag,' I said.

'We wouldn't want to harsh their mellow,' Matt agreed.

'Or even worse, get them all the way downstairs thinking we were their pizza delivery.'

'God, how pissed off would they be?'

We chuckled, but it felt somehow humourless. That glimpse into the strangers' lives, their love, had felt too raw, reminding me of what we'd had in a way that was almost too painful to bear.

If we were going to recapture that feeling, find it again in our marriage, I knew that we were looking in the wrong place.

We turned and walked back the way we'd come, more swiftly now, as if in mutual agreement that coming here had been a mistake; as if our memories were pursuing us, mocking us with the reminder of what we'd had – the love and the hopes and the dreams, all in the past now.

The end of the road approached and we hurried towards it, as if it was a portal into a better, happier present.

But before we reached it, we were distracted.

In the gateway of one of the houses, one that looked as if it had been left to its own devices for years, with a giant laurel bush filling most of the garden and bits of plastic fluttering in its branches, was a cat.

We might not have noticed it if it hadn't called out to us. As we passed, our eyes on the road ahead of us, we heard a plaintive cry.

'Was that a cat?' I asked.

'A baby, I think,' Matt said.

'No, it was a cat.' I stopped and turned around, and there it was. A small, nondescript black-and-white cat, emerging from between the crumbling brick gateposts and walking purposefully towards us, yelling its head off.

'Hello.' Matt bent down, reaching out his hand towards the cat, which extended a cautious nose in return to sniff his fingers.

Immediately, it rubbed its cheeks against his hand, and I could hear it begin to purr.

'Aw, aren't you a cutie?' I squatted down and reached out to stroke the piebald fur. This wasn't a smart tuxedo-style black-and-white cat; it was mostly white, with a black splodge on its shoulder, a black tail and a black nose. White, though – not exactly. Its fur was dusty and its paws were stained yellow, and there were grass seeds caught in its tail.

'You look like you need a good wash,' Matt said. 'Haven't you been taking care of yourself? That won't do.'

I ran my hands over the length of the cat's body, feeling prominent hip and shoulder bones.

'It's quite thin. I wonder if it's a stray?'

'It's got a collar.'

Around the cat's neck was a narrow strap of pink velvet – at least, it had once been pink. Now it was a grubby salmon colour, as neglected-looking as the cat itself. There was no tag on the collar.

'Where do you live, then?' I asked it. 'Have you got a home? Did your humans move and leave you behind?'

The cat, unsurprisingly, didn't answer our questions. It – she, I guessed, given the gendered collar choice – was persistently headbutting Matt's hand, purring loudly as a sewing machine but switching to outraged meows if his ear-scratches stopped.

The evening was still warm. I could hear a bee buzzing as it investigated the marigolds and hogweed in the garden behind us, even over the distant hum of traffic from the high street. I could smell curry cooking somewhere, the tang of diesel fumes and the sickly sweet scent of jasmine.

As I watched, the cat flopped to the ground and rolled over, exposing her white belly to Matt's caresses.

'She reminds me of Woyzeck,' he said. 'Remember how he used to like belly rubs?'

'She's not like a rat,' I objected. 'Besides, they were clean. This little girl's all grubby.'

As if she'd heard me, the cat sat upright and started to wash. But there were burrs in her coat and I could see a clump of matted fur next to her tail.

'She's trying to get clean,' I said softly. 'Do you think she lives outside, with nowhere dry to sleep?'

'I'm sure she's got a home. Besides, they manage, don't they? Feral cats and farm cats and stuff?'

'Maybe she does. But I think we should...'

'Come back tomorrow and check on her?'

I nodded reluctantly. Part of me wanted to scoop the cat up and take her off somewhere safe. But I knew we couldn't do that – for all we knew, she was someone's beloved pet, albeit a scruffy one.

'Let's come back tomorrow,' I agreed.

Matt stood up, promising the cat that we'd see her soon. He slipped his arm around my shoulder and pulled me close, dropping a kiss on top of my head. I wrapped my arm round his waist, feeling the length of his body and the rhythm of his stride as we walked back the way we'd come.

We hadn't found what I'd hoped for at our old home. Whatever I'd been searching for there was long gone, our history erased and replaced with the present of the couple who lived there now, our laughter drowned out by theirs, like a video tape being recorded over.

But I sensed we'd found something else instead, and I knew we'd come here again before long.

SUMMER 2011
ALL I NEED

Matt and Abbie trudged through the mud, so thick and heavy it threatened to pull Abbie's wellies off her feet with every step. Her waterproof poncho – which was printed with bright pink prawns and which she thought might possibly be the coolest garment she'd ever owned – was no match for the driving rain; her jeans were laden with water and sticking uncomfortably to her thighs; sodden tendrils of hair clung to her face and neck, and she was unable to brush them off because both her hands were occupied with her end of the trolley, which they were fighting to navigate through the sludge.

'This is what fighting in the First World War must have been like,' she gasped.

'We'll end up with trench foot for sure,' Matt agreed.

'Picking lice out of each other's hair.'

'Did you remember to pack your gas mask?'

'Why? You're not planning to fart in our tent, are you?'

They dissolved in giggles, the rain putting no damper at all on their excitement. Matt hadn't bothered with a waterproof anything, and his white T-shirt was wet through, moulded to his body in a way Abbie wished she wasn't too soaked herself to appreciate.

'How much further is it?'

Matt dug in the pocket of his board shorts for the map, which he'd consulted so often it had almost turned to porridge.

'I'm not sure. Another mile, maybe.'

'Another mile? In this? Are you sure?'

'Want to stop and take a break?'

Abbie shook her head, grimly adjusting her grip on the trolley. A groundsheet was stretched over its top, but she could see deep puddles of water forming on its surface and felt little confidence that their belongings inside would be protected.

This had seemed like a great idea – the best idea – when Kate had suggested it a year before. The intervening months had been taken up with intermittent bouts of frantic planning, which had ramped up as the date grew closer. In the past couple of weeks, their excitement had reached fever pitch and the dedicated Facebook group had pinged so constantly with comments that none of them had managed to get any work done.

But now that they were here – actually at Glastonbury, the festival to end all festivals – Abbie wasn't so sure. It was exciting – of course it was. The faces of the people around them, some laden with enormous backpacks, some wrestling with festival trolleys like Abbie and Matt's, others mysteriously burdened with little more than bumbags, were alight with eager anticipation.

However, it was also pissing it down with rain that was forecast to go on all weekend.

Abbie had literally never camped before. In spite of all the lists that had been shared on the group page, in spite of all the blogs she'd read, she felt hopelessly unprepared. How would she find the toilet if she needed a wee in the middle of the night? Had they brought enough spare batteries for their torch?

If all her clothes were wet, how on earth would she get them dry?

And what the actual fuck had possessed her to bring a full make-up bag?

They toiled on and, at last, over the heads of the thickening crowd, they spotted a familiar waving arm.

'Hello, hello!' Rowan hurried towards them, her legs as long as a colt's in her denim micro-shorts and sparkly pink wellies. She'd knotted the waistband of her T-shirt so that even if it got wet, it wouldn't flap around. Her hair was in two French plaits on either side of her head. She wasn't wearing any make-up and didn't need any.

'Oh my God.' Abbie let herself be pulled into a hug. 'You look incredible! Like Kate Moss! Where's your tent, and where's our pitch?'

'Just along here,' Rowan pointed into the sea of mud. 'You're next to Kate, and Naomi and Patch are the other side. Wet, isn't it?'

'It's flaming biblical.' Matt kissed both her cheeks, leaving a smear of mud. 'Come on, Abs, let's get this beast of a tent up.'

Far from being a beast, their tent was tiny – a two-person affair with no room to stand up, no room for their belongings, and barely room for their two soggy sleeping bags. They knelt across from each other, faces reflecting the scarlet of the tent's fabric, and raised their voices over the drumming of the rain.

'It's not like we're going to do anything in here except sleep,' Abbie said.

'Really?' Matt grinned at her. 'I was kind of hoping we might do stuff other than sleep.'

'I never knew you had a thing for having sex in knee-deep mud, with a couple of hundred thousand strangers parading past.'

But in spite of herself, Abbie felt the familiar, excited stirring she still felt when he looked at her that way, even after ten years.

'Come here,' he said.

There wasn't far for her to go; he pulled her into his arms and they kissed, their skin still slick with rain. She could taste salt on his skin; his face was wet with perspiration as well as water. He tasted a bit of the motorway service station burgers they'd stopped for on their way. Her body sprang to life at his touch, her breath coming faster, her heart beating like the rain against the tent.

'What are you two up to in there?' Kate's voice interrupted them, and she peered through the tent flap. 'Oh my God. Really? Are you going to christen your boudoir, or are you going to come and get a drink and explore?'

They pulled apart, laughing.

'All right then,' Abbie said. 'Just because you're single and bitter, don't take it out on us.'

Matt folded his long body awkwardly out of the tent and Abbie followed. Kate was wearing a poncho printed with bananas, sister to Abbie's prawn one, and a baseball cap shielded her face from the rain.

'You know, I'm beginning to think this was the craziest idea ever,' she said, as Naomi and Patch joined them and they all set off, labouring through the mud. 'I'm totally not cut out for the outdoor life. I'm already wondering if there isn't a nice hotel somewhere nearby where I can go for a shower.'

'Ah, come on,' Rowan said. 'You brought your dry shampoo and wet wipes, right?'

'I did,' Kate confirmed. 'Along with a family pack of loo roll. I read that list you made.'

'I decanted a bottle of rum into a water bottle,' Naomi said. 'What's the bet I wake up with a mouth like the Sahara Desert in the middle of the night and down a load of Captain Morgan by mistake?'

'Best we finish it tonight then,' Matt said. 'It'll be safer that way.'

'Don't tempt me,' Rowan said. 'Since I dropped Clara off at her dad's this morning I've been promising myself the world's most massive drink. And now it's time.'

'I'm bloody hungry, too,' Patch said. He was shirtless, whether because whatever he was wearing had got too wet to be any use or to show off his amazing gym-honed torso, Abbie couldn't be sure.

'Right, then.' Kate checked the contents of her bumbag. 'Phone, cash, cards, ciggies, lighter, loo roll, hand sanitiser. Anything I've forgotten?'

'Hoodie for later when it gets cold?' Rowan had a leopard-print sweatshirt knotted around her own waist.

Abbie rummaged in the trolley, trying to find her own essentials.

'I think I'm good to go,' she said at last, wrestling the zip of her mini backpack closed and slinging it over her shoulder.

'Booze first, then food, then tunes?' Matt suggested.

'Gotcha,' Patch said. 'Let's get something decent now, because we'll likely be living off chips and cereal bars for most of the weekend.'

The rain was easing now, but the ground was still wet, a sea of mud interspersed with clumps of sodden grass. But, with the prospect of the world's most massive drink and their first evening at the festival approaching, Abbie felt her spirits lift. They were here – this was special and magical and she intended to enjoy every second of it, wet or not.

Two hours later, they were in the crowd at the main stage, satiated by pulled-pork burritos, plastic pint glasses of lager in their hands, their throats already raw from cheering and singing along with the band. Earlier, a rainbow had arched spectacu-larly over the site; now, a pale sliver of moon was edging its way up the darkening sky, obscured sometimes by ominous-looking clouds.

Abbie felt Matt's warm, damp hand enfold her own. He leaned in close, bending to speak to her over the deafening music.

'Having a good time?'

'The best.' She turned to smile up at him. Her cheeks were already sore from laughing, her head already pleasantly swimming from alcohol. 'You're the best.'

'No, you're the best.' They giggled, delighted to be here, to be themselves. 'Fancy going to see the secret act on the other stage later?'

'It's not secret. Everyone knows it's Radiohead – it's been all over social media.'

'We'll have to pretend not to, otherwise we'll hurt their feelings.'

'Poor Radiohead, they'd be crushed if they knew it wasn't a surprise.'

'Like your folks when they clock you know Father Christmas isn't real.'

'Exactly. So let's try very hard to pretend we don't know it's going to be them. Give me your best OMG face.'

Matt widened his eyes and let his jaw drop. 'Holy crap, it's only Radiohead! I can't believe it!'

'No way! Radiohead! It can't possibly be.' Abbie clapped her hands over her mouth.

Slowly, because there was no other way to move through the mud and the crowd, they made their way from one stage to the other, stopping en route to buy cocktails and random sweets, chat to strangers and hug them, and for Abbie to use the utterly putrid Portaloo.

'Okay?' Matt asked, seeing her grimace when she emerged.

'Fine! Just great. I hovered and pretended it was Buckingham Palace.'

Night was falling now. The threatening clouds had receded, clustered on the horizon, waiting to dump their burden of water on the huddled tents overnight. The sky arched above them, navy blue, studded with stars and illuminated by dancing spotlights. The delicate sliver of moon soared high in the darkness, like a smile turned on its side.

Clearly, they weren't the only ones who knew what the mystery act was. The space in front of the stage was rammed, the support act barely visible in the distance. The giant screens gave Abbie a better view, but it wasn't enough.

'Look, they're coming on,' she said to Matt, having to scream into his ear to make herself heard. 'I can't see.'

'Get up then.' He bent down, grasping her thighs and lifting her up, high onto his shoulders like a child at a funfair.

'No! Stop that! I'm too heavy – you'll put your back out.'

But Matt couldn't hear her.

She perched on his shoulders, clutching his head, at once elated, embarrassed and afraid. But then she found her balance. His arms held her legs securely; he was strong and confident even on the uneven, slippery ground. And now she had the best view.

A couple of tracks into the set, she'd begun to relax. She could feel Matt's body beneath her, holding her strongly and easily. The music swept over her as powerfully as the arcing lights. She was at one with it, with the crowd, with the night.

And then they heard the opening chords of their favourite song, the one they'd played over and over in their flat by candlelight, danced to in bars together, made love to in a tangle of limbs and sweat and sheets.

Matt's shoulders under her legs grew still. The crowd silenced. The moon and the stars continued their journey above them, oblivious yet somehow also present in the moment.

And in the instant between the final chord ending and the roar of the crowd beginning, Matt lifted Abbie down from his shoulders as if she weighed nothing at all, but also like she was the most important thing he'd ever held. She wrapped her legs around his waist, his hands supporting her hips the way they did when they had sex standing up, too turned on and urgent to make it to bed.

'Say you'll marry me,' Matt said, 'or I'll drop you on your arse in the mud.'

CHAPTER THIRTEEN

Over the next couple of weeks, Matt and I walked back to the old flat almost every day. The first time, we stopped off at a local supermarket and bought a bag of cat biscuits. We sprinkled some on the pavement and watched as the cat hoovered them up as if she hadn't eaten for weeks – which, for all we knew, she hadn't. The next day we took a cereal bowl from home and gave her her dinner in that, because it didn't seem right to have her eating off the pavement. The following day, we took a plastic container left over from a takeaway, filled it with water and left it there for her.

The next day, we knocked on the doors of a few of the neighbouring houses and asked if anyone knew anything about the cat.

'I've seen it out in that garden for a while now,' said one woman. 'The owners might be on holiday.'

'I think they moved away,' another neighbour said. 'We hardly saw them when they were here; they kept themselves to themselves.'

'I call her Shrimp,' his daughter said, appearing shyly behind her father. 'Because she's so little and scrawny.'

We knocked at the door to the house itself, of course, but there was no answer.

'What are we going to do?' I asked Matt as we headed home through the twilight, about a week after we'd first encountered the cat, who we'd inevitably started referring to as Shrimp. The belongings we'd provided for her now included two stainless-steel cat bowls, a Tupperware box to keep her food secure from the local foxes and an aluminium bottle we used to bring her water each day from home. 'We can't just keep on going there and feeding her.'

'It's unsustainable,' Matt agreed.

'It really is,' I said. 'And she's not our responsibility.'

'No,' Matt agreed, 'I guess she isn't.'

That's what we said to each other, anyway. But I knew, deep down, that I already felt responsible for this little cat, who seemed to have no one to look out for her except us. I knew that the more often we went there, the more we'd start to care. And I was wary of caring too much about anything right then.

So now our afternoon walks took us not along the familiar routes closer to home, past the fluffy grey cat and the cat with the diamanté collar and the huge, regal ginger cat, but the longer route back towards our old flat, to Shrimp.

One morning in early September, we were walking home through the park when a poster caught my eye.

'Look.' I grabbed Matt's arm and he came to a stop next to me. 'There's a festival happening this weekend.'

'It's an annual thing,' Matt said. 'Well, it didn't happen last year, obviously. But we've heard the music from the garden sometimes.'

'We should go.'

'Really? Won't it just be loads of teenagers getting wasted and filming themselves doing the Renegade on TikTok?'

'Not necessarily. Look, it says – "craft stalls, street food, family-friendly". It sounds quite civilised. We could ask if Rowan and Naomi want to bring their kids.'

Matt gave me a curious glance. I wondered if he was remembering that magical weekend at Glastonbury, when he'd asked me to marry him. I had said yes, of course – and this seemed like fate was dangling the opportunity to recreate it right within my grasp.

'Okay,' he said. 'Why not? Let's make a day of it.'

'At least it's near home so we won't have to camp.'

Matt laughed. 'That Glasto weekend was amazing in many ways, Abs, but I have to say the leaky tent wasn't one of the highlights.'

So he had remembered. 'Not to mention the leaky groundsheet.'

'And all our clothes being soaked through.'

'And the toilets – oh my God, I still have nightmares about them. I swear I can still feel the cramp I got in my thighs hovering over the seat to wee.'

'And yet you're still keen to go to this thing.'

'Don't be daft, it won't be the same at all!'

Privately, I hoped it would be a bit the same. Just, you know, the same enough.

Soon after we got home, while Matt was sautéing onions for a spaghetti bolognese, I got on to the Girlfriends' Club WhatsApp and shared my idea.

Kate: Glastonbury 2.0? Sounds like a great plan. I'm in. Who's bringing the Es?

Abbie: We're grown up and sensible now. We'll have prosecco and maybe Pimm's.

Rowan: I'll bring Clara. Might get me some much-needed Cool Mum points.

Naomi: The twins would be smoking weed in the chill-out tent within about three seconds. I'll see if Patch's mum and dad can babysit.

So, on Saturday morning, I shaved my legs right up to the tops of my thighs, which I hadn't bothered to do in months. I put on short denim shorts and a white cotton boho top, and tied a scarf around my hair. I looked for a second at the pair of pink platform espadrilles I'd bought for a holiday in Greece a few years before, then told myself not to be ridiculous and laced up my trainers instead.

Still, when I walked downstairs, Matt's eyes widened. 'Swit swoo. You look about sixteen.'

'Not sure perving over teenagers is the best look, mister.'

'Less of your backchat. Now, what do we need? I've got a picnic blanket, water bottles, bug spray, sunblock...'

'Loo roll?'

Matt grinned. 'Keep it going with the Glasto flashbacks. Condoms?'

'Fat lot of good those did us. We were too wasted and the tent was too wet.'

He slipped his arm round my shoulders and pulled me close, dropping a kiss on my bare shoulder. I felt a fizz of happiness, remembering how nothing that weekend – not the state of the toilets, not our flooded, muddy tent, not the endless driving rain – had been able to dim the sheer joy I'd felt.

Today would be tame in comparison, I knew. But that was okay – it would all work out. At least, I hoped it would.

Kate, Naomi, Patch and Rowan were waiting for us outside the station, as we'd arranged. Kate was wearing a Pucci-print maxi dress and looked like she'd stepped straight out of the pages of *Vogue*. Rowan's daughter Clara had a friend with her, both of them in mom jeans, cropped tops and expressions of careful indifference that I was pretty sure concealed genuine excitement. Naomi and Patch didn't bother concealing theirs.

'A child-free day, what a massive win,' Naomi said, swinging her husband's hand as we walked together towards the park.

'And my folks are having the kids overnight, so we can get completely wasted,' Patch agreed cheerfully. 'No responsible adulting today.'

We followed the crowds of people and the increasing volume of the music towards the festival enclosure. The sun was shining, the occasional white cloud drifting benignly in a cornflower-blue sky. There was just a whisper of a breeze to prevent it being too hot.

We found a perfect spot, not too close to the stage but close enough to see and hear, and spread out our blankets on the dry grass. Patch went to the bar and returned with two bottles of fizz and plastic glasses. Clara and her friend headed off to explore, already followed by a tentative herd of thirteen-year-old boys. I tore open the bags of posh crisps and pretzels we'd brought – there'd be proper food later on, but for now we definitely needed to pre-emptively blot up the booze.

The band that was playing up on the stage was pretty rubbish, really – certainly no Radiohead – but none of us cared much. We lounged in the sun, drinking and chatting. Every now and then one of us would get up, stretch and wander off to the (relatively luxurious) toilet or to the bar.

Towards the middle of the afternoon, Patch volunteered to go and get food, and returned with burgers laden with bacon, cheese and jalapeño peppers and cardboard boxes of waffle fries, at which point Clara and her friend reappeared, inhaled the food with teenage hunger and then disappeared again into the crowd.

I lay back down on the blanket, propping myself up on my elbow, sipping Pimm's and feeling pleasantly full and a bit fuzzy-headed from drinking in the sun. All around us were other groups, either splayed on the grass like we were or strolling around checking out the stalls. Kids paraded past, their faces painted with glittery rainbows and butterflies, eating ice cream. I could hear excited shrieks coming from the fairground rides, and smell candyfloss and freshly fried doughnuts, but I was too full of burger and chips to even consider eating any.

I rolled over onto my back and covered my face with my arm, ready to indulge in a sneaky disco nap. But Matt nudged me.

'Come on, lazybones. Let's head off and explore a bit.'

'But I'm sleepy.'

'You can sleep when you're dead.'

I sat up, laughing, remembering how we used to say that to each other when we stayed late in the pub, even though it was a school night.

'There are many, many hangovers I blame on you saying that,' I told him.

'I never noticed you objecting particularly strenuously.'

'I'm objecting strenuously now.'

'No you're not.'

He was right; I was already lacing up my trainers, which I'd kicked off when we sat down.

'Want to come and have a wander round?' I asked the group.

'Nah, I'm good, thanks,' Naomi said.

'Just bring us back some drinks,' said Kate.

'And Clara, if you happen to spot her,' said Rowan. 'It's getting late. She'll be on the razz all night if I let her.'

So Matt and I headed off into the crowd, hand in hand. Just a few months back, I realised, holding his hand had felt strange, like it was something I'd never expected to do. Now, it felt normal: the calluses on his palm from the gym rough when I caressed them with my thumb; the warmth of his hand always slightly warmer than my own; the way my lilac-painted nails looked against his tanned skin.

Hell, a few months back I'd thought I'd never bother painting my nails again, and now look at me, I realised with a smile.

We passed a stall where a little queue of children were waiting to have their faces painted on one side and emerging as glittery butterflies, stripy tigers or Disney characters on the other. We paused to look at a group of impressively bendy men and women doing yoga, and I told myself I was definitely going to find a local class to join, then remembered that I'd told myself that about once every six months for the past ten years, and here I still was, as unbendy as ever.

As we watched, they all stood on one leg, folding the other foot up to meet the inside of the standing knee, their hands clasped before their chests in the prayer position.

'I can totally do that,' I told Matt.

'You totally can't. You're the most amazing woman in the world but you have the balance of a baby elephant on roller skates.'

'I so don't!'

'Yeah? Prove it.'

'Fine.'

Breathing a fresh prayer of thanks that I'd decided against the platform shoes, I lifted my left leg off the ground, trying to fix my eyes on an imaginary still point in the distance. I bent my knee, attempting to emulate the pose I could see the group in front of me executing so effortlessly. The sole of my trainer met the inside of my thigh, chilly and damp against my skin. I pressed the palms of my hands together and managed the first syllable – although I guess technically there would only ever have been one – of 'Om'. Then, predictably, my balance failed me and I wobbled, tried and failed to save myself, then collapsed in Matt's arms, helpless with giggles.

'Okay,' I admitted, 'you were right.'

'And what does that mean?'

I paused for a second, puzzled, then I remembered the old ritual we used to have, years back, that meant arguments always ended in laughter.

'It means I was wrong,' I said.

'And that means?'

'You can sing the "I was right" song.'

And right there, in front of everyone, Matt did the thing I hadn't seen him do for years – or indeed done myself: hopping from foot to foot, pointing alternating fingers at me, chanting, 'I was right and you were wrong, so I can sing the "I was right" song.'

Giggling like children, our arms wrapped around each other, we continued on our way.

We stopped outside the literature tent, where a table had been set up outside laden with books by local authors, and I wished I'd known that one of them had done a reading and talk earlier in the day.

'It's really impressive,' I remarked. 'Who knew all this was happening right on our doorstep?'

'We'll have to make it a regular thing,' Matt said. 'Make sure you don't miss the intellectual literary chit-chat next time.'

And I realised I could see a future where, in five or even ten years' time, Matt and I would still be living where we were, content with our lives and each other, coming here because it was what we did on the second weekend in September.

'I guess we should get some drinks and go back to the others,' I said. 'They'll all be dying of thirst back there.'

'Maybe we should suggest they come here.' Matt grinned, gesturing to a tent I hadn't noticed, which had a sign outside: '12-Step Recovery Drop-in Centre'.

'Pimm's and lemonade in the middle of the day.' I sucked my teeth. 'It's a slippery slope.'

'Too right. They'll be on the Special Brew at breakfast time next.'

We turned away, but something made me glance back, and I saw a man emerging from the tent. A blond man wearing a hot-pink T-shirt, a jumper slung over his shoulders and sunglasses hiding his eyes. But something about him was familiar: the loose set of his shoulders, the way he walked, fluid and easy, as if just his presence was enough to part the crowds.

I pulled Matt away quickly, dodging behind a stage where a group of traditional African drummers were setting up.

'What's up?' Matt asked. 'You're acting like you just saw a ghost.'

'I just saw Andy,' I said. 'He was coming out of the AA tent.'

Matt paused. 'Right. That's good. I kind of hoped it might stick this time.'

'You knew?'

'I mean, yeah. Last time I saw him, he said he was going to get clean. But, you know, he's said that plenty of times before. And anyway he was loaded at the time so I guess I took it with a pinch of salt.'

My head spun like it was me who'd been overdoing it on the good shit. I'd come to realise, over the years, that while what Andy had done to Matt and me had been a betrayal there was no coming back from, it also hadn't been entirely Andy's fault. I'd tried to imagine what it would take to be so desperate, so far in over my head in a lifestyle I couldn't sustain but also couldn't stop, that I'd steal from my friends, and although my imagination had failed me, I'd realised that was because the desperation Andy must have felt was too enormous for me to comprehend.

Desperation – or just selfishness? I'd never quite been able to work that out, and there was no way I was going to ask.

'Should we tell the others?' I asked stupidly.

'Guess not,' Matt said. 'Alcoholics – or Narcotics, whatever – Anonymous. Clue's in the name, right?'

'Right,' I said.

And we made our way back to our friends, to the close-knit group that had once included Andy but no longer did, the knowledge that there was an important secret I was keeping from them weighing heavily on me.

Perhaps it was because of that that the vibe of the afternoon changed a bit after that. Rowan left in the early evening because Clara and her mate were meeting friends at the cinema, and, without the duty of even vaguely pretending to be responsible adults, the rest of us went a bit feral.

Kate snogged a random stranger she met outside the negroni stall. I smoked the first cigarette I'd had in years – and, I suspected, the last I'd have for years to come. Naomi announced that she was going to be sick, and Patch courteously handed her his baseball cap to use, neither of them realising that its mesh fabric made it as much use as puking into a sieve would have been.

We folded up our blankets and decamped to one of the bars, where Kate bought a round of tequila shots and then another. As evening began to fall, the families departed for bathtime and bedtime, and the venue became more crowded and less serene. The volume of the music increased, and the band playing was significantly better. The face-painting stall had long since shut up shop and most of the food stalls had closed, too. I could smell marijuana smoke, heavy in the cooling air, and remembered Naomi's joke about her twins.

But, increasingly, time was behaving in that strange way it does when you're a bit drunk and a lot irresponsible. I spent five minutes queueing for drinks, which felt like a lifetime, and yet the next thing I knew an hour had passed and it was nine o'clock and almost fully dark, stars glinting in the sky above the lights of the fairground and the stage.

'I don't know about you,' Kate said, leaning in to me to make herself heard over the music, cigarette smoke on her breath, 'but I'm completely shitfaced.'

'Seriously, seriously shitfaced,' Naomi agreed, her teeth gleaming white in a manic grin. 'Patch just went for an al-fresco piss. We're getting too old for this.'

'No we're not!' I pulled them both into a group hug. 'I'm having the best time. I love you guys so much.'

And we all agreed, several times, that we loved each other so, so much and were having the best time, then we pushed to the heart of the crowd in front of the stage to dance.

And then, suddenly, it was midnight.

The music stilled and the lights over the stage dimmed. The roar of voices was suddenly loud, and the press of bodies heading towards the exit was hot, urgent, almost threatening. Somehow, I found Matt, and he gripped my hand firmly in his as we walked. I could see Kate and Naomi just ahead of us, each grasping one of Patch's arms for dear life.

At last, we made it out to the relative calm of the street – although it was littered with discarded cans and plastic cups, and a group of young men looked like they were squaring up to one another for a fight.

'Want to come back to ours?' Matt asked.

'Best not,' Naomi said regretfully. 'We promised the in-laws we wouldn't be too late picking the kids up tomorrow, and if we drink any more, they'll end up staying there until Monday.'

'Aw, come on, they won't mind,' Patch objected.

'No, babe, let's not take the piss.'

'I've got to work tomorrow.' Kate raked her fingers through her hair, shedding glitter onto her bare shoulders. 'God knows how, but I have to. I'm getting an Uber.'

'Come on, let's jump on the Tube,' Naomi urged, and Patch reluctantly complied.

Suddenly, only Matt and I were left, the crowd around us

already thinning. We walked towards our road, my feet seeming to carry me unbidden, the natural homing instinct of the pissed person kicking in. And when we turned the corner, the people and the noise and the detritus behind us, the magic of the day came flooding back.

It seemed like the pools of light from the street lamps were stepping stones, a magical pathway we could follow back to the safety of home. A jasmine bush, flourishing still even this late in summer, enveloped us in its heady scent. An unfamiliar black cat darted across the road, pausing to regard us with searchlight emerald eyes that were like a wish for good luck.

And, next to me, there was Matt. The same man who'd lifted me onto his shoulders ten years before, lowered me back down and asked me to be his wife. I was walking alongside him now; there was no music, no mud and no leaky tent to return to, only the silent streets and the promise of our home.

CHAPTER FOURTEEN

I woke up with a pounding head, a churning stomach, a mouth that tasted like someone had used my toothbrush to clean a festival toilet... and an overwhelming sense of well-being. For a second I couldn't work out why, then I opened my eyes and saw Matt's face on the pillow next to mine, a smile on his lips even in sleep.

With more energy than any hungover person had the right to have, I sprang out of bed, dressed and hurried downstairs. I switched on the kettle, took Matt a coffee and rummaged in the fridge for breakfast. We had no bacon, but there was a pack of smoked salmon I'd meant to use in a pasta sauce earlier in the week, only I'd been too lazy and cooked fish fingers instead. I scrambled eggs, added the salmon and a splash of cream that was nearing its best-before date, toasted two bagels, assembled it all on plates and headed upstairs again.

'Room service,' I informed my husband, who'd evidently woken up to drink his coffee then fallen back asleep.

'Room what?' He sat up, rubbing his eyes groggily. 'I feel absolutely terrible. And that looks seriously good. Hold on.'

He levered himself out of bed, wincing at the sunlight

lasering through the gap in the curtains, and went to the bathroom. I heard the buzz of his toothbrush and water running into glass once, then again and again.

Then he returned, looking slightly less ghostly.

'You made us breakfast in bed. You never do that.'

'First time for everything.' I crossed my legs and forked up some salmon and eggs, not caring if I got crumbs on the duvet. We could change the sheets later on – we probably should, anyway, and run the hoover round, clean the shower, get rid of the wilting contents of the vegetable drawer in the fridge, and...

But that wouldn't do. Thinking about the mundanities of Sunday housework was putting a real damper on my good mood.

Matt took a crunchy bite of bagel, making the precariously positioned eggs wobble dangerously.

'God, that's delicious,' he said. 'So. What shall we do today?'

I pushed aside the intruding thoughts of cleaning. We could go into town and visit an art gallery. We could take a train out into the countryside. We could visit a garden centre and have tea and scones like an old married couple.

But I found there was something we needed to do more than any of those things.

'Come on,' I said. 'We need to go and give Shrimp her breakfast.'

Matt set his empty plate aside and stretched. 'I guess we do. Here I am stuffing my face when we didn't even give her dinner last night.'

'I expect one of the neighbours will have. Still, though.'

'All right, I'll get my lazy arse out of bed. It looks like another nice day.'

And he was right – but by the time we'd showered, dressed and put a load of washing on, a black cloud had appeared on the horizon and a sudden, chilly wind picked up. My choice of a summer dress and flip-flops didn't seem quite so clever now.

'Looks like it's about to piss it down,' Matt said unnecessarily, as the first few raindrops splatted heavily on the street in front of us.

'Should we head back? Try again later on?'

'We're more than halfway there. We'll likely get soaked whatever we do.'

At first, I ducked my head, as if the rain falling on my back would somehow make me less wet than if it landed on my face. But I quickly realised there was no point – it was coming down in sheets. My dress was quickly soaked through, clinging damply to my thighs as I walked, and my flip-flops were so slippery with water I felt like I was walking on an ice rink.

The shower didn't last long – only a few minutes before the cloud, its malicious work done, passed over and the sun emerged again, making the trees overhead sparkle like they'd been adorned with diamonds and painting a double rainbow over the rooftops.

But Matt and I were wet through.

'At least it's not cold,' I said, wringing out my hair and grinning up at him.

'You'd think, after spending our whole lives in this bloody country, we'd have thought to bring an umbrella.'

'Or get a bus.'

'Or stay indoors, like sensible people.'

'Anyway, here we are. But where's Shrimp?'

Right on cue, we heard a familiar cry. From behind a green recycling bin, the cat emerged. Except she was barely recognisable as herself – or indeed any cat. Her small body looked even smaller, her fur soaked through with water, sticking up in random spikes around her scrawny shoulders. Her head looked like that of one of those hairless sphinx cats, all eyes and ears and whiskers.

She trotted towards us, mewing pitifully. Her demeanour

couldn't have been clearer: she was a cat with a problem on her hands – or paws – and she needed us to help her solve it.

'Oh, you poor little love.' I squatted down, reaching out a hand, and Shrimp rubbed her face against it, leaving wet fur clinging to my skin. 'What are we going to do with you?'

Matt joined me, squatting on the wet concrete path, stroking the cat's sodden flanks. Incredibly, we heard her start to purr.

'I'm not sure what we can do,' Matt said. 'We can't exactly take her home with us.'

'But we can't leave her here, either. It might rain again. She must be freezing.'

Just seconds before, I'd been comforting myself with the knowledge that I, although wet through, wasn't at all cold. But I wasn't a little cat, shut out of her home with nowhere to go to get warm and dry.

'Poor baby. Look, her food bowl's full of water,' Matt said.

It was true; it would be impossible to tell which of the small stainless-steel bowls was which, except that one of them had a few soggy cat biscuits in the bottom.

Shrimp miaowed again, as if to emphasise the gravity of the situation.

'You wait here,' I said. 'I'll be right back.'

'What are you—' Matt began, but I was already hurrying away in the direction we'd come from.

On the high street, many of the shops were closed, because it was Sunday. But I bought a towel, a roll of black bin liners, cat food and – in a fortuitously open pet shop – a fluffy pink cat bed printed with paw marks. It might not stay dry for long, but at least it would stay dry for now.

And then I panted my way back to Matt, wishing I had brought him along on my lightning errand to carry the heavy, awkward bag.

'What the hell have you got there?' he asked. 'Planning to set up a branch of Battersea Cats and Dogs Home?'

'Just some bits and pieces to make her more comfortable,' I replied defensively – extra defensively, because Shrimp was perched on Matt's lap, making a pretty good go of drying herself with her surprisingly large pink tongue, aided by Matt's T-shirt, which he'd peeled off, apparently unaware that it was at least as wet as the cat.

'She knows what that is, anyway,' he said.

Some feline instinct appeared to have alerted Shrimp to the presence of food, and she jumped down, rubbing her damp body against my legs and purring furiously in between little cheeps of longing.

'Come on, then.' I tipped the water out of her food bowl, gave it a makeshift wipe with the towel and tipped in some cat biscuits. 'I know this is different from the food we gave you before but it cost a bloody fortune, so it had better be good.'

'Seems to meet with her approval,' Matt said as Shrimp buried her face in the bowl and began crunching enthusiastically.

I nodded, but we didn't turn to leave just yet. We watched as Shrimp finished her food then padded over to the cat bed, sniffed it thoroughly all over, then stepped carefully in, turning around a few times before settling down and embarking on a more thorough wash, paying particular attention to her whiskers.

Then, without saying anything more, we walked away, hand in hand, our clothes gently steaming in the humid air.

I realised I hadn't felt this close to my husband in the longest time. It felt like we were united again, with a common purpose.

CHAPTER FIFTEEN

Monday passed, then Tuesday. We visited Shrimp together each evening, spending a few minutes with her while she ate. Matt knocked on the door of the house again, but again there was no answer. The cat was dry, at least, and we hoped relatively warm in her new bed, but as we walked home together, we talked again about what would happen to her when winter came.

'I called an animal shelter,' I told Matt. 'But they're all full. Absolutely bursting at the seams with unwanted cats. Apparently lots of people bought animals last year, and now they're going back to the office they can't look after them any more.'

'She's all right for now, anyway. We'll keep on trying the door. Maybe the owners are just on holiday.'

'Some owners they are, if they disappear off on holiday and leave their cat behind.'

'Don't be so judgemental, Abs. You don't know what their situation is.'

Over the next couple of days, though, work ramped up to the point where I found it hard to focus on anything else – even

Shrimp – and Matt made the daily pilgrimage to feed her on his own.

A date had been set for the Quim launch, at a super-swanky Shoreditch club, and the invitations were on their fourth draft and counting, which meant the urgency of getting the website live was ramping up even more. The agency was pitching to a new client, a delivery service for carb-less, lactose-free vegan ready meals, and the slide deck was doing my head in. Bastian had finally signed a lease on a new office and was driving the poor office manager mad constantly changing his mind about sign-in protocols and flexible working hours.

Each time I joined an online meeting with him and Marc, their bickering seemed to have escalated further. Marc berated Bastian for failing to win a pitch for a new e-scooter brand; Bastian tore a strip off Marc because the Talon online shop kept falling over. The previous week, I'd noticed that the background on Marc's Zoom image had changed from the wine racks to an empty, industrial-style apartment, and I thought with sadness that, personally if not professionally, they must have reached the end of the road.

It wasn't entirely unsurprising, I reflected – after all, how many relationships could withstand one partner telling the other he was so far up his own arse he needed a candle to read his emails, and the other responding that he'd rather look at the inside of his own bum than his partner's gurning face.

They made Matt and me look like love's young dream. Not that that was a particularly high bar to clear.

When five thirty on Thursday came, Matt didn't suggest a walk as usual. He glanced over to where I was sitting, hunched over my keyboard, came across and briefly massaged my aching shoulders.

'What's another word for "penetration"?' I muttered, my eyes fixed on the screen.

'"Enclosure"?' Matt suggested.

'Fuck no. That sounds like somewhere you'd keep goats.'

'"The act"?'

'What are you, a fundamentalist preacher?'

'"Completion"?'

'Nah, that means shooting your load.'

'God, I don't know, Abbie. You're the expert here.'

I pushed back my hair, which felt like I hadn't brushed it for days. '"Mattress mambo". That'll have to do.'

I heard Matt give a snort of laughter. 'I'll let you get on with it. Shout when you're ready to grab some dinner.'

He closed his own laptop, and I heard his footsteps climbing the stairs. But he didn't go into the bedroom as I expected, or into the bathroom. The other room – the one we didn't use – was right above me, and I heard Matt's tread as he walked in.

The sound of his trainers on the wooden floor came to a stop. I imagined him standing there, looking at the empty room. I wondered what he was feeling – the same sense of loss and failure I experienced on the rare occasions when I opened the door? Grief? Anger at me and my failure to conceive a child?

Or perhaps he was just looking out at the crab apple tree in our neighbour's garden, its leaves just beginning to turn acid green and gold with autumn, the fruit ripening on its branches, and not thinking of very much at all.

I worked on for the next two hours, until my eyes were burning and every word I typed felt meaningless. Then I gave up and logged off.

'Hey, Matt,' I called. 'I think I'm done here. Want to grab a takeaway?'

There was a pause, and then my husband's feet began their familiar series of thuds back downstairs.

'Sure. Chinese? Indian? Pizza?'

'Whatever you want. I'm pretty much brain-dead – even deciding what to eat is beyond me.'

'Indian, then. Samosas, lamb dhansak, garlic naan and that spinach thing you like?'

'Sounds great.'

But I couldn't summon up much enthusiasm for the food when it arrived. We sat opposite each other at the table, as we'd been doing all day, only eating now rather than working – or, in my case, fussing with half a popadom and some chutney. Matt pushed the dish of curry across to me, and I spooned a little onto my plate. The spicy smell would normally have made my mouth water, but all I could think about was the imagined taste of Talon.

Possibly the guava flavour, which, I remembered from our long-ago tasting with the client, had been utterly repellent.

'So I was upstairs just now,' Matt said, scooping up a chunk of meat with a torn-off piece of bread.

I waited for him to carry on, but he didn't, so I said, 'Yes, I heard you.'

'I was thinking,' he said. 'It seems a waste to have that room empty, when we're on top of each other working down here.'

I broke off some bread, looked at it, then put it back down on my plate. 'But you'll be out of the house way more when schools go back, won't you? You won't just be doing random sessions for holiday clubs, but proper regular training.'

'Yeah, sure. But I'm still here most mornings.'

'And I'll be going into the office a couple of days a week. Bastian was saying we'll be there for client meetings and stuff.'

'Still, though. You've been sat here working for over a year, and me too. It's not ideal, is it, when we've got that space upstairs that we could turn into a proper office.'

A proper office. The room I'd imagined furnishing with a white-painted cot, decorating with bunting, filling with the smell of baby wipes. The room I'd imagined entering to be greeted by the smiling faces of an array of cuddly toys, and another face, too, which I'd never been able to picture clearly in my mind.

'I don't want an office. I'm perfectly okay here.'

'Abs, it's… You know it doesn't make sense. When we have people round, it takes ages to clear all our work crap out of the way.'

'We hardly ever have people round.'

'Maybe that's why. And we can't have anyone to stay over without them having to camp on the couch. If you don't want an office, we could turn it into a proper spare bedroom.'

'I don't want a proper spare bedroom,' I said, petulant as a child.

Matt sighed. He dug a spoon into the dish of spinach, looked at it, then put it back.

'I just don't feel ready, okay?' I said. 'It just feels like it's too soon.'

'And I do feel ready. I feel like that room's been there, empty, for five years now, like a shrine or – or a morgue or something. It's depressing.'

I felt anger and hurt flare inside me. 'Too right it's depressing. How many times do you think I've walked past that door and felt depressed?'

'I know, Abs. I understand. I'm here too, you know. I just don't think we can move on properly while we've still got that… that reminder.'

'What if I don't want to move on?'

Matt looked at me steadily. I felt a rush of words building up in my head, crowding into my throat, needing to be said – but I wasn't sure how to say them.

I said, 'Are you done with the food?'

'Yeah. I guess I wasn't that hungry after all.'

I cleared the table, noticing a little row of four coffee spoons on the draining board. But the usual spark of rage their presence would have ignited in me didn't come today. I just wearily scooped all the curry back into its plastic boxes and put it into the fridge, wrapped the bread and put it in the bread bin, and stacked everything else in the dishwasher.

Then I got a bottle of red wine out of the rack, levered out the cork, and plonked it down on the table with two glasses. Matt stabbed the end of the corkscrew into the foil and peeled it away.

'I just don't get it,' I said. 'You wanted a baby. We tried and tried, for years. We spent thousands of pounds. And now you think we should just move on?'

'What choice do we have? We're not getting free treatment and we can't afford to pay. I mean, maybe it'll just happen. It does sometimes. I was reading the other day about a couple who—'

'Matt, please don't tell me you're going to come out with that "just relax and it might happen" bullshit? Because I've spent the past six years relaxing – as much as you can relax when you're having sex you don't want to have because it's the right time and you want to have a baby – and it hasn't happened. So what exactly would be different now?'

He poured wine into our glasses. A drop splashed from the bottle and landed on the surface of the table, a bright stain against the pale wood. 'Do you think I've wanted to have sex when we've been doing it because an app tells us to? Do you think I like it when my wife's lying there crying and I've got to finish because if I don't it will have been for nothing?'

I felt blood rush to my face. I remembered those nights, when we'd been actively trying, having baby-making sex, and how Matt had held me afterwards and said he was sorry. I remembered turning my face away, ashamed of my distress, and asking him to pass me a pillow to put under my hips, guarding whatever might be there inside me to give it the best chance.

How cruel I'd been. At a time when we should have been

holding each other, consoling each other, sharing our fear and our hope, I'd turned away.

Of course he hadn't wanted it, any more than I had. Not for itself, just for the possible outcome, which had never happened.

'I guess I never thought of it that way,' I said.

Matt said, 'No. I guess you didn't.'

'I'm sorry. I should have done.'

He smiled, a crooked facsimile of his usual grin, the one that seemed too wide for his face. 'Nobody's perfect.'

'Maybe just a desk upstairs,' I said. 'I could live with a desk.'

I imagined sitting by the window, looking out at the crab apple tree. There'd still be plenty of space in the room behind me.

'Just say when you're ready,' he said. 'We won't order one until you are.'

'Okay. Thanks.'

'You're welcome.'

We drank some more wine, half looking at each other across the table. I thought again what it must have been like for Matt, as the months of trying for a baby turned into years. I thought of all the pregnancy and ovulation tests I'd taken, how obsessed I'd become with the inner workings of my own body, how everything I'd always taken for granted about it had seemed to fall apart around me.

He must have felt the same about himself, although he'd never said so.

And at some point, the easy intimacy, the flame of desire that had burned so steadily between us, like the pilot light on a gas boiler, flaring into life when it was needed, had guttered and gone cold.

Could we ever get it back again?

NOVEMBER 2008
IF I WERE A BOY

'I'm scared,' Abbie said. 'Are you scared?'

'Shitless,' said Rowan. 'Worse than when I went into hospital to be induced with Clara.'

'But it's going to be worth it, right? Tell me it's going to be worth it.'

'Well, I don't know. That's what everyone says about having a baby and even now I'm not convinced. But Kate says it is.'

'Kate's hardcore though. She does Bikram yoga and goes on holiday on her own and everything.'

'True. Look, this must be the place here.'

They stopped outside the glass door, with its swirly gold writing and ornate handle shaped like a long-stemmed lily. The flower head looked rather like a... but that was the last thing Abbie wanted to think about right now. Not that she'd have a choice in a few minutes' time.

'We could change our minds,' Rowan said. 'We could just have a pedicure or something instead.'

'Won't work. Look, they do the pedicures out the front here and the other stuff... well, presumably.'

'Of course they do. I mean, they wouldn't – would they?'

'No chance. This place has got loads of five-star reviews on Google. They're the best. The woman who runs it is literally Brazilian. They know what they're doing.'

Emboldened by her own words, Abbie pushed open the door and was greeted by a blast of warm, fragrant air.

'Good afternoon, ladies.' The smiling receptionist was heavily and flawlessly made-up, and Abbie was willing to bet there wasn't a hair on her body below the neck.

'We've got an appointment,' Rowan said. 'I mean, two appointments, obviously. My name's Rowan Connell and this is Abbie Saunders.'

'Let me just check.' A shellac-manicured hand tapped a keyboard. 'All good. Welcome, ladies. Abbie, the room's ready for you. Your therapist, Elena, will take you through right away. Rowan, if you wouldn't mind taking a seat for just a few minutes. Can I get you anything? Glass of water? Green tea?'

'I'm okay, thank you.' Obediently, Rowan sat and Abbie cast a last, desperate look at her before being led away by a white-overalled blonde woman, who also seemed to be permanently smiling.

'Is this your first time at Blooming Beauty?' asked Elena, making her way swiftly past the manicure and pedicure stations to a narrow spiral staircase at the back of the room. 'We're just down here. Watch your step.'

'Yes, it is. It's actually my first...'

'And you're here for a Hollywood wax?'

'I...' Abbie hesitated. But it was too late – she was here now. There was no going back. 'Yes, that's right.'

Elena opened a door to a tiny cubicle, containing a treatment bed and a huge machine whose purpose Abbie could only guess at. The smell was stronger in here; on a table, she could see a vat of pale green wax on a burner and a little pot of what looked like ice cream sticks.

'Just slip your things off and lie down on the bed. Cover yourself with the towel and I'll be with you in just a minute.'

'Slip off my…?'

'Everything on the bottom half.' Another bright smile, and Elena whisked out, pulling the door closed behind her.

Shit. *Everything?* Abbie imagined Kate laughing and asking her what the hell she expected – them to wax her minge through her knickers?

Hastily, she unzipped her boots, pulled off her tights and skirt, then paused.

Pants. Off, Kate instructed firmly in her head, and Abbie whipped off her pants, concealed them under the little pile of her clothes (*Like it matters if the woman sees your undercrackers when she's about to see literally everything,* imaginary Kate chided) and lay down on the bed, covering what was left of her modesty with a soft, coffee-coloured towel.

'All ready for me?' Elena reappeared, smile firmly in place.

Abbie nodded, her ponytail pressing into the back of her head against the thin pillow.

'Then let's get started. I try to work quickly, so it'll all be over nice and soon.'

Abbie nodded again.

'Now, if you'll just let your legs fall apart…'

Abbie closed her eyes, like a child putting her hands over her face in a game of hide-and-seek. She felt the first slick of hot wax on her skin, then a sharp rip, and the beautician's gloved hand pressing firmly where her hair had been seconds before. The plinky whale music that had been playing stopped, and Beyoncé came on.

If I were a boy, Abbie thought, *I'd never, ever have to do shit like this.*

Come on, woman up! It's not that bad, is it? asked Kate in her head.

No, but—

It was about to get a whole lot worse. Afterwards, over an enormous glass of chardonnay with Rowan, Abbie would try to work out which the worst bit had been. Was it when Elena took two powerful yanks to remove the thickest bit of hair over her pubic bone? Was it when – oh God, the utter, cringe-tastic humiliation – she had to trim a few of the longer hairs with a pair of nail scissors before ripping them out? Was it the gynae-cological bit when she got right in there – literally right in here – to access bits of Abbie's anatomy that only Matt and the nurse at her GP practice had ever seen before?

No, it wasn't. Unquestionably, utterly the worst bit was when, just as Abbie thought it was all done, the horror over, the glass of wine feeling like a realistic prospect, Elena said, 'Now, if you'll just turn over.'

'Sorry?' Abbie asked.

'Just get on all fours, so we can do the back.'

Oh my God, screamed Abbie's mind. *Please, no!*

Of course she's going to wax your bum, you doofus. Imaginary Kate was uncompromising. *Don't you know that's the whole point? Everything off means everything off.*

And so, dying inside, face flaming, Abbie turned over, spread her cheeks, and waited for it to be over.

'All done,' Elena said at last, once she'd crowned Abbie's humiliation by carefully applying aloe vera gel to what she referred to as the 'treated areas'. 'All clean now.'

Oh God, was I dirty before? Abbie agonised. Had her hasty wash with a pack of baby wipes in the work loo not been sufficient?

Of course that's not what she meant, imaginary Kate assured her. *It's just a thing they say.* Absolutely steeped in misogyny, of course, but here we are.

Elena whisked out once more, leaving Abbie to cast a brief, wondering glance at her denuded bits and wonder if they'd carry on looking quite so angry for much longer, before pulling on her clothes and hurrying back to the reception area, where she paid for her treatment on her credit card and handed over a hefty tip in cash. Rowan was already done, waiting on the peach-coloured chaise longue, looking shame-faced.

In silence, they left the salon together.

'Holy shit,' Abbie said, as soon as the door swung shut behind them. 'Wasn't that just the absolute worst? I mean, it wasn't all that sore – don't get me wrong, it smarted – but the cringe factor was off the scale. How did you get done so quickly?'

'Um.' Rowan looked sideways at Abbie under her fringe. 'Here's the thing. They'd had a cancellation, so they could fit me in for a pedicure instead.'

Abbie's outrage lasted about as long as it took them to reach the pub, and by the time they were a bottle of wine down, she'd forgiven her friend for her betrayal. She'd even forgiven imaginary Kate for forcing her to go through with the whole thing. And now, there was just one more step to be taken on her Hollywood wax maiden voyage.

'Shall we get another bottle?' Rowan suggested.

Abbie was tempted for a second – the wine was doing an excellent job of helping her to forget the pain.

But she said, 'I'd love to, but I'd better get home.'

'To do the big reveal for Matt?' Rowan laughed. 'God, I'd give anything to see his face. It'll be so worth it. Apparently it makes oral sex off the scale. Not that I can really remember what that feels like.'

'Oh, stop!' Abbie tucked her phone in her bag. 'For all I know, he'll be absolutely horrified and refuse to go near me until it's grown back and I can have a normal bikini wax like I usually do.'

Rowan sighed. 'Good on you for bothering. I really don't know why I thought I could be arsed to go through with it, given no one's going to see it, barring some kind of miracle.'

'Yeah, you stick to that excuse. I know perfectly well you just wussed out because you couldn't face the pain.'

'Well, there was that, too,' Rowan admitted, and they left the pub still laughing.

But Abbie needn't have worried about Matt's reaction. She wasn't sure how to do the big reveal, as Rowan had put it. Should she leave her knickers off and cross her legs slowly and alluringly like Sharon Stone in *Fatal Attraction*? Should she warn him first, in case he thought she'd had a dreadful accident with a hedge trimmer or something? Should she go full Ann Summers in crotchless knickers to frame Elena's handiwork?

In the end, she did none of those things. Matt was late home from work, they'd both already eaten, and the stage wasn't exactly set for a romantic evening. But, once they were in bed together, Matt pulled her close and kissed her in a way that made it clear he had other things on his mind than sleep.

Abbie kissed him back, waiting for the moment when his hand would slip under the hem of her nightie to touch her.

When it happened, she saw his eyes widen.

'Oh my God. You're all... smooth.'

'I am.' She smiled, amazed at how different his fingers felt on her bare skin.

He pushed down the duvet and knelt between her legs. 'Let me look. Jesus. You're fucking beautiful.'

She and Matt had been together for a lot of years, and they'd had sex a lot of times. But, at that moment, she couldn't have identified a time it had felt more exciting, or she herself more irresistibly, powerfully sexy.

'Want me to switch the light on?' she asked.

'Damn sure.'

She reached over and snapped on the bedside lamp. Matt's eyes were dark pools of desire; she was sure hers must look the same. She glanced down at her body and saw that the redness had faded – all there was now was smooth skin, pearl-white, never touched by sunlight.

She watched as Matt's hand moved up her thigh, his fingers brushing her skin. Against her pale, soft flesh, his fingers looked almost absurdly masculine. But his lips on hers were soft, his tongue gentle and questing.

Abbie knew what she wanted, and she knew without having to ask that Matt wanted it just as much.

She smiled again, then closed her eyes and lay back on the pillow, letting her legs fall open as she had in the salon, only willingly now. She waited for Matt to lower his head to taste her and heard his moan of pleasure when he did, and her own answering gasp.

And then she stopped thinking – she couldn't focus on a single thought. It was as if everything in her brain had been erased and she was just a body, just sensation, just Matt's lover being dissolved into a puddle of bliss.

CHAPTER SIXTEEN

'So basically, it's working.' Kate said, splashing wine into our glasses, once I'd filled the Girlfriends' Club in on the progress of Operation Memory Lane. 'You and Matt. Talking, having a laugh. It all sounds pretty good to me.'

'It is,' I said. 'Only, there's still the stuff we try to talk about, but it's kind of hard. Like the baby thing.'

I took a deep breath. The letter that had arrived three months before was something I still hadn't told the others about, even though normally I'd have shared just about everything with them. But not that – not yet. It still felt too raw; I still hadn't properly processed it in my own head, not even enough to formulate the words I'd use when I described its arrival to my closest friends.

And our spare room was still just that – a room with no purpose, extraneous and empty, the branches of the tree bare now apart from a few clinging golden berries the parakeets hadn't discovered yet, the desk I'd promised still unpurchased.

But now, looking at their curious, concerned faces around the table, I found I had to.

'It looks like we're at the end of the road. They said we've run out of time – I'm too old for another go at funded fertility treatment. And we can't afford to pay for it privately, even if I thought it might work, which quite honestly, I...'

My words petered out. I couldn't quite bear to say the final one.

'Oh, love.' Kate reached out and squeezed my hand. 'What an utter pile of pants.'

'And,' I went on, my tongue loosened by wine and the company of my friends, 'you know what? When you're trying for a baby, sex is shit. It was for me, anyway. At least after the first few months. It just totally stopped being fun, or even nice. Like how you can love eating salad, but as soon as you're on a diet it's like penance food.'

'Like eating grass,' Naomi agreed. 'Like you're some – I don't know – farm animal or something, and you'll never be able to trough a guilt-free Mars bar again.'

'Was it like that for you and Patch?' I asked hesitantly.

Naomi said, 'Uhhh, yes and no. I mean, we weren't even trying for that long. So it was still fun and everything. But it definitely started to feel like, "Okay, you put the bins out and I'll bleach the toilet and then we'd better have sex, and then we can order a pizza." Even if we did enjoy the sex so much we forgot about the pizza until everything was closed, I still had a few moments when I thought, "Hold on, this isn't great, really."'

'Since we had to stop the fertility treatment, Matt and I haven't had sex once,' I confessed. 'Ever. In almost eighteen months. It's like, we're getting on better and everything, but on the marital unpleasantness front – nada.'

'I haven't had sex in three years,' Rowan said. 'And the last time was a dreadful pity shag with Paul. I mean, what was I thinking? He basically gave me one so I'd have Clara for an extra weekend while he swanned off to Tenerife on a mate's stag do.'

'I have sex all the time,' Kate said mournfully. 'Unfortunately it's with people I hook up with on Tinder who I don't give a crap about. I mean, it's getting my end away – if girls even do that – but it's not ideal.'

'You and Matt, though,' Naomi said. 'You were always total goals. Couldn't keep your hands off each other. All the time I've known you. I thought it was still that way.'

Rowan said, 'You always bought fancy lingerie and stuff, even when you were skint. And had everything waxed – remember that?'

I felt a blush creeping up my neck, not because my mates were discussing my sex life – they were all pretty used to that, and if I'd felt uncomfortable I'd have told them to wind their necks in – but because their words had reminded me just how bad things had become.

I couldn't remember when it had changed. There must have been a point when those monthly waxes became occasional, and then never (to be fair, everyone's personal grooming had been neglected over the past year or so); when those lace and satin bras and thongs gradually made their way to the clothes recycling bank (the trouble with being skint was that I'd only ever been able to afford them in cheap polyester) and stopped being replaced (cheap polyester was, after all, highly unethical, I'd told myself).

But it wasn't about that – or not just that, I thought, taking an outsize gulp of wine. It was about the way I felt about Matt – and about myself. And it was definitely not wanting to waste money on frivolities or a growing awareness of climate change and the wasteful, exploitative nature of garment production that had changed that. It had been the long, gruelling, unsuccessful process of trying to procreate that had stopped me feeling like a desiring, desirable, sexual person and made me feel like an egg-laying chicken in a battery farm – except my eggs were no good, and I'd get turned into pet food even sooner than my fertile sister chickens.

'I need to get my shit together,' I said. 'If we're going to survive. Stay married, I mean – no one ever literally died from not getting nookie. Did they?'

'Not so far as I know,' Kate said. 'Although, looking at some of the desperate bastards on dating apps, you'd think they'd been crawling through the desert for weeks without food or water and your minge was an oasis.'

'What do you do, though? How do you get the spark back?'

'I remember Andy saying once when he'd gone off a bloke that you can't strike the same match twice,' Rowan said. Then she added hastily, 'But I'm sure he was wrong.'

'His relationships never lasted more than a few weeks anyway,' Naomi said. 'He's hardly a beacon of fidelity and marital longevity to which we should all aspire.'

'So what are you going to do?' Kate asked. 'Start tonight? Get home and jump Matt's bones?'

'No,' I said, more firmly than I'd intended. Why did the idea of doing that seem so far-fetched? 'I'm going to need a plan. Starting with booking a wax. Tomorrow. First thing.'

The next day, Matt was conveniently out all day doing a workshop at a school on the other side of London, Marc was off supervising the printing of some point-of-sale material and Bastian was doing a pitch with one of the other account executives. So, at lunchtime, I was able to abandon my post and sneak off to our local high street.

I hurried to the supermarket and bought ingredients for the closest thing to a romantic dinner I could come up with, complete with a pack of candles and a bottle of decent champagne, because obviously the name on the bottle would transform me into an instant sex goddess in a way cava or prosecco couldn't possibly.

Back in the day, I'd had all the boutiques of Covent Garden on my doorstep – or at least the office doorstep, even if I did always end up in Primark. Now, though, I was limited to the retail offerings on the high street, and Agent Provocateur they were not. There were market stalls selling nylon underwear in lurid pastel colours that I was pretty sure shouldn't be let anywhere near a naked flame. There were discount stores whose rails were jumbled with mismatched garments where, if I'd had time, I might have been able to locate a designer bargain – but I didn't have time.

And when I pushed open the door of the local beauty salon – which looked like it mostly specialised in nail art and eyelash extensions so thick and long it was a miracle anyone could see past them – and asked if they could fit me in for a wax, the girl looked at me like I must've just emerged from several months living under a rock and told me they were booked solid for weeks.

Shit. I was meant to be setting the stage for romance, and a couple of steaks and a bottle of fizz was nowhere near good enough.

Then I remembered the box of products from Quim, gathering dust in a corner of the spare bedroom. Since first opening it, I'd barely looked at it. It was too harsh a reminder of where Matt and I should be in terms of the physical side of our marriage, versus where we were. Where we were, versus where we used to be.

But now its time had come.

I raced through my afternoon's work then closed my laptop at five thirty on the dot and had a shower, meticulously shaving my legs and managing not to cut myself to ribbons. Then, wrapped in a towel, I padded through to the back bedroom and squatted down in front of the box. Encased in rustling polythene sleeves, I found the various items of lingerie I remembered glimpsing back when the box had arrived. Handily, each one had a stick-on label identifying its contents.

Naked Desire wet-look open-cup crotchless body – that was way too advanced for me. Fishnet all-in-one catsuit – not a chance in hell. Studded bondage-style basque with suspenders – hard pass. Good grief. What had happened to me? I'd never been the kind of person who wore stuff like this without a second thought, but I'd been a whole lot more adventurous than I was now. Now, the idea of wearing anything so overtly sexy made me do a full-body cringe.

There was also a Love Me scarlet lace push-up bra and French knicker set. I looked at it for a second, then put it on top of the pile. It was going to have to do.

Then I rummaged in the box a bit more. There were furry handcuffs and lubricant applicators and nipple clamps. There were more kinds of vibrator than I'd ever known existed: double-ended ones and app-controlled ones and even a glow-in-the-dark one.

'Don't want to frighten the horses,' I muttered to myself.

And then my hand clasped around a tube. I pulled it out of the carton and read the label: 'Intimate Hair-Removal Creme'.

Right. Waxing had turned out not to be an option, but clearly the gods of minge maintenance were smiling on me after all. I turned the tube over and glanced at the instructions on the back.

'Warning: Perform a patch test 24 hours before use', it said in bold capital letters.

'Yeah, right,' I told it. 'We've got no time for that. Don't let me down – this is not a drill.'

Back in the bathroom, I pulled off my towel, squeezed a dollop of the cream onto my fingers and applied it generously to – well, the relevant area. All the relevant areas. It smelled weird – a bit like the hair salon I used to go to with my mum when I was a little girl, perching on a too-high chair for what felt like hours while the perm lotion did its work on her hair.

I turned back to the label on the tube. 'Wait for five minutes, then use the enclosed spatula' – what spatula? – 'to remove a small test area of creme.' Okay. I checked the time on my phone – it had been on about forty-five seconds, maybe a minute. Only four to go.

But then I noticed a distinct tingling sensation, quickly growing more intense, until it wasn't so much tingling as burning.

Basically, what had happened to my mouth all those years ago when I ate my first ever extra-hot Nando's burger on my first ever date with Matt was happening again, only this time to my fanjo.

And this time, there was no way I was going to tough it out. Impressing my boyfriend with my ability to eat spicy food was one thing – impressing my husband with third-degree chemical burns on my nether regions was right up there with the worst ideas ever.

With speed that would have impressed Usain Bolt, I ducked back into the shower, switching it onto cool and directing the nozzle at my pubic hair. The relief was instant. The water soothed my skin and, not as quickly as I'd have liked, washed away the surprisingly sticky, gloopy cream and a few clumps of hair.

Once I was sure I'd got it all off and the stinging had totally subsided, I stepped out of the shower again and assessed the state of affairs.

'FML,' I said aloud. 'It looks like a wool jumper the moths have got to.'

I picked up my razor, then hesitated. I'd avoided severe skin irritation; I wasn't now going to risk a nasty case of razor burn. So, squatting over the toilet like the absolute antithesis of a sex goddess, I evened things out as best I could using my nail scissors.

Then, before my courage could desert me altogether, I pulled on the scratchy red lace underwear, dragged a black jumper dress over my head and slipped my feet into a pair of black ballet flats, and hurried downstairs.

I'd never been much of a cook. Back in the early days of the Girlfriends' Club, when we'd all been coupled up, we'd gone through a phase of having monthly dinner parties. Andy and Zara had both always shown off massively when it was their turn; Kate cooked as competently as she did everything else; Rowan and Naomi relied on simple recipes they knew well and copious amounts of wine.

I'd just found the whole business massively stressful, spending too much on ingredients I didn't know what to do with and producing results that were – if I was lucky – just about edible. Apart from the memorable time I tried to make a cheese soufflé and ended up with a slab of something like shoe leather, that is. So I knew Matt wouldn't be expecting gourmet cuisine from me, and if I produced anything fancy he would think I'd somehow been spirited away and replaced with a Stepford wife – although, now I came to think of it, the new underwear and spruced-up nether regions might well give him that impression anyway.

I took the pack of fillet steaks I'd bought at the supermarket out of the fridge, dumped some new potatoes into a pan and made a salad – that would have to do. This wasn't about food, anyway; it was about atmosphere. I lit candles, put the bottle of champagne into the copper wine cooler that had been a wedding present from Matt's aunt, then poured myself a glass of chardonnay from the fridge.

I was just taking the first, grateful sip when I heard Matt's key in the door.

'Blimey.' He paused, taking in the scene. 'What's the occasion?'

'Nothing. I just thought – you know – it would be nice to do something a bit special. It's only steak.'

'My favourite. You look beautiful. And' – he rummaged in his laptop bag – 'as it happens, I brought a bottle of your favourite cab sauv. That Aussie one.'

He kissed me, and I had a moment of giddy optimism – *Yes! This is going to work!*

So, when Matt headed upstairs to shower, I followed him and perched on the bed, waiting for him to emerge. Then I heard the shower stop running and a kind of desperation overtook me. He needed to get the message loud and clear; there was absolutely no room for subtlety here. So I peeled off my dress and arranged myself on top of the duvet, wishing I felt more like a glamour model and less like a total plonker.

When he saw me, Matt literally froze in the doorway, his hand halfway up to his head, a towel hanging limply from it. The towel, I couldn't help noticing, wasn't the only thing that was limp.

But that was okay, I assured myself. We could work on that.

'Hey, Abs.' He came over and sat next to me. 'Cop a load of you. What's this?'

'It's new underwear. Well, new from Quim. I thought I'd surprise you.' I reached out and ran my hand over the lean length of his thigh.

But he didn't respond – at least, the bit of him that I'd been hoping would didn't.

'Abbie. I get what this is about. Don't get me wrong, I've been thinking about it too. And you look bloody gorgeous. But it's not going to work.'

My mouth felt suddenly dry. 'What's not going to work?'

'This. The whole seduction scene.'

'Why? Matt, I don't understand. Why isn't it going to work? Is something wrong?'

I sat up, my legs hanging next to his over the edge of the bed, my thighs bare and smooth, his dusted with black hair. He slipped his arm around my shoulder. 'You know something's wrong. Something's been wrong for a long time, and I don't know how to fix it.'

'That's why I – I thought, if I did something like this, we could kind of get stuff back on track.'

'Abbie, our sex life isn't an ad campaign that's running behind schedule. And I'm not a client who you can get into the office for a meeting with Pret sandwiches and a PowerPoint presentation to address the way forward.'

I felt hot colour rush to my cheeks. 'That's not what I think. You know it's not.'

'I'm sorry. That was harsh. It's just – I know you don't want me. Not now, not like that, not really.'

'But I want—'

'You *want* to want me. That's not the same thing.'

I felt tears sting my eyes. Matt knew me, knew me too well. He knew almost everything there was to know. And he was right. He'd been there, all those times when we'd had desperate, passionless sex that we'd hoped would result in a baby. He'd seen me cry as he tried to orgasm inside me. At the time, I'd known it must have been just as awful for him as it was for me, but I'd pushed the knowledge aside – the whole thing was a means to an end, after all.

Except the end hadn't happened – and now I felt like a different end was almost upon us. Everything we'd tried together, everything we'd done to recapture the closeness we'd taken for granted in the past – well, it had worked. I'd felt like it was working.

But there was still this last one, huge thing. And without that, did we have anything at all?

'I don't know what to do,' I said, my voice coming out thin and small, then muffled almost entirely as I pulled my dress back over my head. I thought about ripping off the sexy underwear and chucking it into a corner, but that was the kind of thing I might have done six months before, when I didn't care if my own hurt made Matt's hurt worse.

'I don't know either.' He looked down at his hands, clasped

in his lap, and I wondered if he, too, was remembering how they'd once looked touching my naked skin.

'If we never – if we didn't ever have sex again, would you still want to be married?' I asked.

'Abs, I can't imagine wanting to be married to anyone except you. But I don't know. It's – I mean, sex is great. When it's good, I mean.'

'When it's good, it's amazing.' There was a lump in my throat so big I could hardly get the words out.

Matt nodded.

'I mean, I think it is.' I tried to hide my sadness with feeble humour. 'Other people might be miles better. You might have just been giving yourself great PR all these years.'

It had always been a kind of joke between us that, while Matt had had sex with other girls before he met me, I'd never slept with anyone but him. But now he didn't smile.

'What we have – what we had – it's the best,' he said. 'I can't imagine wanting anyone else as much as you. Because it's you I love.'

That was something. It was a big something. He loved me still. Surely, with love, we could make everything else all right again?

'I love you too,' I said.

Our eyes met and we looked at each other for a long moment. The tears that had threatened to fall receded and I saw in his face the man I'd trusted with almost everything for twenty years. Could I trust him with this one last thing?

'Shall we go downstairs and eat?' I asked.

SPRING 2004

IF I AIN'T GOT YOU

Abbie lay with her head on Matt's shoulder. Their bodies had created a warm cocoon under the duvet, and the rain lashing against the window made it feel even warmer. The door was closed. She could hear her housemates moving around the kitchen and catch the hum of their voices, Alicia Keys playing on the stereo and an occasional shout of laughter.

But they didn't matter either. For now, there was nothing in the world but her and Matt.

It was March, halfway into her second year at uni, and they hadn't seen each other since Christmas. She'd met him at the station and brought him straight back here, straight to her bedroom, and straight to bed. Their getting-to-know-you-again sex had been amazing, as it always was after some time apart, but now – as she always did – she felt awkward with him, almost as if he was a stranger. As if the bridge built between them by all the text messages, emails, posts on Myspace and late-night phone calls was so fragile that, now it had been crossed, it would crumble away to nothing and have to be built all over again.

This was usual, she told herself. This was the way it always was. It would be okay.

Matt gave a soft snore, then jerked awake. Tired from the six-hour train journey from Scotland, he always fell asleep for a couple of hours, as she did whenever she made the journey up north to visit him. She lay still, waiting to see whether he'd fall back asleep.

But now he rolled over, propping himself up on his elbow, and dropped a kiss onto her lips.

'Hello, stranger.'

'Hello, you.'

'So what's the plan?'

'We could order a takeaway. Or go with the others to the pub. Or go clubbing in the gay village.'

'Or go to Pizza Express?' Matt suggested.

Abbie giggled. 'Or, in defiance of all convention, go to Pizza Express.'

Because that, on their first night together, was what they always ended up doing. The first time, it had felt special, like a proper grown-up date, but over time it had become a ritual, a familiar thing for them to do together, with no surprises. And, with that strange not-quite-connected feeling hanging over them still, surprises were exactly what they didn't need.

'I'll just jump in the shower,' Abbie said.

Reluctantly, she eased the duvet aside. The room was cold and the bathroom would be even colder, the boiler reluctantly spluttering as the shower yielded a thin stream of hot water, the shower curtain wrapping her in a clammy embrace if she got too close to it. She'd lived here six months now – it wasn't much worse than the student houses where her friends lived, and by this stage she was used to it. Kind of.

She pulled on a thick towelling dressing gown and fluffy slippers and made the chilly journey to the bathroom, which smelled of Amanda's Calvin Klein perfume and of the patch of black mould on the ceiling, and showered hastily before hurrying back to Matt.

'It's pretty crap,' she warned, 'but there should still be hot water. Just.'

'Hey, I'm not picky.' He folded his long, naked body out of bed and pulled on his boxer shorts and T-shirt. 'The place where I'm living has rats.'

'Seriously? Horrible ones, not like these guys?' She pointed to the cage where Woyzeck and Stanik were sleeping, curled up together in their bed of wood shavings.

'Horrible ones. We don't see them, but they chewed through my housemate's laptop charger and they eat our Pot Noodles.'

Abbie shuddered. 'Don't tell Woyzeck and Stanik that or they'll be wanting some too.'

She heard the familiar creak of the floorboard outside her door, then the boiler's gasps of protest as Matt began his shower, and quickly put on some make-up, then reluctantly shrugged off her robe and pulled on a jumper, denim miniskirt, tights and Doc Marten boots. Not the most alluring outfit ever, but it was too cold to matter. Her hooded parka, hanging on the back of the bedroom door, would hopefully be equal to the weather – the restaurant was just a fifteen-minute walk away, and her only umbrella had blown inside out when she was making her way between lectures the previous day.

While she waited for Matt, she allowed herself to wallow for a moment in happiness. No one had expected that they'd still be together three years later. If she was honest, she hadn't really expected it herself. When they'd accepted university places at Glasgow and Nottingham, which were, if not exactly at opposite ends of the country, certainly distant enough to restrict visits to bank holiday weekends and vacations, they'd done so with excitement for their individual futures, but genuine uncertainty about what it might mean for them as a couple.

Everyone knew how it worked: you promised that you'd be faithful, that nothing would change, that three years was no time at all – and then you shagged someone else in freshers' week. Abbie had seen that happen over and over again, as her new-found uni friends wept on one another's shoulders over cheating boyfriends or their own sudden realisation that what had felt like security and permanence just weeks before now felt suffocating, distant and – well, dull.

But Abbie had never felt that way. She'd met new people, made new friends, danced and got drunk with boys, listened and analysed and sympathised with her mates as they fell in and out of love, and fake-snogged hot Devon Thompson on stage in their university production of *Othello*. She'd even had to tactfully rebuff Ritchie from her tutorial group when he started slipping handwritten love poems into her bag (not hard, since they neither rhymed nor scanned and she didn't appreciate hearing that her breasts were like scoops of pistachio gelato).

But she'd never once been tempted by anyone else. She didn't know why – what it was about them that kept them together when other couples parted ways with varying degrees of relief, sadness and acrimony – but as time passed she'd become more and more certain that the two of them would make it through. They'd still be together when their courses were over, and after that they could be together always.

They'd never said that to each other. They'd never even said they loved each other. But seeing Matt, getting a text or an email from him, hearing his voice, still gave her the same thrill it had when she was at school. Other blokes might be nice enough – objectively even wildly attractive – but they weren't Matt.

And when she'd asked him, tentatively, about his experiences with other girls, he'd shrugged and said, 'What's the point? I've got you. Why would I want anyone else?'

And now, almost halfway through their enforced separation, she'd allowed herself to dare to hope that they'd make it through to the other side.

So long as nothing went wrong.

'You're not wrong, it's baltic in there.' Matt burst back into the room, fragrant with shower gel, dumped his washbag on the unmade bed and stepped into his jeans, hopping on one foot as his wet skin caught the fabric. He pulled on a shirt and jumper, towelled his hair and pulled Abbie into a hug. 'Just as well we already shagged, because my dick's gone into hiding and might never come out.'

'We can't have that.' Abbie wrapped her arms round his waist and they kissed, then she slid her own cold hands under Matt's jumper, pressing them against the warm skin of his back.

'Ow! Get off me!'

'Come on then, get your skates on. I'm starving.'

Wrapped in coats, scarves and gloves, they headed out into the street – which, Abbie pointed out, wasn't actually that much colder than the house. The rain had taken on that semisolid quality that wasn't snow but held the promise of it. Drifts of grit salt crunched damply under their feet as they walked, heads ducked against the rain.

The brightly lit glass front of the restaurant was like an oasis, promising warmth, dryness and food. Then Abbie pushed open the door and Matt followed her in, and they were shown to a corner table, where Matt ordered a beer and Abbie a Diet Coke.

'No red wine?' he asked. 'What departure from tradition is this?'

'I've put on a few pounds. It's so bloody cold in that house I've been mainlining toasted cheese and hot chocolate and none of my clothes fit, so I'm trying to be a bit sensible.'

'You look just the same,' he said. 'Utterly gorgeous.'

'Maybe to you. But I can't afford new clothes, and we can't afford to turn the heating up, so something has to give. And it's not going to be pizza.'

'Thank God for that – you had me worried for a second.'

And he had her worried for a second. But, looking at his cheerful face, she realised there was no double meaning in what he'd said – no inkling that anything was abnormal, except for her not chugging down a large house merlot as she would normally.

They ordered doughballs (whatever the circumstances, those would have to be prised from Abbie's cold, dead hands), a salad as a token gesture to her healthy diet, and pizzas – ham and mushroom for her and the weird one with spinach and a fried egg for him, which she always said was a sign of his total lack of good taste but which she always accepted a slice of, anyway.

As they ate they caught up on the news from the past two months, most of which they'd already shared, but it felt new, somehow, hearing it in Matt's actual voice rather than in typed words, looking at his face as he told her again about the time his flatmate Chris had locked himself out after a night out and they'd found him asleep on the doorstep the next morning and had to rush him to Accident and Emergency in case he had frostbite. But this felt different. She realised that it wasn't just a funny story, that he'd been genuinely concerned. And when he talked about his course, the programming languages he was learning, the challenges he was solving, there was a passion in his voice that no email could have conveyed.

'I've been doing some volunteering teaching coding at an after-school club for kids from deprived backgrounds,' he said. 'It's amazing. Just seeing how they engage, how fired up they get when they realise they can be good at something. It's made me think that's something I'd like to do more of, after I graduate.'

'I thought you were going to earn shitloads as a software engineer and drive a fancy car.'

'I can earn shitloads as a software engineer and drive a fancy car and make the world a better place. Multi-tasking, innit?'

'And I can do my summer internship at an ad agency and still have a totally credible life ahead of me as a long-form essayist and poet, because that's always been a viable way to make a living, right?'

'My lucrative career on the dark side will keep you in the style to which you want to become accustomed, and then when we're properly rich...'

'Like, mortgage-paid-off rich?'

'Maybe mortgage almost paid off. And two holidays a year, one long-haul and one to a nice little villa in France...'

'Where the owner of the local bakery recognises us and keeps fresh croissants for us every morning, even when we've slept in?'

'Yes, but it's really unpretentious and costs next to nothing, and we invite our friends and we all get pissed on rosé round the pool at lunchtime.'

'And then we sleep all afternoon and I cook something amazing for dinner and we drink more rosé.'

'And our kids run riot and learn to like olives and we have to nag them to put on sunblock.'

Abbie felt the smile on her face freeze. This was a game they played every time – it was one of the ways they'd found to reconnect after these long absences from each other – something they never, ever talked about on email or Myspace but kept for when they were actually together. It had never felt serious before; never felt like anything much except an imagined future in which they were so different, so adult, that they were barely recognisable as themselves.

Now, it felt both impossible and terrifyingly real.

Still, she gave it her best shot. 'And I wear floaty dresses that I've bought from Net-a-Porter...'

'What's that?'

'It's an online designer fashion retailer. God, don't you know anything about the internet?'

'You lost me at designer fashion. Tell me more about the floaty dresses, though. Are you wearing them with those sandals that lace up around your ankles, and do they have slits right up your thighs and show lots of cleavage?'

Abbie laughed, but she found herself unable to remain in their fantasy adult world.

'Matt?'

'Speaking.'

'Listen. The dresses and stuff – I'll tell you about them another time. Right now, there's something else I need to tell you.'

He took a sip of beer and reached out his hand across the table, placing it on top of hers, which was hovering over the doughballs she suddenly no longer wanted to eat.

'There's something I need to tell you, too.'

She felt a heave of sick fear. Now the doughballs hadn't only lost their appeal but were threatening to reappear. She dabbed her mouth with her napkin and took a gulp of her drink, and the sickness receded a bit.

'Abs? It's okay. You go first.'

'No.' Her voice sounded reedy and strange. 'You go first.'

Matt cleared his throat. His grip on her hand tightened. She saw a flush spreading over his pale skin and felt dread crawling over hers at the same time.

He's met someone else. He's going to dump me. Or he's decided to spend a year working at a start-up in San Francisco after uni and we'll be apart for a whole extra, endless year.

'I love you, Abbie,' he said. 'I'm sorry it's taken me so long to say it. It felt like such a massive thing. But I really, really do.'

The anxiety that had been churning inside Abbie's stomach, mixing uncomfortably with doughballs and cola, melted away, replaced with a warm glow like she'd just downed a shot of Jack Daniel's. The weight on her mind was still there – she didn't know if it would ever go away – but it felt lighter now. She knew this; she could deal with whatever happened next.

So, awash with relief and happiness, Abbie said the same thing – the only true thing that was in her heart at that moment.

'I love you, too.'

CHAPTER SEVENTEEN

'Wow, this is a bit posh compared to my old student house.' I lifted my wheelie suitcase onto the king-size bed and looked around. 'You'd never guess we were even in the same city.'

The hotel room wasn't particularly luxurious – standard conference-hotel stuff, I guessed, not that I got to go to many conferences – but it was nice all the same, decorated in shades of oatmeal and sage green, with an abstract painting that looked like it might represent a forest hanging over the bed and a white-tiled bathroom with piles of fluffy towels and full-size bottles of locally made toiletries.

And it felt like a treat – the first time we'd spent a night in a hotel together in absolutely ages. Never mind that it was just a dull convention about levelling up computer literacy in schools, at which Matt was giving a presentation and to which he'd suggested I tag along. After asking the neighbour to look in on Shrimp and feed her for two days, I'd happily agreed.

'Not bad, is it?' Matt said. 'I'm pleasantly surprised, actually – I've had to stay in some right dumps when I've done these gigs before.'

'And you say there's a spa?'

'There is. And you'll have plenty of time to enjoy it, because this lot want their pound of flesh – I'm booked from coffee at eight to the networking drinks that finish at seven thirty.'

'Don't worry, I'll have a great time. Massive lie-in, all-you-can-eat hotel breakfast, spa, then a bit of a wander round my old stomping grounds – I might even see if I can find that house; I bet it's been chi-chi-ed up beyond recognition now – and maybe afternoon tea somewhere if I'm not still full from breakfast.'

'Sounds idyllic. I'll think of you while I'm sitting through other people's presentations and drinking bad, lukewarm coffee.'

'And shall we meet somewhere for dinner, or do you think you'll be dragged out with the other presenters?'

'Doubt it – they were pretty clear that they're wrapping up after the drinks. And if they do ask I'll say I've got other plans.'

'Pizza Express?'

'Of course.'

Matt kissed me and we finished unpacking, then had dinner in the hotel restaurant and went to bed early, surprised how exhausted we were by the excitement of being in an unfamiliar place.

The next day, true to my promise to myself, I slept in, not even waking up when Matt left for the conference, and almost missed breakfast. Still, I was able to do justice to a mountain of bacon, eggs, fried mushrooms, sausages and coffee, and even squeeze in a croissant I neither needed nor wanted. It was the kind of breakfast you crave after being up all night having sex, which I hadn't, but I made the most of it anyway. Afterwards, I made my way to the heated indoor pool and lay on a lounger for a couple of hours before having a massage.

Then I made my way out into the city.

The fact I'd lived here for three years seemed strange now – and stranger still was that I'd never been back, except one final

time to collect the last of my belongings and return the house
keys to the estate agent. I'd loved Nottingham – loved the
glorious architecture of its old town; loved the city's compact
size, which meant I'd never got lost, not even making my way
home late and drunk after a night out; loved the friendliness of
the people.

But there had never been any question of my living here
after I graduated; I'd always known that home would be in
London, with Matt.

All told, we must only have spent a handful of weekends
here together – mostly, we'd returned to our parents for holidays
or gone abroad on cheap Interrail tickets to explore European
cities; occasionally, I'd made the long trip to Scotland to visit
Matt. So although the streets, the university's main building –
Hogwarts-like, reflected in the lake over which it stood – and
the jumble of streets at the city's centre were filled with memories, few of them were of him and me together.

I easily found the house where I'd lived, which had indeed
been done up and now had wooden shutters in the windows
and a BMW parked outside. I considered knocking on the door
and telling whoever answered that I'd lived there as a student,
but abandoned the idea almost immediately. I found the high
street, where my friends and I had eagerly browsed in Topshop,
trying on clothes and occasionally buying a cheap top or pair of
earrings before a night out. I found the All Bar One where I'd
worked as a waitress in my third year and the Wetherspoons
outside which my friend Lucy had vomited all over a police-
man's boots on her twenty-first birthday.

I'd shown Matt all these places – I must have. But my
memories of that were scant. I must have walked with him along
the canal, shown him the castle and the cathedral and the old
abbey where Lord Byron once lived, like a proper tour guide.

But all my memories of us there together seemed to be of
the house: of us in bed together, us frying eggs on the wonky

spiral hotplate in the damp-riddled kitchen, us drinking frozen margaritas in the garden on a sunny evening. But mostly us in bed together.

How I'd craved being with him, back then. But how careful I'd been not to seem needy or clingy – to be fun and cool, available but making no demands. I wondered how I'd have reacted if I'd known a time would come when we would spend months and months almost exclusively in each other's company, and whether I'd have believed how suffocating that would become.

I suppose it must have concerned me – or at least have crossed my mind – that Matt and I wouldn't stay together, wouldn't last the distance. I might have thought that once we were living together properly, as adults, cracks would appear in our relationship – we'd grow apart, as people did in their twenties. But I don't think I would have believed it if someone had suggested that now, at thirty-seven and after nine years of marriage, I'd find us deep in crisis.

And yet, here we were. And in just a couple of hours, we'd be back in the very same restaurant where, all those years ago, Matt had told me for the first time that he loved me, and I'd said, giddy with elation and relief, that I loved him, too – even though it wasn't what I had been meaning to say.

I retraced my steps to the hotel, showered and dressed, then went to have a drink in the bar while I waited for him. I'd never travelled much for work, so it felt sophisticated and even a bit intimidating to be sitting there on my own, a gin and tonic and a bowl of rice crackers in front of me. I glanced at my phone occasionally, but not enough that anyone would think I'd been stood up on a date or was a high-class call girl waiting for a client – not that high-class call girls met their clients in jeans and trainers, as far as I knew.

As he'd promised, Matt wasn't late. It was just before eight when I saw him enter the room, look around, spot me and then smile that magical smile that I couldn't help responding to. I finished my drink and hurried over to him.

'How did it go?'

'Okay. They seemed to like my presentation and there were loads of questions afterwards, which is always good. I'm knackered, though. All talked out.'

'Would you rather get room service than go out?'

'No way. Got to have our blast from the past. Let's head out now, though.'

We walked through the streets, hand in hand. So he didn't have to say too much, I told him about my morning in the spa and my afternoon wandering round the city. I pointed out the sights as we passed them, even though I'd done so before.

And as we walked, memories began to return. Us snogging in the cathedral, Matt's face illuminated in purple and yellow by a stained-glass window, until the actual bishop had appeared behind us and discreetly cleared his throat, and we'd scuttled off in shame. Dancing with him in a nightclub in a skirt so short it barely covered my knickers, knowing other men were watching me and Matt was watching them watch me but only having eyes for him.

And that other night, when Matt hadn't been there. When I'd woken my flatmate Sarah at four in the morning to tell her something was wrong, and I needed help.

I remembered, as clearly as if it was happening right now, walking to this same restaurant on that rainy March evening. Matt's hand in mine felt just the same. The streets beneath my feet were familiar. Even the sense of hollow anticipation – of dread, really – in my stomach was the same.

And I knew suddenly that, although I hadn't planned or intended it at all, tonight I was going to tell Matt what I hadn't been able to tell him then.

He was oblivious, though. For now, he was relaxed and

cheerful, pointing out things he recognised, ordering a beer for himself and a glass of merlot for me, perusing the menu.

'Oh my God, haven't they moved with the times? Look at it – vegan this, gluten-free that. Blimey.'

'You can still have your one with the fried egg though, if you want,' I said. 'Weirdo.'

'You know what, I think I will. I haven't had one for years and I used to love them. Wonder if it'll taste the same?'

'It'll either be a blast of pure nostalgia or the biggest disappointment of your life,' I warned.

'I'll risk it. You've got to take chances in life, right?'

You've got to take chances in life. I was certainly about to take one.

I didn't order my old favourite pizza with the ham and mushrooms – I might as well have stabbed the menu with a pin for all the thought that went into my decision. I was pretty sure that whatever the waitress brought me, even if it was the most delicious thing ever, I wouldn't be able to eat it.

But I did take a huge gulp of my wine, and then another.

Then I said to Matt, 'You remember that time we came here just before Easter in my second year of uni?'

'God, we must have come here – what – a dozen times? Maybe even more. Was that one different for some reason? Did we not have doughballs?'

'It was the first time you said you loved me.'

'Oh!' His face softened. 'God, I was a soppy git, wasn't I? Now you just have to make do with me telling you I can tolerate you, just about, if I'm in a good mood.'

I tried to laugh, but I couldn't quite manage it. 'There was something else I wanted to tell you that night, but I never did.'

'What? Don't tell me you were going to dump me, and I dropped the L bomb so you stuck around, and you still haven't got around to it?'

'No, not that.' I drank some more wine. The waitress brought our pizzas, but neither of us ate.

'Oh God, sorry, Abs. It's something serious. I'll stop taking the piss. Do you want to tell me now? Cos if it was, like, that you'd cheated on me, I'd honestly rather not know.'

If it had been that, and he'd guessed, it was a bit late now for him not to know, I thought, and the absurdity of that almost made me laugh again. But, again, I couldn't.

'I was pregnant.' I took another big swallow of wine, but my throat still felt dry and tight. 'I wasn't drinking, remember? I made up some story about putting on weight, which I guess I had, but not for the reason I said.'

Matt had picked up his beer to take a sip, but now he put it down again, the glass rattling on the table.

'Shit, Abs. What did you— I mean, did you—?'

'I didn't know what I was going to do. I thought you'd think I was trying to pressure you into something, that I'd done it on purpose. I mean, I didn't think you would, but it was a possibility, and I was just really scared and mixed up. I was going to tell you, but then you said what you said and I just couldn't. It made me so happy, you see.'

'And...?'

'I thought about... you know, terminating. I pretty much decided that was what I was going to do. I wasn't ready for it and nor were you. I thought if I had a baby, we'd never last together. I was going to tell you, I honestly was. I just didn't know how. But then...'

Matt's face was still, caught somewhere between shock and sadness. 'Then what?'

'I had a miscarriage.' I'd never said the word out loud before; it sounded strange coming out of my mouth, like a foreign language. 'I don't know why. They said at the hospital it happens a lot, it's common, blah blah blah. You know. But I was just so relieved it was over I barely heard what they were saying.'

Matt's face was a blank mask. 'And what about when we were having all that treatment? You never mentioned it?'

'I did,' I said in a small voice. 'Just not when you were there. They said it was nothing to do with us not being able to have a baby. They said it was a totally separate thing.'

'So you thought it was okay to never tell me?'

'I didn't mean to hide it from you. I just – I felt so awful, Matt. So guilty. Because I could have had that baby and then when I didn't it was just the biggest weight that had been lifted off me. It would have been so hard, back then. I was so young. We both were. Even though people never think of themselves as young when they are, you know, I just knew it would've been too soon. Too soon for us to be parents together and definitely too soon for me to be one on my own.'

Matt nodded, but didn't say anything, so I carried on, the words spilling out of me like I was trying to explain it all to myself as well as to him.

'I thought it might be too much for our relationship, back then. I still feel like it would've been. But then when we were, you know, trying, I felt like no matter what the doctors said, it was my fault we couldn't, because I never wanted that other baby.'

'Right.' Matt took a gulp of beer and looked down at his untouched pizza.

'I'm sorry,' I said, even though I knew I wasn't really at fault.

'Look, Abs, I need some time to process this. It's a lot. I might head back to London tonight, while you stay in the hotel.'

I shook my head. Right then, like a frightened animal, all I wanted was the safety of home.

'You stay. I'll go. I'll head to the station right now, if you don't mind bringing my stuff with you when you come back.'

If you've got my stuff, you'll have to come back, I thought.

Matt said, 'Okay. I'm pretty much done here, are you?'

I nodded. Matt put his credit card on the table next to our untouched pizzas, and the waitress hurried over.

'Is everything okay here?' she asked.

'Yes,' Matt said. 'Everything's fine.'

CHAPTER EIGHTEEN

After all the months in the flat with Matt, being there without him felt beyond strange. As I sat at the kitchen table working, I kept thinking I could catch a glimpse of his face out of the corner of my eye. When I saw he wasn't there, I imagined I could hear the tread of his feet on the landing upstairs. When I got up to make myself a coffee, I automatically took a second cup out of the cupboard.

I found myself unable to focus, pacing up and down, walking upstairs to look into our bedroom, the bed neatly made with no indentation from his head left on the right-hand pillow. I walked into the second bedroom, which seemed even emptier and more forlorn now. And, finally, I found myself resigned – if not reconciled – to the fact it would never be filled.

Not by a child of ours, at any rate.

I imagined finding myself single, moving on. I imagined signing up for online dating, for the first time in my life. I imagined having sex with a man who wasn't Matt, which proved totally impossible because, after all, I'd never had sex with a man who wasn't Matt. What if I'd been doing it all wrong, all along?

What if I did meet someone and things got frisky and he was like, 'You like *what*?'

The thought was too cringily awful to contemplate, never mind how sad it made me feel.

I found myself browsing the internet for flats like ours for sale, imagining another couple moving in here, filling these rooms with their furniture and laughter and hope, as we had done. Maybe they'd have a third member of their family, to fill our spare bedroom as we'd once hoped to fill it. Because, if we were to split up, that's what would have to happen – neither of us could afford the place on our own.

I looked, with a kind of grim self-harm, at one-bedroom flats nearby. Even those were way beyond my price range. I knew what a sensible person would say if I explained my dilemma: *Move into a flat-share – that's what other people have to do. And you're working remotely anyway. You can do that anywhere. Move somewhere cheaper.*

But that would mean moving away from my friends, the Girlfriends' Club, my life support.

But you communicate with them online all the time, anyway, insisted the sensible voice.

And then I realised that, actually, I hadn't. They were utterly unaware of this turn things had taken in my marriage.

Part of me wanted desperately to tell them, to get their advice on what I should do (which I was fairly sure wouldn't be the coldly practical words of the sensible voice in my head). I wanted to feel their virtual arms around me, even to arrange an emergency extra-curricular drink with someone – or, even better, all of them – so I could explain everything and maybe have a much-needed cry.

But I also felt ashamed. Over the years, we'd shared so much – virtually everything. When Kate got sacked from her job because she hit reply to all on an email meant for a trusted colleague, revealing exactly what she thought of her boss ('sexist dinosaur with the charisma of a bowl of cold porridge'), she told us about it straight away. When Naomi found out she was having twins and felt terrified instead of joyful, she spilled out her fear to the group. When Rowan ran up a load of credit-card debt and didn't know how to pay it back, she came to us not for financial support – although we'd gladly have given what we could – but for advice.

And yet, I'd never told them about that long-ago pregnancy, which had come to nothing. It was before I met any of them – no doubt, if I'd known them at the time, I'd have spilled out all my messy, ambivalent emotions about it. But since then, my silence and shame about it had become so huge a secret, hidden even from Matt, that it had never occurred to me that I didn't have to bear the burden alone.

But I didn't. Of course I didn't. I tried to imagine how I would feel if something like this had happened to one of them, and they felt unable to talk to me about it, but it was impossible. There was no way they would keep quiet if they needed me or one another. And there was no way they'd judge me for something that had happened so long ago, which hadn't even been the direct result of a choice I'd made.

I sat back down at the kitchen table, and this time I reached for my phone. The WhatsApp group had been quiet over the past couple of days – Naomi had said that, seriously, if she had to endure another night with less than three hours' sleep, she'd gouge her own eyes out with a teaspoon, and Rowan had offered sympathy and to have the twins overnight, and I'd said I had a teaspoon handy, actually, as Matt had left his by the kitchen sink as usual.

Kate had asked me to ask Matt for his extra-spicy chicken madras recipe for a dinner party she was having, but I hadn't seen the message and now, of course, Matt wasn't here to ask.

Abbie: Hey gang, sorry I missed all the messages. Kate, when is dinner? Hope it hasn't already happened and left your hostess-with-mostest reputation in tatters.

Kate: Nope, no crisis – it's not for two weeks. You know how I like to plan ahead. How was Nottingham?

Abbie: Awful. It's all gone tits up.

Kate: Oh no, what happened?

Rowan: Oh no, love, are you okay?

Naomi: Shit. Do you want to talk about it?

And feeling their concern and love radiating off the screen like warmth from a radiator on a cold day, I found that I did want to talk about it. Over a few messages, I spilled out the whole story: how I'd arranged to recreate that long-ago date, how I'd realised this was the best opportunity I'd ever get to tell Matt what had happened, and how it had left me feeling in the intervening years. That I'd found out I was having a baby when I was at university but lost it, and how my guilt over the relief I'd felt at the time had intensified to an almost unbearable level when Matt and I were trying to conceive.

Abbie: And he was – I mean, I expected him to be hurt, but he was like beyond hurt. He was gutted that I never told him. And I can see why. I should have done. I've been a fool. But I felt almost like telling him would have jinxed the whole fertility thing even more than it was jinxed already – like it would be admitting that it was my fault.

Naomi: You know it's not your fault really, don't you?

Abbie: A bit of me does. But I was so relieved when I had that miscarriage. I mean, it was awful and painful and grim, but mostly I was like, Thank God, I don't have to make a decision about this. I don't have to decide to abort Matt's baby, and I don't have to face going ahead and having it when I'm not ready.

Rowan: Sounds like a totally normal way to feel. I had to make that decision when I was pregnant with Clara. I don't think I've ever told you guys this, but I seriously thought about not going ahead with it. I did in the end, but sometimes – even though I'd die for her – I wonder what my life would have been like if I'd made the other choice.

There was a pause. I knew how much it must have taken for Rowan to admit that.

Rowan: Don't hate me.

Naomi: Of course we don't hate you! If how Abs felt is normal, so is how you feel.

Kate: So where's Matt now? Are things okay with you guys?

Abbie: Nope. He's staying in Nottingham for a couple more nights to think about his options. And then he said he might go and stay with Ryan for a bit.

Naomi: Oh shit. Do you think he just needs a bit of time to process it all?

Abbie: I hope so. But then – he was horrible to me. He was so cold. It made me feel even worse about the whole thing, like, great, I told my husband this massive secret and now he hates me.

Rowan: He doesn't hate you any more than you guys hate me. He's just taking a bit of time to adjust, I'm sure.

Naomi: What Ro said. Give him a chance to have a think about it, realise he's overreacted and been a knob, and then talk to him.

Abbie: Well, one thing's for sure. This whole recreating memories thing has massively backfired and I'm totally done with it. No more trips down memory lane with my husband. If I even still have a husband at the end of all this.

Kate: You know what, I wouldn't be so sure about that.

Abbie: About me having a husband?

Kate: No, doofus! About it having been a bad idea. Think about it – would you ever have told him about your miscarriage if you hadn't gone back to that Pizza Express?

Abbie: No, I guess not.

Kate: And telling him was totally the right thing to do, right?

Abbie: I'm really not so sure about that.

Rowan: Kate's right. It's awful that you coped with that on your own for so long. You shouldn't have had to.

Naomi: No, you shouldn't.

Abbie: But what if it means it's all over between me and Matt?

Kate: If he ends it over that, he's a fool.

Naomi: Exactly. A right dick.

Rowan: And I genuinely don't think he is.

With their kiss and hug emojis still illuminated on my screen and their kind words bringing me a measure of comfort, I turned back to my laptop and the slew of emails that had landed in my inbox.

I read them, prioritising those that needed answering, like, now, ignoring those in which I'd merely been cc-ed for no particular reason that I could see, and setting aside the rest to deal with as soon as I could. But I was struggling to focus on anything – anxiety over what was happening with Matt, where he was, what he was thinking and feeling, fought with guilt over not being able to give a hundred per cent to my job, with the Quim launch rapidly approaching.

You've worked your arse off the past few months, Abbie, I told myself firmly. *Stuff happens – people have problems. You took two days off work – you've still got a pile of holiday you haven't used. What do they want, blood?*

But it was no good. The more I tried to focus on work, the more my brain kept returning to Matt, like a fly bashing help-lessly against a window, unable to find the gap to the outside world.

Just before five thirty, I gave up, closed my laptop and headed out into the darkness, thinking of the long winter that lay ahead for us – and for Shrimp. I could feel the wind biting through my coat and sending spatters of drizzle onto my face, and I wondered how well her fur would protect her. She'd put on a bit of weight since we'd been feeding her – that would surely help. But Matt had been right when he said the situation was unsustainable.

When I approached the house, I saw Shrimp curled up in her pink cat bed, but as soon as she heard my footsteps, she stood up, stretched and came running to greet me, mewing furiously.

'Did you think we'd forgotten about you, little girl?' I asked. 'We'd never do that. Come on, let's get you some dinner.'

I tipped cat biscuits into her bowl while she clawed impatiently at the legs of my jeans.

'Steady on,' I told her. 'Food's on its way. Just a bit of patience.'

As soon as I put down the bowl, she buried her face in it, crunching enthusiastically.

The misty street was filled with shadows and random patches of light. A fox trotted along the other side of the street, seeming almost to float on its noiseless paws, and I wondered whether foxes ever attacked cats. Shrimp was so small, so defenceless. Bonfire Night was just a few days away – what if she was terrified by the bangs and flashes of the fireworks?

'We can't carry on like this,' I told her, bending down to stroke her as she wound herself around my legs, purring happily now that her dinner was finished. 'We're going to have to find a home for you.'

I stood up and turned to leave her, reluctantly, because I knew I wouldn't be repeating this ritual for much longer. I'd try the local pet shelters again in the morning, I resolved – with winter coming, surely one of them could be persuaded to take her in. And she was a lovely cat, and appeared quite young. Someone would give her a loving home.

If only it could be us, I thought fleetingly. But how could we, with our marriage at risk of shattering?

The drizzle had cleared and a brisk wind had begun to

blow, making me clutch my coat more tightly around my shoulders.

I walked more slowly than usual, and it was almost an hour before I reached home, after stopping at the corner shop to buy a bottle of white wine and a packet of cheese-and-onion crisps, which was all I could face in the way of dinner.

When I approached the flat, I noticed a light burning in the kitchen window. I was sure I'd switched it off before I left, and hope leaped in my heart.

Matt was home.

Still, I hesitated for a second before fitting my key into the lock, as if the blank blue paint of the door would give me some clue to the atmosphere inside. Would he still be angry with me, cold and bewildered as he'd been in the restaurant? Would I have to apologise again for my silence over the past seventeen years about something so important?

Should I even have to apologise? I reached my key towards the lock but, before I could insert it, the door opened, making me jump backwards in fright.

Matt stood there, silhouetted in the light from the hallway.

'I thought I heard you outside,' he said. 'I thought maybe you'd forgotten your keys.'

I shook my head, holding them out to him. 'I was just...'

'Standing in the cold. Come inside.'

I followed him into the kitchen and put the thin blue plastic bag containing my purchases on the table.

'Wine and crisps,' I said.

'Two essential food groups.' Matt opened the bottle, poured pinot grigio into two glasses and tipped the crisps into a bowl.

We sat down at the kitchen table, facing each other, the way we'd spent so many days.

'I've just been to see Shrimp,' I said. 'I was thinking. You're right, it's not sustainable. We can't leave her there.'

'I guess not.'

'It was so dark there today. I kept thinking about her there alone all night. People aren't always kind to animals. Anything could...'

My words tailed off and I drank some wine, wanting to look at Matt, to hear words of reassurance, feel his arm around me, see the way his forehead wrinkled when he was worried about something.

But I couldn't bring myself to meet his eyes. I knew that by sharing my worries about Shrimp, I was hiding deeper worries from him.

'We'll try the shelters again. Maybe space will have opened up somewhere,' he said.

'We could take her to a vet and say she's been abandoned. They'd have to do something, surely?'

'We'll make some calls tomorrow,' he promised.

I nodded.

'But first, I wanted to talk to you.'

My throat tightened. 'I wanted to talk to you, too. But you weren't here.'

'I'm sorry. I should have been here. I should have been with you, instead of going off in a strop like a teenager.'

'Funny,' I said. 'You didn't used to strop when you were a teenager. Maybe you've been working up to it.'

Now I did look at him, and there was a flicker of a smile on his face. I took a crisp from the bowl and bit it in half, the crunch sounding implausibly loud in the silence as I waited for him to speak.

'Seriously, Abs,' he went on. 'What you told me the other night... I mean, I was shocked, obviously. Because it's a big thing, and you kept it to yourself for so long.'

'How long would have been too long, though?' I echoed the thought that had come into my mind while I stood outside the flat. 'What if I'd told you a week after, or the next time I saw you, or a year later?'

'Or never,' he said. 'I suppose you could have never told me.'

'I think if I hadn't, I couldn't have carried on with this. With us, I mean. It was... It was casting a kind of shadow over everything. You know, I've been trying to make things better. To remind us of when things were good, and see if we could get that back. But...'

'But what?'

'But as long as we weren't talking about the big things, things like that, it felt like all of the other stuff wouldn't make a difference.'

Matt drank some wine and heaved a long sigh. 'There's a big thing I didn't tell you either.'

The tightness came back around my throat, like I was wearing a scarf wound too snugly.

'Do you want to tell me now?'

He nodded. 'Us trying to have a baby. I know how much you wanted that to happen. But I never really did. Not like you did. I thought if it happened I'd be happy, but actually I was terrified witless of it the whole time.'

I felt the breath leave my lungs in a long, slow trickle, as if my throat wasn't being squeezed any more but my stomach was.

'It's a scary thing,' I said carefully.

'Yeah, course it is. I chatted to Patch about it and he was like, "Mate, you'll be shitting yourself the entire nine months, and then the sprog arrives and you're so busy cleaning up its shit you forget all about it."'

I laughed. 'Sounds like Patch.'

'Yeah. But he said that, for the longest time, he's been able to imagine being a dad. And he's great with the twins.'

When he's not at work, or at the gym, or out cycling, or too tired from doing those things to get off the sofa, according to Naomi, I thought.

'You'd have been great, too.'

'Maybe. But every time I thought about it, I thought about

what our life is like now – well, what it was like before we started all this – and I thought, do I really want this to change?'

'Go on,' I said.

'So when you told me about the – about losing the baby, back when we were at uni, and how relieved you'd felt, I realised I'd felt relieved, too, when we couldn't have kids. And when that letter came back in August, I read it and part of me was practically punching the air, because the decision had been made for us, in a way.'

I imagined him sitting on the sofa in the dark, waiting for me to come home, trying to process those feelings. I remembered how I'd felt, gutted for us both but mostly almost drowning in a fresh wave of guilt because in my heart, too, there'd been an echo of the relief I'd felt back at uni, when I'd woken in the small hours of the morning feeling cramp twisting in my belly and blood seeping into my bedsheets and knocked on Sarah's door, toilet paper bunched between my thighs, calling her name in a thin, frightened voice that didn't sound like mine at all.

'I wasn't sure I could go through with it either, by then,' I admitted. 'I get what you mean about it not being our decision any more. I felt like once we'd started trying, we kind of had to carry on until either it happened or we'd exhausted all avenues.'

'Like we'd stopped being a couple and become an infertile couple.'

'God, that's a hideous word.'

'Sure is. But that's what we were. And there were only two ways to stop being one.'

I nodded. 'Have a baby, or stop trying to have one. Become a childless couple.'

'Or a child-free couple.'

'That sounds a bit better.'

'It does, right? Do you think we could do that? Be that?'

'Do you think we'd be happy?'

'Abs, I don't know. I don't know whether having a baby would have made us happy. But what I do know, one hundred per cent, is that trying to have one didn't.'

'It made us fucking miserable.'

Matt reached across the table and took my hand. There were crisp crumbs on his fingers, but I didn't care – it was like we were connecting again, in a way that we hadn't in the longest time.

'Shall we try, then? Try and get – not back to how we were, but to make things work again now?'

'A new normal?'

I shook my head, looking at the table holding our two closed laptops, the tangle of chargers, the wine and the crisps.

'Us sitting here day after day – that was the new normal,' I said. 'I reckon it's time for a different normal.'

'I reckon it's time to order a pizza,' he said. 'These crisps aren't hacking it.'

And then I burst out with the idea that had been in the back of my mind for ages, which I'd rejected over and over again but which now seemed like the most logical thing in the world.

'Matt? Could we take Shrimp and bring her here to live with us?'

CHAPTER NINETEEN

For the first time in months, I was actually dressed for work, although admittedly only in a smart-ish jacket over my jeans. But still – I'd blow-dried my hair. I was wearing make-up and carrying a proper work bag, with a pair of proper work shoes in it. I was giddy with excitement at the prospect of a Costa coffee at my desk and a Pret cheese and pickle baguette for lunch.

Forty-five minutes later, I emerged from the Tube station into the bustling streets of Soho. London was busy – not as busy as it used to be, but almost. People were struggling to get their umbrellas open amid the press of other umbrellas. There was a small queue outside Flat White. There were even a few bewildered German tourists huddled together over a map on their phone.

I needed the map on my own phone to locate the new office, which was down a narrow alleyway I'd never noticed before. But there was a bar a few doors down that looked like it had potential, I noticed approvingly, and a boutique next door with a gorgeous tan trench coat in the window. Maybe in a few weeks it would have a sale on.

I ran my finger down the row of buzzer buttons and pressed

the one with a Cardew Henderson tag next to it. In due course, I'd be issued with a security code and could come and go as I pleased, but for now I was still a visitor. I signed myself in at reception, making sure to ask the woman at the desk her name as well as giving her mine, and caught the lift up to the sixth floor.

Another sign directed me to turn left. But I didn't need a sign: Marc and Bastian's voices could be heard, quite clearly telling me where I needed to go.

And by the sound of things, any minute now they'd be telling each other where to go.

'Whose daft idea was it to get balloons, anyway?' Marc was saying. 'Don't you know how terrible they are for the environment? Choke sea turtles to death if that's your thing, but if our Green Team client hears about this, we'll lose the account for sure.'

'It's a celebration,' Bastian replied. 'For God's sake, can't you take any joy in anything, ever? Have you always got to be so bloody worthy? And besides, last time we went to Green Team HQ for a meeting, there was bottled water on the tables and I happen to know their CEO drives a Maserati.'

Ignoring the point Bastian evidently felt he'd scored, Marc went on the attack again. 'And I still think that artwork behind the reception desk is the single most hideous thing I've ever seen in all my born days. It looks like Picasso puked on it, possibly when he was going through his blue period.'

'It's an up-and-coming local artist. The dealer said it's likely to rocket in value in the next few years. And if we're not about supporting home-grown talent then exactly what the hell are we about?'

'Making money, rather than spaffing it on a load of pastries no one will eat. And champagne – at nine thirty in the morning? What were you thinking? Do you want our entire contingent of staff to be utterly wankered before they even start their first day back? And you know croissants set off my IBS something dreadful.'

'Don't eat any, then. You've properly porked up over the past few months – it'll do you good to try a spot of intermittent fasting. And it's not just champagne – there's bottles of Talon there too, in case you hadn't noticed that I was giving the team a chance to get a sneak preview of the product they've been working on for the best part of a year.'

'That's even worse! That stuff is lethal. I had two bottles last night and I was puking my guts out at eleven o'clock.'

'That's more likely to have been the extra-large stuffed-crust double pepperoni you had with them.'

How did he know that if Marc's moved out? Are they back together?

'It didn't have a stuffed— Oh, good morning, Abbie. Welcome to Cardew Henderson towers. What do you reckon? The interior design team did a cracking job, didn't they?'

'Morning, guys. It all looks great. Can I get the grand tour?' I accepted hugs and air-kisses from both of them, then looked around.

The new office was pure ad-agency chic: banks of desks made from what looked like upcycled pallets, polished concrete floors, glass-walled meeting rooms, a chill-out area with a vintage pinball machine, an enormous, squashy yellow sofa and, of course, the art hanging behind the sculptural stainless-steel reception desk.

Vishni, the office manager, hurried past, a tea towel draped over her arm and threads of grey in her black hair that I'd have sworn hadn't been there the last time I saw her and laid blame for squarely at Marc and Bastian's door. I waylaid her, hugged her and congratulated her on how hard she must have worked and how great everything looked.

But before I could venture further into the new premises and find my desk – at least, the desk that would be mine today, since a strict hot-desking policy had been introduced along with the new hybrid-working one – the last junior designer rushed tardily in, saying he was awfully sorry to be so late on our first day back but he'd just had to stop and smell M&Ms World, because it had been so long.

'People, people.' Bastian pinged one of the artfully arrayed champagne bottles with a teaspoon.

'May we have your attention, gang.' Marc stepped up next to his business partner and former life partner and deployed a fork to pop one of the balloons that someone – probably poor Vishni – had carefully strung around the reception desk.

Everyone jumped.

'What the flip did you have to do that for?' Bastian demanded. 'Are you trying to make our colleagues think they're in Kabul or something?'

'Don't be absurd. Are you going to give the guided tour or am I?'

'You do it. If I do, you'll only say I'm doing it wrong.'

'Right. So I'd like to welcome you all, officially, to our new home. It's been a long time coming and we're delighted to be here at last. We'd both like to thank you, first and foremost, for your patience, dedication and hard work over the past—'

'Oh, for God's sake, do get on with it.'

'Eighteen months, and on that note, I'll hand over to Bastian to show you all around the new office.'

'But you were going to do it.'

'But you said I was doing it wrong.'

'Fine.' With a resentful glance at Bastian, Marc embarked on the official tour, interrupted by frequent digs from his partner and occasional questions from their staff.

It should have been awkward AF, but not only were we all used to their ways, we were all so giddy with goodwill and excitement that we'd have put up with anything.

Once the last personal locker had been pointed out, the last rule about how to use the communal microwave explained, the importance of topping up the beans in the coffee machine if they ran out when you were using it reiterated, we all crowded around the food and drink trolley once more.

'And we have one final announcement to make,' Bastian said, taking a bottle of champagne out of the cooler and opening it.

'God! You know you're not meant to pop the cork, you utter Visigoth,' said Marc.

'So what the eff did you want me to—'

'Ease it out. Just ease it out. A mere hiss.'

'As. I. Was. Saying,' Bastian went on.

'Before you were so rudely interrupted,' interrupted Marc.

And then the two of them looked at each other with such pure, searing passion it took my breath away.

'We invite you all to join in this celebration.' Bastian took a Liberty-print silk square out of the breast pocket of his suit and dabbed his temple. 'And there's another piece of good news, too.'

'We have sign-off on the Quim project!' Marc shook another champagne bottle, sending its cork ricocheting off the Picasso-puke artwork and foam cascading everywhere.

Vishni blanched and hurried over with her tea towel.

'The whole team has worked incredibly hard on this over the past five months, from inception to delivery,' Bastian said. 'Abbie and Craig on the copy. Marc and the art team on the stunning website design and accompanying print collateral, and of course all of you who've given your time and support to the project.'

'And it's going to be a while until any of us need to look at an apple slice that looks like a pussy again,' Marc went on triumphantly.

'And best of all, we've cracked an invite to the launch party in December. The whole team is invited, and there will be free drinks, canapés and goodie bags all round.'

'Oh great, more caramel-latte-flavoured lube,' muttered Craig.

Everyone erupted into startled cheers. I accepted a glass of fizz and a pain au chocolat and perched on the edge of a desk. I ought to be feeling proud – and I did feel proud of what I'd achieved. I'd given the project my all. I'd immersed myself into the ins and outs (ha!) of the brief, zhuzhing up my copy on command, spending far longer than I'd ever wanted to thinking about the satisfying and adventurous sex lives enjoyed by other people.

The client had been particularly pleased with my line about the Magic Mercury slimline clit stimulator – 'Ride this silver bronco all the way to paradise' – and would probably have been even more pleased if I'd revealed that, one afternoon when Matt was out delivering a workshop, I'd done some hands-on research and discovered that the device did exactly what it said on the tin.

But, really, what did I have to show for it all?

Well, I still had a job. That was definitely nothing to be sniffed at. I might even get a Christmas bonus if the performance of our other accounts had been equally strong – hopefully not in the form of another crate of free hard seltzer, period pants or sex toys.

I still had a marriage. Matt and I were in a different place – a better place, that was for sure – to where we'd been before. I'd told him a secret I'd held on to for years, letting it fester inside me and carrying the blame alone for something I could now accept had never been my fault. I felt like we could move forward now more honestly and lovingly than I could have dreamed of five months ago.

Through some of the memories we'd recreated, Matt and I

had recaptured the love and closeness I'd taken for granted for so long.

But I knew there was still something missing – something that wasn't right, which I had no idea how to make right.

Marc appeared at my elbow, interrupting my musings. 'I've been meaning to ask what you thought of my new Zoom background. It's not one of the standard ones; I made it myself in Photoshop.'

My mind reeled. I knew this stuff could be done – of course I did. Only in my mind, things between my bosses had been terminal, and the end of their relationship inevitable.

'So you haven't... I mean, you and Bastian are still...?'

'Oh my God! You thought he'd chucked me?' He roared with laughter. 'I just thought given we're working on a hard seltzer account, the wine was a bit off-message.'

'Oh,' I said. 'Right. Of course. That makes sense.'

'In fact' – he leaned in confidingly – 'we're getting hitched. Bas popped the question last weekend and – obviously – I said, "Hell, yeah."'

'T-That's wonderful,' I stammered. 'Congratulations. I hope you'll be very happy.'

If the recipe for a happy marriage was barely being able to say a civil word to each other, I reckoned they'd nail it.

'We're having a little celebration din-dins after work at Café Boheme,' Marc went on. 'Assuming Bas hasn't ballsed up the booking as usual. Just the senior management team. I hope you'll be able to join us?'

'I'd love to,' I said. 'But I've got a date with my husband.'

AUTUMN 2012
CHASING CARS

Abbie lifted her hand and touched the mass of curls at the back of her head. She could feel the rounded ends of hairpins through the lacquered rigidity of her hair; even the 'soft' ringlets on either side of her face were stiff with spray. A diamanté tiara perched above her wide, frightened eyes. Underneath the flawless, glowing make-up, she imagined her skin was ashy white.

'Oh my God,' Naomi breathed. 'You look so beautiful.'

'Only shit-scared,' said Kate. 'Try and smile – you're going to get married to the love of your life, not be executed by lethal injection.'

Abbie managed a shaky laugh.

'Just look this way for a second.' Abbie turned her face to the window so the low autumn sun illuminated it, and Rowan plied a giant brush, sweeping extra translucent loose powder over her skin. 'Seriously, can you please stop sweating? This is industrial-strength slap but even it might not be able to withstand that.'

'I'll try.' Abbie wiped her hands for the millionth time on the flannel she was clutching. They were ice cold and clammy.

She could feel her teeth chattering and her knees trembling. 'It's not even cold. It's gorgeous out there, I don't know why I'm...'

'Shush, sweetie.' Her mother ran a gentle hand down the lace-clad length of Abbie's arm. 'The nerves will melt away as soon as you get up the aisle, just you watch. Remember how you were at your graduation?'

'Not really.' Abbie's voice sounded hoarse. 'I think I've blotted it out.'

'Well, for God's sake don't blot this out,' said Kate. 'It's your special day – you need to enjoy every minute of it.'

'I certainly intend to,' Rowan said. 'It's a bridesmaid's first duty to get drunk and get off with the best man, right?'

'Only the best man's Ryan,' Naomi reminded her.

'I mean, he's lovely and everything, and you're more than welcome, but wouldn't snogging my ex be a bit weird?' asked Kate.

'Okay,' Rowan agreed. 'Maybe not the best man. There must be plenty of other hot single men around, though.'

'Only fifty guests,' Kate said. 'So you're not exactly spoiled for choice. But I'm sure you'll find a way.'

'Do you think Zara minds not being a bridesmaid?' Abbie fretted. 'I mean, I did ask, and she said no because of working away so much, but I wonder if I should have pushed harder.'

'Well, it's a bit late now.' Her mother glanced at her watch. 'Unless you know someone who can run up a cerise satin shift in... two and a half minutes.'

'Two and a half minutes? Does that mean there's no time for me to be sick again?' Abbie stood up, her knees feeling almost liquid under the full white satin skirt. Her breath was coming in tight gasps, which had nothing to do with the rigid boning in her dress's bodice.

'Definitely no time.' Kate gave herself a final, cursory glance in the mirror. 'Come on, chicas, let's do this thing.'

They left the room and walked slowly down the carpeted

corridor towards the lift. A couple of American tourists who were waiting insisted they go ahead, and wished Abbie all the best. Her mouth was too dry to thank them.

Downstairs, Abbie could smell the lilies that stood in tall vases on either side of the entrance to the function room, mingling with the odour of toast and bacon left over from the hotel breakfast. Her father waited next to them, immaculate in a charcoal-grey suit, looking almost as nervous as Abbie felt. Her stomach gave a loud, embarrassing rumble and her bridesmaids giggled.

'I'll take my seat, then.' Abbie's mother paused, then pulled her into a hug. 'I love you, my darling girl. You look very beautiful. Be happy always.'

Abbie watched her mother's elaborate hat, cream straw laden with coral silk roses, make its way to the front of the room. Rowan handed her her bouquet and she buried her face in the strangely scentless magenta gerberas.

'Deep breaths,' Kate said. 'You've got this.'

'Wait, wait! Don't go in yet!'

Abbie jumped like she'd been stung and they all spun around. Hurrying through the lobby on impossibly high, pearl-studded stilettos was Zara, her dark hair flying behind her like a banner. She was wearing a full-length white satin dress, the heavy fabric suspended from spaghetti straps, the back hem dragging slightly on the thick carpet like a train.

Abbie saw surprise, then shock, then outraged amusement on her friends' faces. They all knew what Zara was like – always late, always wanting to be the centre of attention.

But even for her, this was going some.

'Don't worry, I'm not going to walk down the aisle with you,' she said airily, leaning in to kiss Abbie on both cheeks.

Rowan hastily wiped away the scarlet prints her lips had left.

'I'll just take my seat and then you're good to go.'

With a dazzling smile, she turned and swished through the doors. Abbie saw heads turn, heard the room erupt in whispers and saw, briefly, Matt's bemused face as he turned to see what the fuss was about, before Naomi pulled her out of sight.

'Did that just happen?' Rowan marvelled. 'I mean, seriously?'

'I can confirm that that did indeed just happen,' Kate said.

'Is she for real?' asked Naomi.

As the four of them dissolved into aghast laughter, Abbie felt some of her nerves melt away.

'Come on, Dad,' she said. 'Time to go in.'

'I'll just cue the music,' said Kate.

She hurried in, conferred briefly with Paul, and then returned. The first notes of the 'Wedding March' swelled in the air.

'Wait!' Rowan said. 'Hold on!'

'What?' Abbie asked.

'Arms above your head – now!'

Bemused, Abbie raised her bouquet high into the air. Rowan reached into the neckline of her dress, first on one side and then on the other, and held aloft two soggy tissues.

'We put them there to soak up the sweat,' she said. 'Just as well I remembered.'

They were laughing in earnest now, until Rowan told Abbie to stop that right now or her mascara would run. She gave a few final hiccupping giggles, then took her father's arm, her bridesmaids falling into place behind her.

She was okay now, she realised. Not nervous in the slightest. Everything was going to be fine – she was going to marry the person she loved best in all the world, she looked as good as it was possible for her to look, everyone was here because they cared about her and Matt and wanted them to be happy, and her best mates had her back.

Feeling as if she was floating on a cloud of joy, she made her way towards the man who was about to become her husband.

Afterwards, Abbie barely remembered anything about the next two hours. She had to watch the video (which she and Matt did, obsessively, over and over, reliving every single detail of the day) to remind herself of her saying her vows and reassure herself that she had, definitely, promised to cherish and respect Matt throughout their lives together, be faithful always and never let the sun go down on a quarrel – not that she could imagine ever not doing those things. She was able to confirm that she'd got through them with barely a blip (just one horrible moment when she almost got the giggles again at Matt's middle name, Justin, remembering that it was the answer to an old, bad joke: what do you call a guy with a tiny penis?).

Her happiness was written all over her face as they made their way back down the aisle and through to the room where the champagne reception was held, but her clearest memory of that was that, strangely, no one seemed to want to talk to her – she supposed it was because, as the bride, they assumed that she had other, more important people to mingle with.

The official photos seemed to take hours, and they were worth it – Abbie and Matt gazing up at each other under a bronze-leafed tree in the hotel garden; Abbie's bridesmaids laughing hysterically at something one of them had said as they toasted each other with glasses brim-full of champagne; Matt and Ryan and their parents standing in a formal row, all looking as if they might burst with pride.

Somehow, the photographer must have tactfully arranged the shots – or perhaps just done a drastic cull of the resulting images – so that in none of the pictures were Zara and Abbie next to each other, and nor were Zara and Matt. Zara herself featured in loads of others, though, impossibly beautiful in her white dress as she mingled and laughed. If it hadn't been for the pure happiness that shone from Abbie's face in every picture, Zara would have upstaged the bride for sure.

There was one photo of Abbie with Andy, which she remembered being taken. They were looking at each other, quite serious, glasses in their hands. Andy's arm was draped around Abbie's shoulder. It looked like a touching moment between two close friends, but the reality had been a bit different.

Just before they were due to go into the wedding breakfast, Andy had approached her, glass in hand, his tie already pulled to half-mast.

'I just want you to know,' he said, 'how happy I am for you guys.'

Abbie beamed at him. She'd beamed at everyone that day. 'Thank you. I'm happy for us, too.'

'I know you're not going to forgive me for what I did – ever,' Andy went on, leaning in close.

His eyes had a familiar glassiness and seemed unable to meet Abbie's own, sliding away like two green marbles.

He's absolutely off his face, she realised.

'But maybe you can forget. Maybe we can go back to being mates, all of us. We were the best mates. I fucking loved you guys. I still love you. I want to make things right. I—'

And then Ryan, kind, loyal Ryan, came and whisked Abbie away on the pretext that the photographer wanted to get a pic of her with her parents.

After that, some carefully planned operation was put in place to prevent Andy getting her alone again. Every now and then, she'd spot him approaching her through the crowd, but he was always waylaid – by Ryan, or by Kate, or by Rowan. She remembered feeling a deep appreciation of her friends' desire to protect her, to prevent anything from happening that would spoil her big day.

And nothing did. Not Zara's dress, not Andy having fallen

spectacularly off the wagon (again), not little three-year-old Clara having a spectacular tantrum just as the speeches were about to begin – nothing could have dulled her happiness that day.

Not even Matt making a complete pig's ear of his speech.

When they watched the video afterwards, that was the moment when Matt would get up to open another bottle of wine, or go for a piss, or – conveniently – the takeaway delivery guy would arrive just then.

And if fate failed to intervene in the form of Deliveroo, an empty bottle or Matt's bladder, or if Abbie just said, 'Oh come on, stay and watch! It's the best bit!' Matt would hunch over on the sofa, his hands over his eyes like a child watching a scary *Doctor Who* episode, and say, 'For Christ's sake, tell me when it's over.'

Abbie would lean in, saying to whichever long-suffering friends were there, pretending they wanted nothing more than to replay the day for the fifth time, that this was her favourite bit and promising that, honestly, after this they could switch off because the first dance was a bit shit and boring.

Their friends would say, 'We love that bit! It's "Chasing Cars" by Snow Patrol!'

And Abbie would say, 'Fine. Matt's speech, then you get Snow Patrol.'

Then they'd press play on the remote control again, and the picture would resume: Matt in his suit, his cravat askew, the carnation long gone from his buttonhole, his hair standing up at odd, jagged angles because he'd run his nervous fingers through it so many times, a fingerprint-smeared champagne flute in his hand. Abbie gazing up at him, waiting for the words of love, the special moments that her new husband would recall on this most special day, the tears that would be dabbed off her friends' cheeks as they listened.

It didn't quite go to plan. Matt had written and rewritten his speech many times, draft after draft being reworded and then discarded. Unknown to Abbie, the night before, he'd embarked on a new master version, bringing together all the best bits of the previous ones, and texted Abbie at almost midnight in triumph, saying he'd finally nailed it and was printing out the final draft.

But something had gone wrong. Abbie watched as Matt stood next to her, nervous, of course, but also quietly confident that the speech he'd laboured over would bring the house down. She heard him clear his throat, watched as he took a final sip of champagne and then saw with horror the dawning panic in his eyes as he patted first one pocket and then the next.

But she heard no reassuring rustle of paper.

Matt sat down again, leaned over to his brother and whispered something. Ryan shook his head.

Abbie didn't need to hear to know what the conversation was.

I don't suppose you thought to print off a spare copy of that speech?

Sorry, mate. I was in bed by the time you finished it.

Well, I forgot to bring it. It's back at the flat, on top of the bloody printer.

I don't know what to suggest. Wing it?

And then, a trickle of perspiration running down his temple, Matt stood up.

It was at this point, when they watched the DVD back, that they'd pause and wait for anyone who was in the loo or shout for whoever was getting fresh drinks to hurry up.

'It's almost Matt's speech!' Abbie would say.

'Oh God. I don't have to watch that again, do I?' Matt would groan.

'Of course you do! It's the best bit.'

The truth was, Abbie didn't need to watch the DVD to

remember what had happened. She could replay it in her mind, almost word for word, without even trying.

She remembered sitting there, watching her new husband, first with expectation and then with mounting concern.

Matt wasn't just nervous. He was panicking. This man, who could stand up in front of a room full of teenagers – the ultimate tough crowd – and explain variables and data structures in clear language, with a few laughs thrown in, was paralysed by a room full of their friends and family.

He was drying up, as they used to say in Abbie's university drama society, right before her eyes.

Come on, they willed him. *Come on! Just get started and you'll be fine! Everyone loves you!*

Matt pushed his hair back again and cleared his throat. His fingers twitched as if trying to summon from the ether the sheet of paper that should have been there but wasn't. He opened his mouth and closed it again.

Abbie caught Ryan's eye and a silent message passed between them: *Shit. What are we going to do? I don't know! What are we going to do?*

And then, quite suddenly, Abbie knew. This was the man she loved – she couldn't bear to watch him suffer for another second.

She stood up, almost shoulder to shoulder with him in her high heels.

'Ladies and gentlemen, family and friends,' she began. 'It seems Matt isn't in a position to speak right now, so I'll take over. First of all, Matt would like to thank his new in-laws, John and Carol, for welcoming him so warmly to their family. He's grateful that they've had plenty of time to adjust to the idea of him marrying their daughter, since it's been more than ten years since he and I – I mean, he and Abbie – first met at the school bus stop.

'Matt's own parents, Tony and Julia, have been equally

welcoming to Abbie. And why not – they couldn't possibly have asked for a more accomplished, charming daughter-in-law.'

There was a wave of laughter. Abbie felt confidence surging through her – she'd got this.

'Matt would like to thank his best man and brother, Ryan, for being his closest friend and partner in crime all his life, and especially while planning this wedding. He's particularly grateful to Ryan for his discreet and diplomatic handling of the stag night – the bill for the total refurb of the Tiger of India is on its way to you in the post, Ryan.'

More laughter. Matt reached out his hand and squeezed Abbie's tightly. His fingers were ice cold and clammy.

'Matt knows that Abbie couldn't have got through planning this wedding without the love, support and heated rollers of her best friends, Kate, Rowan and Naomi. Not only do her brides- maids look absolutely stunning today, they've helped Abbie with everything from calming her nerves with copious fizz to holding her skirt while she had a wee.'

Abbie paused while the murmur of laughter rose and died away.

'And finally, Matt would like to say how excited he is about his future with Abbie. If it's anything like their past has been, their marriage will be full of laughter, adventure and love. So Matt would like to propose a toast to me – I mean, to Abbie. And I guess Abbie – I mean I – may as well propose one to him, too.' That wouldn't have been in the script, she knew. But the whole room rose to their feet. There was a bellow of, 'To Matt and Abbie!' 'Abbie and Matt!' 'The bride and groom!' and the music of clinking glasses filled the air.

At last, Matt found his voice. 'To Abbie, saving my arse since 2001.'

As the room exploded into laughter, Abbie's knees suddenly felt like jelly and her hand as sweaty as Matt's had been. Relieved, she sank down into her chair next to him.

'Thank you,' he whispered.

'Any time,' she replied. 'I've always got your back. I love you.'

'I love you, too.'

'See?' Abbie would say, pressing rewind on the DVD while Matt asked if it was safe to open his eyes again. 'That's the best bit of all.'

CHAPTER TWENTY

'Not wearing your bridal gown, then?' Matt quipped, as I pulled a black satin cold-shoulder top over my charcoal coated skinny jeans. My outfit was a good three years out of fashion, but I couldn't think what else to wear – a frantic ten-minute rummage through my wardrobe had drawn a blank.

'As if! Anyway, I got rid of it years ago. I donated it to one of those charities that repurpose them for stillborn babies. I thought it was a nice thing to do.'

He touched my bare shoulder. 'It was a nice thing to do.'

'Black boots or red shoes?' I asked, holding up the options for his inspection.

'Neither of them look very comfortable.'

'Yeah, they aren't. But we're not doing comfortable. We're doing Proper Fancy.'

'Red shoes, then.'

'Done.' I sat down on the bed and carefully buckled the straps around my ankles. The shoes were high, pointy and as dated as the rest of my outfit, but they – and I – would have to do. At least I'd been to the hairdresser and had my ends trimmed and a deep-conditioning treatment applied.

Matt had made an effort too, I noticed: his purple paisley shirt was one I'd given him for Christmas, which he'd barely had the occasion to wear, and was freshly ironed. His face was smoothly shaved, and he smelled of the sandalwood cologne he knew I liked.

'Tube or Uber?' he asked.

'Tube there, Uber back. I can walk in these shoes now but I won't be able to after we drink all the champagne.'

'We're going to drink all the champagne?'

'That was my plan.'

He grinned, but said nothing, throwing his battered leather jacket over his shoulders and tucking his keys and phone into his pocket. I gave my lipstick a final blot, ran a brush through my hair and picked up my handbag.

When I'd suggested to Matt a week or so before that we visit our wedding venue for dinner, he hadn't seemed surprised – but he hadn't seemed particularly enthusiastic either. To be honest I could see why.

Our wedding day had been fabulous, magical, but that had been because we were in love and surrounded by people celebrating that, not because the hotel itself was particularly outstanding in any way. It was a mid-range, comfortable place, near where our parents had lived at the time and mine still did, although Matt's mum and dad had pursued their lifelong dream of moving to a tumbledown cottage in the depths of the Dorset countryside when Tony retired.

But there was more to it than that. We ate out in mediocre places all the time – mostly it was all we could afford. Matt's ambivalence about the idea – and my own, if I was honest – was down to something else: a feeling that, when it came to Operation Memory Lane, this was the last roll of the dice. We'd tried lots of things and mostly they'd worked. We'd recaptured some of our feelings for each other and discovered new ones. We'd unpicked and made peace with the biggest issue that was coming between us and blocking our happiness.

But what if all that wasn't enough?

Sitting next to Matt on the Tube, I wondered if he could feel waves of tension coming off me, because I was fairly sure I could feel them coming off him. Maybe it was the chilly autumn air, but my shoulders were actually shivering inside my too-thin fake leather jacket.

Half an hour later, we stepped into the hotel lobby. I felt the strangest sense of déjà vu – if you'd asked me to describe it, just a couple of hours earlier, I wouldn't have known where to begin. The days when Matt and I had watched our wedding video over and over were long gone, after all; I couldn't even remember the last time we'd taken the photo album out of its duck-egg-blue cardboard box and opened it. And the picture we kept on permanent display was of us in the hotel garden, kissing under a pergola festooned with autumn leaves, glasses of champagne in our hands.

Yet now, I could remember the place as if I visited every day. The marble steps were the same ones I'd worried about slipping on in my wedding shoes. The deep carpet was the same one that had trapped my heels back then. The place even smelled the same – of potpourri, or more likely potpourri-scented air freshener, and cooking, only now it was roasting meat that wafted through the air, not toast and bacon as I remembered.

Back then, our choice of venue had been dictated mostly by finances and time. We'd planned our wedding in a hurry, because neither of us saw the point in being engaged for ages and we didn't want a massively elaborate do anyway. And although Matt's parents had offered to foot the bill for more guests and a swankier location, we'd declined, just as we'd declined their offer of help with our flat deposit.

So this place wasn't exactly The Ritz – not that our trip

there had been all that, either. It was comfortable, it had good locations for photos, the staff had seemed friendly and helpful, and that had been good enough for us.

And, like everything else, that last quality didn't seem to have changed at all. The woman who greeted us smiled with what seemed like genuine enthusiasm, saying that our table was ready, but we were welcome to have a drink in the bar first, and asking if it was a special occasion.

'It's our wedding anniversary,' Matt said. 'Well, almost.'

'We got married here nine years ago,' I explained. 'Actually, nine years and two months. We kind of forgot about it, this time round.'

'Well, you're here now,' she said, ushering us through to the bar and showing us to a small, polished table, flanked by two squashy cocktail chairs. 'What can I get you?'

'Champagne?' Matt said.

'Of course,' I agreed, and two glasses appeared with welcome speed, together with a little dish of olives, apparently on the house.

'Well, this is civilised.' Matt crossed his legs and leaned forward, holding out his glass for me to clink.

'To us,' I said. 'Happy not-quite-anniversary.'

I took a sip of cold bubbles, wiping away the imprint my red lipstick left on the glass. I remembered how I'd felt on that magical day: the sense of infinite possibility, the giddy happiness, the certainty, when I looked at Matt, that I was making a decision I'd never regret – once I'd got over totally bricking it with nerves, that is.

Could I recapture all that tonight? Could he?

'Your table is ready, if you'd like to come through to the dining room?' The nice maître d' had dialled up the smileyness even more now that we'd shared the significance of the occasion.

'I think we're ready,' Matt said.

'We've put you in the best table.' She leaned in confidingly.

'The one by the window. We had to shuffle things around a little bit.'

'Thank you,' I said, a grateful smile spreading over my face.

We followed her through to the room I remembered from our wedding reception. Then, it had been decked out with flowers and candles and even a balloon arch; now, it was a bit more restrained, but there was still no shortage of starched snow-white napery, glowing lamplight and hovering, solicitous waiters in bow ties.

The table she escorted us to clearly was the best in the room, in an alcove by a window overlooking the garden. Not that we could see the garden now – beyond the window, there was only blackness and the reflection of my pale, anxious face looking back at me. Somewhere, though, in the dark beyond, would be the pergola under which we'd kissed, the rose bushes that had still borne a few last, tenacious blooms back then naked now, pruned back ready to flower again next spring.

We sat down and smiled at each other across the table, which was laid with ornate silver cutlery, gold charger plates and a pink rosebud in a crystal vase. Glasses of water appeared, leather-bound menus were placed reverently in front of us and Matt ordered a bottle of champagne – the same mid-range brand we'd had on our wedding day.

'You remembered.' I felt a melting softness in my heart, and I'm sure my smile grew a bit wider.

'Of course. Didn't I swear the next day that I'd never touch the stuff again, my hangover was so brutal?'

'I guess nine years is enough to recover from that trauma.'

'Nine years and two months. Back in September it would still have made me want to spew.'

We giggled, a bit too loudly for the formal atmosphere of the room.

'Behave yourself. No trash talk here – this is a respectable establishment.'

'Sorry. Shall we order oysters?'

The famous aphrodisiac. God knew we needed that. But I didn't want to go there – now when we were so relaxed and happy together.

'Absolutely,' I agreed. 'Fillet mignon, dauphinoise potatoes – the works.'

'Gotcha.'

Matt placed our order and we drank some champagne and tasted the warm bread, which came cocooned in yet another pristine white napkin alongside a little dish of butter that had apparently been smoked then whipped, or whipped then smoked, I wasn't sure which. Under the table, I felt Matt's ankle brush against mine, and I returned the pressure, meeting his eyes and smiling.

'So,' he said, sprinkling lemon juice on an oyster, easing it loose from its shell and passing it across the table for me to eat. 'Where do we go after this?'

'Literally or metaphorically?' I slid the oyster into my mouth, savouring its taste for a moment before I swallowed.

My words were light, but my question was serious. Was he suggesting we go out for a drink after our meal, or even book a room here for the night? Or was he talking in the wider context of our marriage? Did he mean to tell me that we'd tried everything and now we'd reached the end of the road?

'A bit of both,' Matt said. 'I wanted to talk to you about the baby thing. If you still want to try again, we can make it happen somehow. Mum and Dad would lend us money. Give it to us, even. They love being grandparents.'

I felt a twinge of the old bitterness. Tony and Julia had loved me and accepted me as part of their family for twenty years, and I couldn't do this one basic yet hugely important thing for them, while Ryan's wife Eleanor had effortlessly produced two babies in the space of as many years.

'I don't think so,' I replied slowly. 'It's not about the money –

okay, it's not just about the money. It's about how it made me feel. So desperate and resentful and sad and fucking angry all the time. I hated feeling that way. It wasn't like me at all. I was horrible to you.'

'You were hurting,' Matt said. 'I was too. And you were holding on to that other thing – the pregnancy you lost, and all the guilt and misery of that. Having secrets is hard. It sucks the life out of you.'

Our oyster plates had been taken away, and now perfectly crusted, juicy steaks were being placed in front of us, the cork being eased from a bottle of claret, a few drops poured into Matt's glass for him to taste.

I waited for the little performance of service to be over, but I didn't taste my food.

I looked across the table at Matt and said, 'When you say secrets, you're not just talking about mine, are you?'

He took a big gulp of wine, so big it left red stains at the corners of his mouth so it looked like he was smiling, until he dabbed his lips with a napkin.

And then he shook his head.

'Whatever it is, you can tell me,' I said. 'We've been through so much together. Whatever it is – as long as you're not... not ill, or something dreadful like that – we'll get through it. Even if it is that, we'll try.'

Matt smiled, for real this time. 'I'm not ill. Apart from having sperm that won't win the four-hundred-metre freestyle at the Olympics any time soon, I'm grand. So don't worry about that.'

To my surprise, I felt relief wash over me. I hadn't really worried that he might have some horrible, deadly illness he was about to tell me of – not really. But in the few seconds the idea had spent in my mind, the awfulness of it had almost taken my breath away. Whatever this was, whatever he was going to tell me, we'd both still be here afterwards, and so I could deal with it.

'Well, that's a relief,' I said lightly. 'But whatever it is, you may as well hit me with it.'

I cut into my steak and ate a piece. It tasted as good as it looked, but I knew I wasn't going to make much headway with it just yet.

'You remember that school reunion thing we went to back in July?' he asked.

I nodded. It had been that which had kind of kicked off the whole idea that, somehow, by recapturing our past, we could make our present bearable.

'Did Chloe say anything to you that night?'

'Chloe?' I echoed. 'Not really. Just about her kids and stuff. I can't really remember.'

'But you remember what she was like at school?'

'Yeah.' I smiled, remembering the girl who had been my best friend. Bookish and shy, like me. Never part of the in-crowd that centred around Rosie and Amber. Her friendship had kept me afloat, in those early weeks when I'd been new and awkward, surrounded by kids I didn't know and rules I didn't understand. And I'd continued to value it, even though it had never had the intensity my relationship with Matt did. 'She was sweet. I guess we didn't have enough in common to stay close mates after school though.'

Matt looked down at his plate. He picked up his knife and fork then put them down again and looked at me.

'There's something I need to tell you about Chloe.'

I waited for him to carry on then realised he was hesitating deliberately, as if asking my permission to share something I might not want to hear.

'It's okay,' I said, taking a deep breath that I hoped would slow the pounding of my heart. 'You can tell me.'

As if he'd been practising them for a long time, composing

and revising them like he had his wedding speech, Matt's words came out.

'There was a party at Rosie's parents' place, a couple of weeks before you started at school. Like the one at Andy's. Lots of booze, people smoking weed, all that stuff. Chloe was there.'

I nodded, surprised. I remembered phoning Chloe, the afternoon before Andy's party, to firm up the story I was going to tell my parents about where I was and trying to get her to change her mind and join me. But she'd refused adamantly, saying there was no way she was going near any dodgy house party with people leaving cigarette burns on the sofas and puking on the bathroom floor.

Clearly that hadn't always been her policy.

'Everyone was drunk,' Matt went on. 'I was, Chloe was. I didn't even know her that well, but we ended up hooking up.'

'You and Chloe?'

Matt nodded. 'It was... Abs, we had sex. In a bedroom on a pile of coats. We weren't the only ones – at the party, I mean, not in that room. It was that kind of night. We were only in there for, like, ten minutes, and then we went back to the party like nothing had happened. And then she left.'

In my mind, I could picture it as easily as if it was a film playing on a screen right in front of me. The dim lights, the dancers, the bottles of alcopop everywhere, the overflowing ashtrays. The couples kissing, moving away from the crowd to the edges of the room and then out, somewhere else. Behind closed doors. And then emerging shortly afterwards, ashamed or triumphant, blissful or in tears.

That was just what happened back then. For all I knew it still did if you were seventeen.

But Matt and Chloe? I felt like I wasn't in the staid dining room of our wedding venue but in one of those revolving restaurants they have in places like Dubai, and what I'd seen out of the window when we arrived would be completely different now.

'She talked to me about it at school on the Monday,' Matt went on. 'She was crying. She felt so ashamed. I tried to tell her it was okay, we hadn't done anything wrong, but she was just really scared people would find out. Because she wasn't...'

'That kind of girl?' It was true. I knew what had happened to girls who were somehow the wrong type if it was discovered that they'd had sex. They wouldn't be treated like they were the hot ones all the boys wanted; they'd be vilified as sluts. I could totally imagine that happening to Chloe.

Matt nodded. 'So she made me promise not to tell anyone – ever. And I said I wouldn't. I felt sorry for her. I didn't want to be the person who made bad things happen to her. It wasn't even a big deal – it wasn't like I was going to brag to my mates about it, anyway.'

'And then she and I got to be friends,' I said slowly. 'And then you and I...'

'Got together,' Matt went on. 'And a few weeks after that – it must've been after we had that date at Nando's – she spoke to me again. And that time she begged me not to tell you, especially, because she thought you wouldn't want to be her friend if you knew.'

I thought back, trying desperately to become seventeen-year-old me again. But I couldn't. The way I felt about Matt was so different now, my doubts and insecurities about our relationship like night and day compared to how they'd been back then.

Would I have been angry with Chloe? Hurt? Would I have ended our friendship over something that had happened before I even met her? Before I even knew that Matt existed?

I didn't think I would. I hoped I wouldn't. But could I really be sure?

And what about Matt? If he'd told me, for instance when we'd kissed by the pond after our first date, that he'd hooked his fingers in the studs of the belt I was wearing before, when it had been around Chloe's waist and not mine?

Again, I couldn't be sure. I was in over my head with him by then already. I was in love for the first time. But that love was fragile and raw and new and vulnerable to damage. I could easily have panicked and ended it.

And then what? What about the next twenty years? What about all the memories I shared now with Matt, which would never have happened?

'Why didn't you tell me?' I asked. 'Not then. I can see why not then. But all this time...'

'I know. Believe me, I've thought about it. But there was never a right time. At first, it would've been breaking a promise that was really important to Chloe. And later – I mean, when could I have told you? When should I?'

I thought of the secret I'd carried alone, all those years. There'd been plenty of times when I could have told Matt – when I should have. But I hadn't. I couldn't blame him for his silence, not when my own had been so deep and corrosive.

And could I blame him for a few minutes in a bedroom on a pile of coats with a pretty girl, more than twenty years ago? Of course I couldn't – that would be absurd. Seventeen-year-old me might have minded; for thirty-seven-year-old me, those few minutes were far too distant to cause me jealousy or hurt.

I said, 'Now. Now was a good time to tell me. I'm glad you did. Thank you.'

CHAPTER TWENTY-ONE

It was still dark when I woke up. I could feel cold radiating from the closed window, because we hadn't shut the blinds the previous night. The swishing of cars' tyres on the street outside told me that it had rained during the night – or was still raining.

But despite all that, I felt a deep glow of well-being.

It took me a moment to remember why. Matt – Matt and me. There he was, next to me in bed, one arm thrown up above his head, his hair spread over the pillow like a raven walking on snow. I edged closer to him and fitted my body into the curves of his in the warm hollow under the duvet, and he stirred in his sleep and flung the arm that had been on the pillow over me, squeezing me tight.

I felt like the distance there had been between us, the huge gulf of sadness and secrets, was gone now.

'Hey, you,' I whispered.

'Good morning, beautiful.' He opened his eyes and smiled, and I smiled back, my whole body feeling lighter, freer than it had for the longest time.

Then my happiness was dampened, as if a cloud had crossed the sun – only of course there wasn't any sun, there was only an icy November morning. And a little cat out there, cold and wet and alone.

'Matt? We have to go and check on Shrimp.'

'Not just check on her,' he said. 'I think we should bring her home.'

'Really? Today?'

'No time like the present,' he said, yanking the duvet off me.

I thought about snatching it back, burrowing into the warm for a few more precious moments, but instead I grabbed my dressing gown off the back of the door and hurried to the bathroom.

Half an hour later, we were walking briskly through the drizzle, the hoods of our coats pulled up, the plastic cat carrier we'd bought from the pet shop gripped firmly in Matt's hand.

'We're going to have to take her to the vet so they can see if she's microchipped,' I said.

'And we'll knock on the door one more time, just in case.'

'Of course we will. It's the right thing to do.'

There'd better not be any bloody answer when we knock. The idea of leaving Shrimp there, with people who cared so little for her welfare that they'd leave her to fend for herself for weeks, made me feel sick.

'We're kidding ourselves, aren't we?' Matt said. 'We're bringing her home to live with us.'

'I think we are.' I reached out for his free hand and gripped it, feeling the warmth of his fingers through my glove. 'I mean, maybe if it turned out she had a really loving home somewhere...'

'But there were no posts about her on social media or anything. I spent hours looking.'

'And I posted myself, and the only person who responded was that neighbour, who said what she'd told us when we knocked about the cat having been outside for as long as she could remember.'

'If you were Shrimp, what would you want to happen?' Matt asked.

'I mean, I'm not a cat so I'm not in a position to tell, really. But I think I'd want to go where it was warm and dry and there was chicken.'

'There's chicken?'

'I bought some yesterday. Organic chicken breasts. I thought we could have them for dinner.'

'Looks like we're going to need to learn to share,' Matt said.

We'd reached the house now and, as usual, Shrimp came out to greet us, yelling her head off for her breakfast. But this time, we put the bowl of cat biscuits inside the carrier, right at the back, left the door open and stepped back.

Shrimp looked from us to the food with an expression that I thought conveyed deep misgivings. But she was hungry enough for that not to last long. She stepped inside with first one paw and then the other. I realised I was holding my breath as I watched her extend her neck as far as it would go – but it wasn't far enough. She put one back leg inside too, and then, with reflexes that would have done credit to a scrum half diving onto a rugby ball, Matt shoved her gently in the rest of the way and closed the door behind her.

An hour later, we were home. The vet had confirmed that Shrimp had no microchip and hadn't been reported as missing to her practice; the neighbour had told us that there'd been no sign of the inhabitants of the house. And Shrimp herself was hiding under the sofa.

'Do you think she hates it here?' I asked. 'Do you think she hates us?'

'I think she's just getting used to us,' Matt said diplomatically.

So instead of working at the kitchen table, that day I took my laptop and sat on the floor, my back against the sofa and my legs extended under the coffee table. It didn't take long for

Shrimp to emerge, and by lunchtime she was draped across my lap, one of her paws resting on my keyboard, occasionally blanking the screen or turning up the sound or typing random things in cat.

During the afternoon, Shrimp moved again, this time onto the sofa, where she curled up in a tight black-and-white ball, her paws crossed over her face, and fell fast asleep.

At five thirty we both logged off, suddenly feeling at a loose end. There was no Shrimp to go and feed, because she was here with us. There was no walk to go on, because it was dark and raining outside and there'd be no cats for us to fuss, and anyway we'd found the one we were meant to have – or she had found us.

Matt came over and joined me on the floor, his hand covering mine. I rested my head on his shoulder, breathing in the clean smell of his hair. I kissed his neck above his jumper, then his cheek, and then he turned and his mouth met mine.

The kiss felt strange, almost tentative after so long. But we'd known each other twenty years; we'd kissed more times than I could count. Our bodies remembered what to do even if our hearts had forgotten. Matt's hands slipped under my T-shirt and stroked my back, warm and strong and familiar. I felt the hard length of his thighs through his jeans, and then the swelling hardness of his cock.

And then, just like that, my body pinged into arousal, as if I'd been asleep for months and now I was awake. I pulled off my top and then his, and moved to sit astride him, kissing him on and on, his skin hot against mine, beginning to feel slippery with sweat in the warm room.

We broke apart, pulling off our jeans. My legs wrapped around his waist and I felt his hands under my hips, lifting me up to him.

His eyes were dark with desire. His skin smelled like the sea. I found his cock with my hand and pushed my knickers aside, guiding him inside me, because I was ready even though he hadn't touched me.

And we fucked like that, on the floor of our living room, in a way we hadn't done for years, our cat sleeping on the sofa, oblivious and indifferent to the momentousness of the occasion. And even though it only lasted a few minutes, we were able to say, over and over again, 'I love you.'

AUTUMN 2015
THINKING OUT LOUD

They arrived at the estate agent's office at the same time, Abbie breathless from hurrying from the station, Matt jumping off a bus that had just pulled up at the stop outside. They stopped together outside the shop, its windows arrayed with carefully staged pictures of properties, and gripped each other's hands.

'Look.' Abbie pointed into the window. 'There's our one.'

'And it says "Sold",' Matt confirmed.

'I guess that means it's really happening.'

'It was really happening a week ago, when we exchanged contracts,' Matt reminded her. 'Now it's a done deal.'

'Too late to change our minds.'

'So I guess we go in.'

'Unless you want to leave the keys there and tell them we've changed our minds.'

'Hell no.'

Matt pushed open the door and Abbie followed him inside, trying to look calm and professional, as if buying a flat was something she did every day of the week. But when the estate agent handed over the keys, her composure deserted her and she pulled him into a hug.

'Thank you so much! Seriously, thank you. This is just the best. We've waited so long for this.'

The young man – he looked barely more than a teenager – pulled his tie away from his throat and coughed. 'Don't mention it. All part of the service.'

'So what happens now?' Matt asked. 'I mean, do we...?'

The estate agent chuckled. 'You move in, mate. Unless you've got a better idea.'

Abbie felt a tide of giggles rising in her throat. 'We could just leave it. Turn it into a museum.'

'Conduct a social experiment to see how long it took to be taken over by squatters,' suggested Matt.

'Leave the windows open and sprinkle bread everywhere and start a pigeon sanctuary.'

'Uh... will that be all?' the estate agent asked.

They stifled their laughter, thanked him and burst out into the crisp autumn sunshine, the keys clutched tightly in Abbie's hand.

'He thought we were completely mad,' she said.

'Absolutely barking. A pigeon sanctuary? You total nutter.'

'There's no way we're grown-up and responsible enough to be homeowners.'

'Never mind parents.'

'Oh God. Maybe I should ask Mum and Dad to let me move back in,' Abbie said. 'I could play CDs in my bedroom all night and hog the bathroom for hours.'

'And I could come and take you out on dates.'

'And we could drink cider in the park and then go home and snog under the duvet.'

'You know, that doesn't sound too bad.'

They beamed at each other. Abbie's heart felt as light as a helium balloon, as if it might burst out from under her jumper and float away, scarlet against the sapphire sky.

The next few days would be a nightmare of box-packing

and furniture-assembling, she knew, but today was all about the sheer joy of stepping together into the next phase of their lives. Okay, the flat was smaller than she'd dreamed of. Granted, the area wasn't all that. Admittedly, it was desperately in need of a new bathroom and a decent kitchen.

But all of that would come in time. It was theirs. It was where they'd start to raise their family. With a lurch of excitement, Abbie remembered the half-empty pill packet she'd handed to Matt the previous night, the two of them standing over the bathroom waste bin going, 'You chuck them,' 'No, you do it,' for ages, until they were so weak with laughter the blister pack slipped from Abbie's fingers as if of its own accord.

'It's the next street, right?'

'Or the one after.'

They kept walking, almost skipping down the pavement as if there were springs under their shoes, Abbie's mustard-yellow scarf flying out behind her. Then Matt's steps slowed.

'Hold on, this is Wilton Road,' he said.

'And the previous one was Hazel Street.'

'It must be the one after.'

They carried on, more slowly now. But the following street wasn't Rushmore Road either.

'Matt?' Abbie asked. 'We couldn't possibly have bought a flat that doesn't exist, could we?'

'Of course not, you lunatic. We've seen it twice, the surveyor's seen it, the agent gave us the keys to it. Our solicitor's got the deeds to it.'

'Then where is it?'

They stopped. A woman pushing a buggy almost collided with Matt, and he jumped aside, apologising, pulling Abbie with him.

'It's definitely here somewhere. Let's try the next street.'

'Matt, it's not the next street. I timed the walk from the station, in high heels and everything. It was only ten minutes.'

'Then where...?'

Abbie took her phone out of her bag and tapped the map icon. Then she burst out laughing.

'We went the wrong way. We turned left outside the estate agent instead of right.'

'Oh my God.' Matt pressed a hand over his eyes. 'And we're meant to be responsible adults.'

'We can't even find our own bloody flat.'

'That guy must've seen us go the wrong way and thought, *What the hell is wrong with them?*'

'And I don't blame him.'

Still giggling, they retraced their steps, stopping this time at a corner shop to buy a bottle of cold cava and paper cups.

A few minutes later, they were slotting the key into their very own front door.

Abbie pushed it open and they stepped over the threshold. A handful of golden leaves had blown in and were scattered on the wooden floorboards. A tongue of lining paper drooped off the wall. Dust hovered in the sunlight that streamed through the window. The air smelled slightly of unemptied bins.

Their footsteps loud in the stillness, they walked cautiously in.

'Hello, home,' Abbie said. 'Remember us?'

'It says it thought we'd never show up,' Matt said.

They passed through the narrow hallway and into the living room.

'We can put the sofa against that wall,' Abbie suggested.

'And the TV in the corner next to the window.'

'And there's room for a table and chairs in the kitchen.'

'Shall we go upstairs?'

'Let's open the fizz first.'

Matt twisted the cork out of the cava bottle, and bubbles frothed out. Abbie caught them in her mouth just in time, and Matt poured two cups for them.

'Oh my God. They've taken the fridge,' she noticed.

They looked at the empty space where it had been, between the cooker and the kitchen window.

'It was ancient anyway,' said Matt. 'We can buy a new one.'

He started up the music app on his phone and propped it up on the worktop. Ed Sheeran began to play tinnily through its speaker, a love song about growing old together. The music followed them as they walked upstairs, clutching their drinks. The stair carpet was grubby, Abbie noticed, and her foot caught in a tear on one of the treads. That would need replacing too, at some point.

The bedroom window looked out on a huge chestnut tree, magnificent now in its amber foliage. But it would be bare in a couple of months, and the windows of the house opposite would be like watching eyes.

Curtains, Abbie added to her mental list.

At least there was nothing to do in the smaller, back bedroom. That could stay as it was for now, bare and empty, or be used to store stuff that wouldn't fit anywhere else, like Matt's collection of DVDs and the doll's house Abbie had treasured since her sixth birthday.

Some day, she thought, another little girl might peer into its wallpapered interior, carefully rearranging the delicate furniture and tiny plates and ornaments, imagining in minute detail the lives of the porcelain-faced family who lived there, the crab apple tree in the next-door garden casting the shadows of its branches over her face.

She turned away and joined Matt in the bathroom, noticing for the first time the broken door handle and the rust stain in the bathtub. But who cared? She and Matt wouldn't need to close the door when they were in the bath, and when it was full of bubbles, they'd hide the stain.

'Shall we go and look at the bedroom again?' she asked.

Matt nodded. 'I should've brought a tape measure. We'll need to go to IKEA and buy a wardrobe.'

'And a chest of drawers.'

'Plus a new mattress. Ours is only fit for a skip, really. It's gone all lumpy.'

'Who are you, the princess with the pea?'

They laughed and Abbie felt her mood lift again. She moved over to the window and looked out at the tree, imagining it naked in winter, then new acid-green leaves unfurling in spring. A magpie alighted on one of the branches and gave its cackling call, and then another joined it.

'One for sorrow, two for joy,' Matt said.

'Three for a girl, four for a boy,' Abbie added.

'How does it go after that?'

'God, I've no idea. Let me check.' She tapped at her phone and seconds later read aloud, 'Five for silver, six for gold, seven for a secret never to be told.'

'Oh,' Matt said. 'Man. That's kind of deep.'

Abbie felt a shiver run down her spine. The flat was chilly, she reasoned.

'Hey, it's just a silly nursery rhyme. And anyway, there's two of them. That's joy, right?'

Matt turned to her, put his arm round her waist and pulled her close. Their cups were almost empty, but they tapped the soggy rims against each other and sipped the last of the cava.

'Cheers to us,' Abbie said.

'Happy housewarming,' Matt said.

And in the golden light that filtered through the smeared window panes, they shared their first kiss in their new home.

CHAPTER TWENTY-TWO

I was up on a stepladder painting the wall of the study – what we used to, tentatively, call the baby's room, then the spare room, then barely mentioned, as if even naming it could harm us – when the doorbell rang. The paint, a gorgeous dark teal blue, was going on beautifully, even and smooth as, well, paint. But the shrill buzz startled me and the roller jerked in my hand, sending a shower of droplets onto the white ceiling.

I let loose a string of swear words I was surprised didn't turn the air blue, too, and called, 'Matt! Get the door please?'

Then I remembered my husband wasn't home; he'd gone off in an Uber to collect the vintage mahogany desk we'd found on Facebook Marketplace, which we agreed was the perfect centrepiece for the 'serious but effortlessly chic' look we were aiming for in the room.

'Bet he's forgotten his keys again,' I muttered, climbing down off the ladder. The relief at being annoyed with Matt over small things, but it being only annoyance – no more and no less, with no undercurrent of rancour – was so great I almost took pleasure in it.

Just a couple of days before, I'd grabbed the teaspoon off the draining board and marched up to him, wagging it under his nose.

'What does this look like to you, now?' I demanded, trying to look stern but mostly failing.

'A teaspoon?' he'd answered, all wide-eyed innocence.

'And where do teaspoons go when they've been used?'

'On the edge of the sink, in case I want to use them again.'

'No they don't! They go in the dishwasher, and if you need another one, you take a clean one and put that in the dishwasher too when you're done with it.'

'What? But that's an insane waste of teaspoons.'

'Waste of... What the actual...? Do you think they get worn out stirring coffee or something?'

'Nah, not really. I just forget, sometimes. Same way you forget to close cupboard doors and I have to do a daily tour of the flat, shutting things. It's the highlight of my evening. Every door I close, I think of my beautiful wife, who drives me absolutely crackers.'

And I'd laughed and kissed him, and earlier that day I'd found the teaspoon wedged between the sofa cushions and spent about half an hour with a cheesy grin on my face, remembering.

I hurried to the front door and tugged it open, hoping that Matt had offered the cab driver a hefty tip to stick around and help get the desk upstairs, because if it was genuine mahogany it would weigh a ton, and my arms were already aching from painting.

But there was no Matt there, no Uber driver and no desk.

On the doorstep, wearing an ankle-length leather coat, a grey knitted scarf and sunglasses, was Andy.

When he saw me he took a step back, almost falling backwards down the steps but catching himself just in time.

'Careful!' I reached out a hand, but he didn't take it.

I realised that, whatever had made him come here, he'd

somehow assumed it would be Matt who answered the bell and not me, and that he was jolted, almost afraid.

'Hello, Abbie,' he said warily, looking past my shoulder as if hoping my husband would appear behind me like Captain America turning up to rescue him from the situation he'd found himself in.

'Hey. You should come in – it's bitter out here.'

It was true – an icy wind was whipping down the street, stripping the trees of the last of their foliage. As I watched, a leaf scudded down from the chestnut tree and landed damply on the shoulder of Andy's coat, almost blending into the worn brown leather.

'Tall Matt not home?'

I smiled at the school nickname, which I'd all but forgotten. 'Not right now. He should be soon, though.'

Andy hesitated, then he said, 'Okay. Thanks. I'll come in.'

I turned, and he followed me through the narrow hallway. He'd never been here before, I realised – this home of ours had never been his.

'Shall I take your coat?' Now that he was here, facing me, so close I could smell the Guerlain aftershave he'd always worn, heady with violets like a summer day in a forest somewhere, I felt awkwardness creeping over me.

'No, I'll... all right. Thanks.'

He unwound his scarf and slid the coat off his shoulders. Without them, he looked much more normal: just a guy in jeans and a varsity sweatshirt, his blond hair thinning slightly at the temples.

I hung up his things and said, 'Can I get you a d— a cup of coffee or something?'

'Tea would be amazing, if you have it? Builder's, with milk and three sugars.'

'Sure.' I waved Andy over to the sofa and ducked into the kitchen, where I flicked on the kettle and put a teabag in a mug, pouring a glass of water for myself. After a quick rummage in the cupboard, I found a packet of chocolate biscuits and tipped some onto a plate.

Then I made Andy's tea and carried everything through to the living room. Shrimp had hopped onto the sofa and was curiously sniffing Andy's fingers.

'New arrival?' he asked.

'Yeah, she kind of adopted us. We're one hundred per cent under the paw now.' I passed Andy his mug of tea and put the biscuits on the coffee table.

'Cheers.' He blew on the tea, then picked up a biscuit and dunked it. 'How did you know?'

'Know what?'

'People in recovery live for biscuits. I swear meeting attendance would halve without them. You could call it cross-addiction, but we prefer to stay in denial about that. Except the Overeaters Anonymous lot, obviously. They stay away from the confectionery.'

'So you're...' I began.

'Off the drugs. Yep. I've been clean for four months. Being stuck alone at home made me realise how bad it had got. I was using non-stop, more and more. They say you've got to hit rock bottom, and I did. When I realised it had been six weeks since I'd spoken to anyone except my dealer, I knew something had to give. I told myself I could cut down, but that didn't work, so I went the whole hog and turned up at a meeting.'

'That's good,' I said. 'I mean, I don't know what you say to someone in recovery. Congratulations?'

'One day at a time?' he suggested, with a lopsided smile that suddenly made him look like the old Andy.

'One day at a time, then,' I said, raising my water glass to him in a gesture I hoped wasn't wildly triggering.

'So I guess you must be wondering what I'm doing here,' Andy said, taking another biscuit and dunking it.

'It's always good to see an old friend.' But I winced at my own lie, because, after all, I could have seen Andy any time if I'd wanted to. Matt had – he'd met up with Andy at least twice a year, even though he knew Andy was likely to be a coked-up mess. Matt had insisted Andy come to our wedding, and even though I'd objected at first, Matt convinced me that it was the right thing to do – the compassionate thing.

And now I could see that he'd been right.

'Frankly,' Andy said, 'I wouldn't have blamed you if you'd slammed the door in my face.'

'I wouldn't do that.' But I realised that, just a few months ago, I might.

Andy took a slurp of tea. Again, I saw a flash of the old him – the man who'd opened a bottle of Advocaat, one late night when we'd run out of wine, poured it into a tumbler and drunk it down like it was medicine, then repeated the process until the bottle was empty.

'Are you familiar with the twelve steps?' he asked.

'Yeah, kind of. I mean, about the same amount as anyone is.'

Anyone who's never needed to follow them, I thought.

'There's a lot of guff in there about God. I don't have a religious bone in my body, but you're allowed to substitute the higher power of your choice. So long as it's not blow, obviously.'

I couldn't help laughing. 'Obviously not.'

'I won't bore you with the details. But I've worked my way through them and I'm up to number nine.'

'Wow. That's good going.'

'They don't get any easier, I can tell you. But here I am.' He took a deep breath and another gulp of tea. 'So step eight is: "We made a list of all persons we had harmed, and became willing to make amends to them all." My list's a long one, I have to admit.'

I wasn't sure whether to agree or not – I was fairly certain Matt and I hadn't been the only victims of Andy's addiction, but it seemed unkind and judgemental to say that. So I found myself making a random gesture with my head that was half 'yes', half 'no' and an extra bit of 'go on', and probably made me look like one of those nodding-dog toys people used to have in their cars.

Andy took a big, trembly breath and went on. 'Step nine: "We made direct amends to such people wherever possible, except when to do so would injure them or others." That's why I'm here.'

'I'm glad you came,' I said. 'I appreciate it. It can't have been easy.'

'Hey, coming here was the easy part. That and troughing your biscuits. Here's where it gets tough.'

A big part of me wanted to come over all British and say something like, *Think nothing of it, Andy. It's all in the past. Let bygones be bygones.* I knew that hearing what he had to say would be almost as awkward for me as saying it would be for him.

But I also knew that this was important for both of us.

'It's okay,' I said. 'Take your time. I'm listening.'

'Abbie, I'm sorry,' he said. 'I came into your home and I took advantage of you and betrayed you. I stole your money and I stole your trust. I didn't set out to hurt you, but once I'd started doing it, I didn't care enough to stop. There was only one thing I cared about.'

This time I did nod, properly, but I found I couldn't say anything.

Andy went on, 'Matt told me about the... issues you two have had. That's on me, too. I took your chance of having a family and that's the worst thing of all. Not that you'd have asked me to be fairy godfather or anything like that.'

Now I found my voice. 'Andy, I really, really appreciate your apology. It means the world. But you can't blame yourself for – the other thing. That's not your fault. It's not mine either –

or Matt's. It's just one of those things that happens. Some people can't have babies. All the money on earth might not have changed that.'

Andy leaned forward too, meeting my eyes. His were steadier than I'd ever seen them, a clear bright green like a pond shaded by trees.

'I haven't finished. There's still the "make amends" bit. My granny died last year. It took forever for probate to go through and she wasn't exactly minted but I've inherited some cash. Thank God it took so long for me to get it or I'd have stuffed the lot up my nose. But now I can pay back what I took from you and Matt, with interest.'

My mind whirled. I thought about the sum of money Andy was talking about. It would be enough for another round of fertility treatment for us. But I didn't need to think for long. I imagined accepting Andy's offer, going through the horrible, painful process we'd been through before. I knew what the odds were of it succeeding, and I knew we'd most likely end up with the same devastating, predictable result.

And I realised – or let myself realise, for the first time – how unfair it had been of me to blame Andy for everything that had happened. It had been our choice, after all, to wait to try and start a family – until our careers were established, until we'd got married, until we'd bought our own home. If we'd started earlier, we'd have known sooner that everything wasn't right and perhaps the outcome would have been different.

That was on us, not on him.

I imagined how trying yet again to have a baby through medical intervention and failing would make me feel – what it would do to Matt and me; how it would fracture the fragile foundations of our marriage, on which we'd just begun to build stability again.

Frankly, I thought, *it would be no better than Andy spunking the whole lot on cocaine.*

'Andy, I don't want your money,' I said. 'Thank you for offering, from the bottom of my heart. But we've moved past that now. There was a time when we'd have used it, but we won't now. We're okay. It matters far more that you're here, you're taking care of yourself and that you've said what you said. Use it for yourself – there must be lots of things you've missed out on. Or give it to charity – maybe something your granny would have supported. But it's yours now, not ours.'

I stood up, and Andy did too. We moved around the coffee table, and I took him in my arms, holding his slim body close, patting his back like he was an upset child.

I'd never loved Andy like Matt did. I'd never been close to him like Kate and Rowan were. But now I knew that I could forgive him and I hoped I could learn to trust him. Now, perhaps, we could be friends – proper friends in a way we never were before.

I heard the scrape of Matt's key in the lock, but we didn't move. Over Andy's shoulder, I saw my husband enter the room and stop, looking at us with first surprise then understanding.

'Mate!' he said. 'Great to see you. Any chance you can help me get this bloody beast of a desk up the stairs?'

DECEMBER 2021

OH MY GOD

I'd never actually been inside a private members' club before, but if I'd allowed myself to imagine what it would be like, it would be like this. The lights were dimmed, but I could make out velvet-covered chaises longues in jewel colours, rich as stained-glass windows in a cathedral, catching the glow from the sleek, modernist chandeliers overhead. The floor was marble tiles, white or perhaps silvery grey, with occasional deep, plushy rugs laid over them, either vintage or aged to look as if they were. In one corner of the room, I could see a grand piano, a vivid shade of lime green that I was willing to bet it hadn't been when it started life.

Music was playing, but I could barely hear it over the excited hum of voices. Behind the bar, bright spotlights illuminated glass shelves bearing bottles of every spirit known to man.

Around the room were glass display cases, each one spotlit, each one holding a carefully curated selection of Quim merchandise. In one, a mannequin stood clad in a leather catsuit and crotch-high boots, a spanking paddle in her hand. In another, a selection of dildos and vibrators were artfully arranged like something in a museum. Another held bottles and tubes of lubricants, massage oils and even a bottle of the hair-removal creme I'd tried with such disastrous effects.

They ought to have slapped a massive warning label on that, I thought.

I took a sip from the glass in my hand – a cosmopolitan, which I'd ordered for old times' sake. It was already slippery with condensation, and I prayed it wouldn't slip through my fingers and disgorge its sticky contents on one of the expensive carpets. I hitched up the strap of my pink jumpsuit, wishing I'd thought to attach it to my skin with a bit of tit tape, and flicked my newly balayaged hair over my shoulder.

I'd taken the afternoon off work to get ready, once Marc and Bastian had assured me that everything was under control and, if it wasn't, the blame would lie squarely on the shoulders of the events management company. I'd had my hair and my nails done and even had my make-up professionally applied by a lovely girl at the Chanel counter in Selfridges, who'd assured me that it was guaranteed not to shift all night, however much I danced. When I took another swig of my drink, the rim of the glass was reassuringly lipstick-free.

Where was Matt? His name was on the guest list and he'd promised me he'd be here tonight, even though he'd taken some persuading to come. First he'd said he didn't want to leave Shrimp in the flat alone, then argued that it was my big night and I wouldn't want him cluttering up the place, then, when I reminded him that I'd be a guest too and not expected to do any work, he'd protested that he was far too uncool for such a gathering. But when I'd eventually overcome all his objections (including arranging babysitting for the cat), he'd admitted that, actually, it sounded brilliant and he couldn't wait.

And now that I was here, I found I was having a totally brilliant time, too. I moved through the room, drink in hand, chatting to a few of the people we'd worked with on the campaign: Craig the copywriter, Marc and Bastian, and, of course, Kendra the client, who was holding court in a corner surrounded by PR minions. Her main job appeared to be using the word 'orgasm' as many times as she could in the shortest time possible.

But my thoughts didn't dwell on them for long. I was here, at the end of a successful and stressful campaign, looking my best, enjoying myself, properly *out* out.

And then I saw Matt. Once my eyes had found him, I couldn't believe I hadn't noticed him straight away. He was leaning against a pillar, a bottle of Talon in his hand (passion-fruit flavour – I could have warned him that was a strategic error), his head clearly visible above the throng. His dark hair shone under the light of a standard lamp, taller even than he was. He was wearing a new dark-red shirt that made his shoulders look impossibly broad and strong, and black jeans that made his legs look endlessly long. He was chatting to one of the celebrity guests, a comedian who was on the *Strictly Come Dancing* line-up and who I'd nurtured a not-so-secret crush on for years.

But as far as I was concerned, the comedian might as well not have been in the room at all. It was as if there was no one there at all, in that moment, apart from Matt and me.

I felt a dizzying surge of happiness, a lightness filling my entire body as if I might suddenly start to dance, or even be able to fly.

I walked slowly across the room to join him, spinning out the moment, not minding when people waylaid me to say what a great evening it was, what a huge success, wasn't it wonderful to be able to bring so many people together to celebrate the launch. I was happy to linger and chat, smile and laugh and drink, because I knew that every second, every step, was bringing me closer to my husband, and he wasn't going anywhere at all. I saw the comedian guffaw at something Matt had said and felt a glow of pride – *He even makes people who are paid to be funny laugh.*

Then he looked up and saw me, and my happiness ramped up a notch. His smile lit up his whole face, just the way it always did. I noticed his white, even teeth, his dark eyes crinkling up at the corners, the dimples in both his cheeks that I'd run my fingers down so many times, as if I was seeing him for the first time. If I got closer, I knew I'd see other things, too: the threads of grey in his hair, the creases on his new shirt, which he wouldn't have bothered to iron after taking it out of its packaging, the scratches on his wrist from an overenthusiastic game of pounce with Shrimp. Everything about him was familiar, yet every day there was something new about him to discover.

'See, I made it,' he said.

'I'm so glad you did.' I leaned in close for a kiss. He introduced me to the comedian and I wondered whether Matt had admitted that he'd seriously considered sacking off this glamorous event in favour of watching telly on the sofa with a cat. Maybe that was what had made the comedian laugh.

'You've got a drink?' I asked.

Matt nodded, holding out the half-empty bottle of passionfruit Talon, too diplomatic to admit that it tasted like the stuff we used to disinfect our kitchen worktops. I reached out my own bottle and we clinked.

'Want to explore a bit?' I asked.

'Sure. This place is off the scale.'

'Isn't it? Or maybe it's just that we haven't been anywhere posh together for so long.'

'We've forgotten how to do fabulous.'

Our eyes met and we both laughed, remembering that what we'd done together in the morning had been pretty fabulous, even with Shrimp watching us disapprovingly from Matt's bedside table. We excused ourselves and made our way back into the crowd, hand in hand, not caring if we were being unsociable. The strap of my jumpsuit had slipped down my shoulder again, but I didn't care about that, either.

'Listen,' Matt said. 'They're playing Destiny's Child.'

'Of course they are. It's a 2000s-themed event, after all.'

'Oh, right! I wondered why the waitresses were all dressed like the girls in our sixth form on a night out.'

'It's the cutting edge of retro fashion now, I'm told.'

'How can it be retro? It was, like, a couple of years ago.'

'A couple of decades ago, old man.'

We giggled again. A waiter offered us glasses of champagne, and I took one in return for my empty cocktail glass. Then a waitress passed with a silver tray laden with canapés, and I helped myself to a smoked salmon blini while Matt had a sun-dried tomato and anchovy pinwheel.

'See?' I said. 'Retro.'

'I don't know what you're talking about. Isn't this the very cutting edge of culinary fashion?'

'You're asking the wrong person,' I admitted. 'I still think artisan Scotch eggs are a bit advanced.'

'Speaking of which...' Matt nabbed two breaded, sausage-meat-encased quail eggs from a platter and passed one to me.

We'd crossed the whole room by this point. The DJ was continuing with a series of decade-appropriate hits, and more people were beginning to move onto the dance floor. A neon light arced over us, and a mirror ball cast rainbows over the crowd. I paused, wanting to take it all in for a second, but Matt squeezed my hand tighter and urged me on.

'Hey,' he said. 'What do you think is up there?'

In front of us was a door, just ajar, with a bare concrete staircase leading up from it.

'No idea. I've never been here before.'

'Come on, then.'

'Matt, I'm not sure we're...'

But it was too late. He'd pulled me through the door, and together we ascended the stairs. We reached a landing, with a closed fire door opening off it. Matt pushed the handle, but it didn't budge.

'Onwards!' he said, turning the light of his infectious smile on me and pulling me towards the next flight of stairs.

'Matt, I'm really not...'

'Sssh. Come on.'

We climbed another flight. I could feel my breath starting to come in gasps – I'd forgotten how hard it was to walk in high heels. But we'd reached the top – there was nowhere further to go, only one closed door opening off the bare landing.

'Right, Abs. We're going in.'

'Are you serious?'

'Absolutely.'

He pushed the steel rail that bisected the dark green paint of the door, and this time it swung obligingly open.

I felt my lungs take in a deep gulp of air, and next to me I heard Matt gasp too.

In front of us was a swimming pool, open to the winter night air, a haze of steam rising off its surface. Its water was luminescent blue in the darkness, illuminated by small spotlights beneath the surface. Teak sun loungers stood around it, bare of the canvas cushions they'd no doubt hold when it was in use. Tropical plants, their leaves so lush and verdant they must surely have been plastic, cast jagged shadows over the charcoal slate surrounding the water.

The heady smell of chlorine filled the air, reminding me of holidays in hot places, the pool at our local leisure centre where I'd embarked on a soon-abandoned get-fit campaign a few years back, and something else, another part of the past I couldn't quite place.

'We totally shouldn't be here,' I whispered.

Matt grinned, his smile almost devilishly infectious in the semi-darkness. 'We totally should.'

'Want to swim, then?' I asked.

Matt's grin widened, then faded away. 'A bridge too far.'

'I think so,' I agreed. 'We haven't got towels or anything. And if we got caught it would be major awks.'

'There are towels there on the sun loungers. Look.'

'Matt, we really can't. We should go back to the party.'

But we didn't retreat down the stairs the way we'd come. We stood there, in the gleam of the sapphire lights, surrounded by the lush foliage and the smell of hot summers, even though it was cold enough for gooseflesh to pop up all over my bare arms.

Distantly, I could still hear the sounds of the party: the voices, louder now as the drink flowed; the occasional shriek of laughter; the music.

'Yellow', by Coldplay.

I remembered that long-ago night – how part of me had longed to plunge into the warm water of the pool with Matt, but I hadn't had the courage. I wasn't that seventeen-year-old girl now. I was older, wiser, braver.

And saggier, but I didn't care about that.

'Go on then,' I said. 'Unzip me.'

'Seriously?'

'Seriously.' But I didn't feel serious – not one bit. I felt giggly, elated and irresponsible, like I'd necked a flight of cocktails and a whole bottle of champagne instead of just a glass of each.

I turned round and felt Matt's fingers grip the zip between my shoulder blades and tug it downwards. There was the familiar moment of resistance at my waist, then the zip yielded and slid all the way down. I kicked off my shoes and stepped out of the jumpsuit, turning to smile at my husband.

'Holy shit,' he said. 'What are you wearing?'

'Just one of the client's garments,' I said. 'Doing my bit for the cause, you know.'

He'd never seen me in the strapless black lace basque before; I was gradually working my way through the box of samples that had moved from my office to our bedroom, and this was its first outing.

'You look...' he began.

'Never mind how I look,' I teased. 'Get your kit off. I'm not going in there on my own.'

He didn't need telling again. He pulled his clothes off, right down to his boxer shorts, and then reached for my hand.

'Come on,' I said. 'On the count of three. One, two...'

But before I could finish, Matt had pulled me forward and we jumped together into the pool, sending up a shower of droplets that sparkled like diamonds in the darkness above us. I kept my face above the water (my hair and make-up had taken ages and what was I, some kind of fool?) but Matt didn't. He ducked fully beneath the surface, a shoal of bubbles surrounding his grinning face as he resurfaced.

Then he reached out for me and I stepped into his arms. His skin, and mine, and the water, were all the same temperature, so I could barely tell where one ended and the other began. I felt his fingers reach around my body for the clasps of my basque, unhooking them with only a bit of fumbling.

'What are you doing?' I gasped, half-laughing.

'Undressing you. You said that jumpsuit looks best with nothing underneath it, and you look best with nothing on.'

'But what are we going to do with it?'

'No idea. Leave it here?'

'They'll think there's been a murder.'

'No they won't. They'll think someone got jiggy in the pool.'

Seconds later, I was naked. Turned on and furtive as a teenager at a party, only with a man I'd known for twenty years and trusted with everything. There was nothing between us now – no sadness, no secrets, only millimetres of blood-hot water.

I was going to kiss him. I was going to kiss him and I wanted it more than I'd wanted any kiss ever – not the ones I'd offered when a fight was looming, not the ones he'd comforted me with after those horrible, sad, desperate trying-to-conceive shags; not the one he'd given me at the altar after we'd said our marriage vows.

Even more than that first ever kiss, brought into sharp focus now by my memories and the music.

The Coldplay song had ended; a new tune was playing: the latest release from Adele's new album. I barely heard it – all I was aware of was Matt and me and the water, and our bodies so, so close together – but I knew that the next time I heard Adele blasting out this anthem about love and desire and taking risks, it would transport me straight back to this moment.

Memories mattered – of course they did. But now, I knew that new ones were happening to us all the time, flowing into the whole being of us and becoming part of us like I felt we were part of the night, like the love we felt for each other was merging with the music and the water and the winter darkness above us.

I'd kissed Matt often enough to know that this kiss wouldn't disappoint me.

And it didn't.

As his lips met mine in the glowing, secret space where we were alone together, I felt my heart and my body sing along with the music.

I'm so glad I'll get to kiss him whenever I want, for the rest of my life, I thought.

A LETTER FROM SOPHIE

Dear reader,

I want to say a huge thank you for choosing to read *P.S. I Hate You*. If you did enjoy it, and want to keep up to date with all my latest releases, just sign up at the following link. Your email address will never be shared and you can unsubscribe at any time.

www.bookouture.com/sophie-ranald

I'm writing this on a blustery, wet December afternoon, with just over two weeks to go until Christmas. By the time you read it, it will be spring: the days will be getting longer again, the first green haze of new leaves appearing on the trees, some hardy early daffodils already turning their bright faces to the sky.

But now, it still feels like there's a long haul of January and February ahead – cold, dark evenings, mashed potato cravings and a cat permanently attached to my lap.

For me, writing a book often feels like being in the depths of winter with the promise of spring almost unimaginably distant. I know that, somehow or other, it will get done; the last words tapped away by my weary fingers; the final checks of the brilliant editorial team complete; and the moment will come when you hold this book in your hand and start to read.

And it will all have been worth it – I hope!

One of the most enjoyable parts of telling Abbie and Matt's story for me was creating the soundtrack to their relationship, rediscovering songs I loved during those heady years of the noughties and beyond (with a couple of old-school faves thrown in). If you'd like to listen to the *P.S. I Hate You* playlist, you can find it on Spotify by searching for my name or the title of the novel.

Thank you for reading *P.S. I Hate You*, and thank you for making it this far. I hope you enjoyed Matt and Abbie's love story, and had a few laughs along the way. If you are able to take the time to leave a review online, I'd be hugely grateful – it doesn't have to be long, and I love hearing what my readers make of my books.

Until next time, take care and happy reading.

Love from Sophie

facebook.com/SophieRanald

twitter.com/SophieRanald

instagram.com/sophieranald

ACKNOWLEDGEMENTS

I may have mentioned this before, but during the process of writing a novel, I complain. Like, a lot. My writing is no good, I can't do this, it will never be finished, all my readers will hate it and it will sink into well-deserved oblivion.

I'm like a one-woman Greek chorus.

Fortunately, I'm surrounded by amazing people who not only put up with my whinging, but reassure me that I can do it, I've got this, and it will all be okay in the end.

I sometimes wonder what they put into the water coolers over at Bookouture Towers. It's an absolute joy to work with a team of such supportive, kind, clever and upbeat people: my wonderful editor, Christina Demosthenous, who is meticulous, motivating, inspiring and above all great fun to work with, and who has improved my writing beyond recognition; Noelle Holten, Kim Nash, Peta Nightingale, Alex Holmes, Lauren Finger and Alex Crow, who have kept everything running like oiled silk behind the scenes on publicity, production and promotion; my brilliant cover designer Lisa Horton, cracking copy-editor Rhian McKay and eagle-eyed proofreader Laura Kincaid. Thank you all.

Also huge thanks to the lovely Alice Saunders at the Soho Agency, which has represented me throughout my writing career. Your support has been invaluable as always, and there aren't enough thank yous in the world to express my appreciation.

And finally, thanks and love to my fabulous friends, who make me laugh every single day, my darling Hopi and precious cats. Love you all.

Made in United States
North Haven, CT
03 March 2022